MOONRISERS

NOVELS BY JERI WESTERSON

Paranormal

BOOKE OF THE HIDDEN SERIES

Booke of the Hidden

Deadly Rising

Shadows in the Mist

The Darkest Gateway

A MOONRISER WEREWOLF MYSTERY SERIES

Moonrisers

Medieval Mysteries

THE CRISPIN GUEST MEDIEVAL NOIR MYSTERIES

Veil of Lies

Serpent in the Thorns

The Demon's Parchment

Troubled Bones

Blood Lance

Shadow of the Alchemist

Cup of Blood (a prequel)

The Silence of Stones

A Maiden Weeping

Season of Blood

The Deepest Grave

Traitor's Codex

Sword of Shadows

Historical Fiction

Though Heaven Fall

Roses in the Tempest

Native Spirit, writing as Anne Castell

Moonrisers

A Moonriser Werewolf Mystery

JERI WESTERSON

Tina,
Keep howling for
good books!

Dragua Press

Cover design by Mayhem Cover Creations

Book design by Jeri Westerson

ISBN: 978-0-9982238-2-7

No werewolves were harmed in the writing of this book. The publishers do not recommend the use of silver or wolfsbane when engaging with a werewolf. Always use caution.

Sign up for my newsletters at
BookeoftheHidden.com
JeriWesterson.com

Dragua Press
PO Box 799
Menifee, CA 92586

To Craig, not a wolfman…but something of a zexy beast anyway. Rawr.

AUTHOR'S NOTE

MOONRISERS is a spin-off mystery trilogy from the Booke of the Hidden series. It isn't absolutely essential to have read that first, but I'm sure it would enhance the experience. Plus, there might be a few spoilers ahead. In any case, happy reading! See it all at BOOKEoftheHIDDEN.com

CHAPTER ONE

℃

I RAN ON all fours. I could feel the cold air through my fur, the forest floor under my paws, the scent of damp and animals in the dark, and I just ran.

There was no other sensation like it. Such freedom. A sense of wildness like no other. Totally sick. The closest I could get to this feeling was hitting the backdoor of a wave on my board. Yeah, surfing was almost the same. Almost. But not quite.

It was okay to go with my wild side, wolfing out, because to repress it was just as bad as doing it without the wolfsbane potion, and I didn't want to do that because I might kill someone. And that was not me. Not the me I used to be anyway.

But that was back in Maine. Don't get me wrong. Maine was a beautiful state, but man, it wasn't California.

It took some time — months! — but I finally got up the courage to leave the east coast and return to SoCal.

I breathed in the salty air of the Pacific with relief, waved to the surfers along the sidewalk, and made the turn at Main toward my place. Bar, souvenir shop, bar, restaurant, taco shack, bar, coffee place, chain restaurant...two blocks up from Pacific Coast Highway and the pier, and there she was. My brick building. Surf City Boards then The Organic Leaf: Spice and Teas, my little home away from home...soon to be my home *below* my home again.

I turned down Walnut and went to the alley in the back and parked in front of the garage/storage. When I flipped off the engine and sat back, I listened to the sounds of Huntington Beach. Home.

I went into the shop by the backdoor and inhaled the scents of the old place. It was all dark wood and driftwood shelves. I had

1

squared glass cannisters for my tea and the herbs, all labeled nicely. One shelf was devoted to mugs, stainless-steel and plastic go-cups, and HB mugs. I had a few teapots—mostly modern because no one around here wanted the traditional type that my ex was able to sell in Maine—and there was even a glass case of colorful bowls, lighters, and pipes for the other kind of herb I didn't sell. Hey, you had to cater to all clientele, right?

Luis was there, opening a package of Royal Robe Oolong and funneling it into a cannister. His brown hair went to his shoulders, and he favored cowboy boots and skinny jeans, with black studs in his ears. Thank goodness the big cross he wore around his neck was on a gold chain, not silver.

Even Cam, his boyfriend, was there. He was only eighteen or nineteen but was totally trustworthy. Blond hair in a crazy cluster on top and flopping over his eyes, and shorter on the sides and back. He wore tees of every description, from bands to sayings to anime characters. He was a hodad; liked to hang on the beach with surfers but didn't ride. That was okay. He was still righteous.

I stood in the back for a long time, till Cam noticed. "Jeff!"

Luis swung around and saw me. "Hey!" They both converged, slapping hands with me.

"Homey," said Luis. "You're so pale. Don't they have sun in Maine?"

"No, man. It just never comes out there. I feel so out of it. Can't wait to get to my board."

"We missed you," said Cam. "Marlene. She's like someone's angry grandma."

"I appreciate your still hanging around."

"Oh, she's okay. She was just worried about you. Did you get Kylie back?"

I offered a smile. "Well, no. She's settled pretty well and has another guy in her life."

"That's harsh."

I shrugged. "Time to move on for the both of us. I'm chill with it."

There was a shuffling at the door and speak of the devil, an older woman wearing a gauzy long skirt with scarves and necklaces that you could barely see behind the bags she clutched in her arms, scuttled in. "Cam! Cam! Take these, please!"

"Yes, ma'am," said Cam, hurrying forward. He scooped the bags from her arms. Marlene, an *actual* hippy from back in the day with long gray hair, some in braids, stood there. She wore no make-up — didn't approve of it — but had colorful reading glasses perched on her nose. She wore tie-dyed skirts and gauzy tops and vests. She probably invented them. But once she caught sight of me, she screamed and threw herself forward, enclosing me in a hug. "You're back, you're back!" She hugged me and bawled.

"I'm okay. I told you. It was just a little problem and it was all cleared up. Doctor fixed me up." I had to give her some excuse for being gone so long. Told her some vague story about my health. After all, I was never sure if I was going to be able to return. By the looks on the guys' faces, she hadn't told them that part.

She pushed me back to look at me. "You're pale, but you look good," she said, really digging her nails into my arms. I peeled her away from me and gave her a solid-gold Jeff-smile. "I'm fine, Marlene. You've been a gem taking care of things."

"Don't ever leave me like that again. I'll have all the books for you to go over. I'm sure I made a hash of it. But Luis' been in charge of making sure the bills were paid. I just couldn't do it alone."

"Luis, my man!" I fist-bumped him.

"I could use a rest," she said, collapsing onto a bar stool at the counter.

"And you deserve one. Take a week off. Take two."

She clutched my cheek. "You are a dear boy. Your dad would have been proud."

It wasn't as if he was dead. He was in Boca, retired. But he didn't do a lot of communicating.

"You know I'd much rather grab my board and hit the waves, but...damn. Responsibility."

"You should go," said Luis. "Cam and I got this. Another few hours on our own isn't gonna make a difference."

For a second, I was ready to take him up. It had been six months! But I thought, no. But then, they kept telling me to and...it had been *six months*! "You guys. It's probably no good out there today."

"You'd better go," said Cam, "before you forget how."

"That's a challenge. Okay, an hour tops, then I'll be back to work."

I ran outside, dug my keys out of my pocket, and took the outside stairs up to the apartment. I cracked open the door and realized no one had been in the place since Marlene did me that solid of locking it up. It smelled musty, hot, and unused. I looked around. Boxes, furniture stacked up. I had no business running off. I had stuff to do. But when I spotted my board, all bets were off.

I slipped out of clothes and found the box with my wetsuit. It was March and still cold out there. I found some wax, grabbed it, and took the board down to my California ride, my tricked F-150, black with mag wheels. "Sheila, babe." I ran my hand over her fender. The boys kept it washed for me. It was good to see her again. Maybe I'd give Cam the Riviera, the car I bought in Maine.

I loaded in the board and drove it quick down to the beach. It was amazing how fast I could be, waxing, getting it together, and rushing out across the sand. Salty wind in my hair, yeah. I could smell the whole beach, from all the food places to the bathrooms. Damn. Wolf nose was sometimes a hinderance, but I ignored it, and when I dove for the first time in a long time into the cold Pacific, I wasn't even thinking about the wolf anymore.

I paddled out, feeling the surf. It was flat, really no waves to speak of. A few breakers but mostly against the pier. I still took it out, laying on the deck.

A seal popped its head up, staring at me not more than a few feet away. I smiled at it and waved. "Hey, dude. Can *you* tell me where the waves went?"

It bobbed in the water, flaring his nostrils at me. My nose was full of sea water and I couldn't smell him back, but he circled me, real close. I never saw a seal do that before. Maybe it smelled the wolf. It reminded me that seals used to be called sea wolves by sailors who never saw them before.

It dove, flipping its tail up with a splash.

Looking at the sky, I figured I should get back. I should check the inventory, make sure I had all the ingredients for the wolfsbane. I was loaded with potion, though, so even if we were out I could order it quick.

Reluctantly, I paddled back, let the tide take me in and I jumped off the board, tucked it under my arm, and headed for the parking lot.

There were a group of surfers by my truck. Two were blond, the other was dark-haired. They all had tats on their pecs and arms, and shiny gold necklaces and earrings. When I approached, waving, they all turned to me with a frown.

"'Sup?" I said, pushing my wet hair back.

"What's up is you surfing where you don't belong, brah," said the dark-haired guy.

I turned back toward the beach and looked up and down the coast. There weren't any coves in our stretch of the beach, not like Laguna or other spots. You had to have a feel for where the waves were, but it was all good, usually. That's why they call it "Surf City." I turned back and laughed. "Hey, I've only been gone six months, but I don't see your name on it around here."

I can't believe he tried to throw a punch at me. But the wolf instincts were strong in this one, and I grabbed his fist before it landed. I squeezed it just to let him know I wasn't a weakling, even though wolfing out gave me a more buff look I was rather pleased with.

He stared at me, and his Barney bros took a step back. I tossed the fist away from me. "Dudes, no one owns this stretch of sand."

"We do," said Dark-Hair, trying to hide the bruise I gave him by rubbing his fist with his hand. He was Mister Square Jaw, probably a babe magnet. I knew the type. Hell, I *am* the type.

I shook my head and nudged them out of the way with my board. "You'll have to take that somewhere else, gents. I'm not buying what you're selling."

"You'd better watch yourself. We surf here now."

"Who's *we*? You three?" I snorted as I stripped the wetsuit off.

"No. Just you be on the lookout for the Cutback Boys. We don't take any shit from no Bennys."

"Dude, I'm no Benny. I've lived here all my life. And I haven't heard of any 'Cutrate Boys'."

"Cut*back* Boys." Mister Jaw was trying to get up in my face again.

"Whatever." I toweled down and slipped on my shorts and shirt before pushing him away with the back of my hand. "I'm not looking for trouble. But I've surfed this beach since I was ten and I'm not going away anytime soon. So back off."

Dude looked like he was going to rush me…or Sheila, since he had his keys in his hand and I knew he was aching to mess up her paint job. I stared him down. Maybe my eyes glowed just that much, or he sensed the wolf in the background because he looked startled and backed away. They all did as I got in, started her up, and headed back.

"Bunch of losers," I muttered, shaking my head.

☾☾☾

WHEN I GOT back to the shop, I poked my head in. "Hey!" said Cam. "How was it?"

"Total shorepound. But it was good to be out there. Then I ran into some surf gang trying to impress me."

Luis and Cam looked at each other. "Not the Cutbacks?" said Luis.

"Yeah. Bunch of namers, trying to take the beach by the pier. By the *pier*! Where do they think they are, LA?"

"I wouldn't mess with them," said Cam. "They are bad news. There've been some break-ins along Main. The police haven't done anything, but everyone knows it's them."

My hackles were up, just the hairs on the back of my neck, but the rest wanted to sprout. "Did they bust in here?"

"No, man," said Luis. "We got cameras up now. But I still wouldn't mess with them."

"If they don't mess with me, I won't mess with them." Or my shop. Nothing was as important as my shop these days, unless it was the people in it. "Look," I said, changing the subject, "I gotta sort out my stuff upstairs. Groceries, that kind of stuff."

"Sure, Jeff. No problem."

"Thanks. Catch you later."

I stumped up the stairs, not happy at all with these surf bastards as well as my having to get organized...again.

My ex took her stuff which I guess wasn't much. I was left with a beat-up dresser, a mattress with no frame—since she took that—and so I aired out the sheets. I found a pillow, made the bed, and covered it with my old eternal-tree coverlet.

I put the dishes—what I had, anyway—in the cupboards. Had a flatscreen, an X-box, an amp and that was kind of it. The fridge was plugged in and it hummed along but it smelled inside so I cleaned that, and then left to get some food. Milk, cereal, meat—lots of meat—eggs, cheese, some frozen pizzas, and beer.

I was stocked for now, and by then it was closing time. The boys locked the place and I retreated to the back room to look at the books with a tall mug of masala chai. Just as I thought, Marlene had made some dubious purchases, but my boys seemed to try to fix it. They left some Post-Its with explanations. We were fine for inventory, in the black this month, and doing okay. The other apartment upstairs was rented so I had income from that. I owed Marlene a lot for taking care of it all. I wondered what would make a good gift for an old lady.

I switched off the light and the place fell to darkness. It didn't matter because I could still see just fine. Wolf vision. But when I got to the backroom and the door, I stopped.

Hair sprouted on the back of my neck suddenly. I listened and my ears started to grow, making my hearing sharper, more defined.

7

Something was snuffling outside my back door. I felt it. Heard it. Who...*what* was it? My heart pounded and I slowly and carefully reached for the knob, my hand halfway from human to paw. In a flash, I twisted it and threw it open.

Nothing was there. But I could smell them. They *were* there. Two of them. *Just* been there and gone.

Two...werewolves. "Oh my God." I'd hoped this would happen and I'd never been sure it could be true. But there it was.

Bracing myself against the doorframe, I sniffed again, just tasting the flavor of their scent at the back of my throat, turning it over and over. Two males. Two real, live...*wolfmen*.

For the first time in my life...well, since the First Werewolf bit me, that is...I knew I wasn't alone. There were more. And they were here. Right here in Huntington Beach.

And they knew *I* was here.

I didn't even stop to think it over. I shed my clothes and shifted. Blond-furred surfer wolf. As a wolf and standing on all four paws, I sniffed the air for their scent, caught it, and took off.

CHAPTER TWO

℃

THE SIDEWALK UNDER my pads felt weird, foreign. I wasn't used to concrete. The smells were full of the beach and its shops and restaurants. It wasn't the dank earth of Maine. It wasn't the pine forests. It was a different forest of concrete, palm trees, eucalyptus, and a ton of other perennials I didn't know the names of, but I could sure smell them.

I lifted my head, sniffing the breeze, following the invisible trail of the evidence of their existence. I might have yipped a little, jumped in the air, sort of like kicking up your heels. It was the most exciting thing to *ever* happen to me. Like...maybe when I was ten and learned to be one with the board and hit an aerial for the first time. I had felt like I was master of the universe, that I could do anything. And it was like that again. Werewolves, man! Right outside my door!

I could smell just a whiff of their scents like an elusive memory, like *hearing* a color. It was hard to describe, hard to put into words. If I could explain it in werewolf talk it would make perfect sense. But in people talk? It lacked...precision.

When I shoved my snout near the sidewalk, I could pick it up even better. Like a bloodhound, I followed it across the asphalt and I pulled up short as a car screeched to a stop in front of me. I looked up wide-eyed right into the headlights and then I bounded onto the sidewalk and down an alley. I loped down that alleyway all the way to the pavement strand that followed the shore, over the low wall that separated sidewalk from beach, and ran along the cold sand. It was weird between my paws, not at all like the feel of it between my human toes because of the fur. Once I got to the surf, I lost the scent...just as they intended. I instinctively knew that. They wanted to ditch me. Maybe they were scared. Maybe they thought I was here to take over their pack. Maybe they thought I was the enemy.

Maybe...they were *my* enemy.

I didn't like the feel of that thought. I just imagined all werewolves were like me. Happy to wolf, but happy to have that human life too. And something else. They smelled...off. Like they weren't taking wolfsbane. I shivered at the idea. I knew what it was like not to. I thought I could go without it and tried to in my early days wolfing out. But it was bad. Worse than bad. I almost attacked my ex, Kylie. I couldn't even remember who she was. All that consumed me was the smell of blood and how I wanted more of it. And if these weredudes didn't have Wiccans like Doc or Seraphina to make wolfsbane for them, didn't even know about it, they had to be killing people.

Shit, I whispered in my head. That was not good at all. I never even thought of that.

Whoa, dude. Hold up. Maybe they're cool. Just cautious. Do you blame them? I didn't. It had to be scary to suddenly smell a new wolf in town. *Chill, Jeff. Just...be chill.* I didn't have any doubt I'd meet them soon. Just not tonight. Damn. And I'd really been looking forward to it. Like...a *lot*.

I stood there sniffing for a while. Even paced up and down the surf line, foam cresting over my paws, wetting them. Nothing.

Damn.

So they knew I was here. But, with a resurgence of excitement burning in my chest, now I knew *they* were here.

☾☾☾

I COULD BARELY sleep. Werewolves. They *were* here. I was going to find them. It was going to be easier than I thought.

Maybe I should have tried harder, but I knew it could wait. They'd be back, probably, or *I* could find *them* somehow.

I lay awake on top of the coverlet almost all night...till I did fall asleep, because I woke somewhere around seven. I fixed myself steak and eggs. There was a time when I only ate vegetarian, but those days were gone. I was on full red meat status now. That was going to be weird in front of my crew. I wondered what I was going to tell them.

I got dressed, excited to get back to the shop. But looking around at my place, I had to get rid of the boxes and get some grown-up furniture, since I'd had that stuff since college. My ex was the one who bought the bed frame, and now my mattress was on the floor. If I was going to get back into the romance game, a thirty-year-old dude with a mattress on the floor was not going to cut it.

"No use wondering." It was time to get to work. I locked my door and headed down the stairs to the shop. I was the first one there. It was cool being home again, smelling the competing aromas of herbs and varying teas. And with wolf senses it became all the keener in my nose.

I was alone for now, just running my hands over the shelves — nicely dusted. Good one, boys. I unlocked the safe, got out the money for the register, and got it all ready. The water was on automatic heat up, so I prepared some ginger spice and some formosa oolong for samples. My place. Yeah, it was good to be home.

By the time the teas were ready, I unlocked the front door and waited for my clientele. I put on some tunes. I liked a little hip-hop to jazz up the place and I felt like cutting some moves. I gave a twirl and did a little of the strike, and then a two-step hip-hop.

Of course, that's when she walked in.

I heard the bell above the door jangle and turned in time to see *the* prettiest woman to walk in. She was African American, with hair shorn close to her scalp, big hoop earrings, and wearing some sort of gauzy, flowy, brightly-colored short dress that showed off her gorgeously long legs. I think my mouth fell open as I stood there like a donk before I got my act together. I moved to the counter and messed with some stuff there, all nonchalant. She was wearing strong perfume. Usually I didn't much like it, especially now that my nose was so keen, but it was like sandalwood, and on

11

her, I liked it. "Hey there," I said, casual as I could. "Can I help you with anything? Would you like a sample of our brew?"

She raised her eyes to me — dark brown, amazing — and looked me over. 'Yes, the ginger, if that's okay."

She had a Jamaican accent or something. I might have donked out again before I scrambled to the samovar and got her a little paper cup.

"Here you go. It's our very own ginger spice, one of the teas we blend ourselves."

She sipped and gazed at me from under her long lashes. I was realizing it had been a long time for old Jeff, girl-wise. And she was *hot*. The accent sounded good to me, too.

"So...I can tell you're not from around here. Where are you from?" I winced a little. I was so out of practice.

She looked at me curiously, cocking her head to one side. "San Fernando Valley."

I froze for half a second and then laughed. "I meant...before that. They don't have that wicked accent in the Valley."

She smiled, a thing to behold. "Oh. *That*." He eyes were shaded, amused. She was probably asked that a lot. Instead of being rude about it, she squared with me and said, "They don't have beaches in the Valley either. That's what brought me here. I'm originally from Haiti."

"Cool," I blurted, not really knowing what else to say. I didn't know anything about Haiti except, vaguely, something about an earthquake?

"Yes. It is...cool," she said. "But only in the sense of being interesting. Because it is very hot there. Not like these beaches in Cali."

"Oh, miss, no one from southern California ever calls it 'Cali'. If you want to sound like a native, you gotta call it SoCal."

That smile again. "I shall."

"Now, besides my scintillating conversation that sounds like I'm in the third grade, is there anything particular I can help you with? I'm Jeff, by the way."

"Jeff." When she said it, it sounded exotic. Until she said her own name; "I'm Nadège," in a slightly French-sounding pronunciation, like "Na-DEZH".

"Well, welcome to my little shop, Nadège."

"Your shop?"

"Yeah, she's all mine. I scour the world for the best, most interesting teas, and hard-to-find herbs and spices."

"I am most interested in your herbs. You see...I belong to a coven of sorts," she said carefully. She seemed to be waiting for the usual eye-rolling. But not here, not anymore.

"Oh cool. I have friends in a Wiccan coven in Maine. They're all straight up dudes."

"They are all men?"

"Naw. In California, anyone is a 'dude.' It was a coven of men and women. And they know their stuff."

"So you were not a part of their coven?"

"No, just a friend of the family, so to speak. Anything you guys need, you just let me know. I can order a lot of stuff, too." She peered over my shoulder at the cannisters. I stepped out of the way. "Be my guest. Look at what we've got. Feel free to open the cannisters and take a whiff of the merchandise. All high quality here."

I let her browse. We had plenty of Wiccans and pagans of all stripes come through over the years. Never much thought about it. But now that I saw how it all worked for real, I had a lot more respect.

I tried not to stare, but man! Even the way she moved was like a slow dance. "Like I said, I can special order anything you don't see. Anything that's important to your particular form of witchcraft or Wiccan."

"Actually...we practice Voodoo. It's not so much a coven as a group of practitioners."

I might have frozen, blinking at her. I was a little like *whoa*. I had seen a lot of stuff back in Maine. Stuff I'd rather forget I saw, to tell you the truth. But being a supernatural now myself...well. Who was I to judge?

"I've, uh, never encountered anyone who did real Voodoo. That's...cool. I guess." Stuff was going through my mind, like sacrifices. Chickens, maybe, but still. Blood sacrifices were a no-no from my experience.

She must have seen the change in my demeanor and frowned. "It's not as scary as it sounds. I know you must have misconceptions about it."

"Oh, sure. Probably. I mean, I'm thinking of all the movies I've seen, for sure."

"*Bon sang*," she muttered. "It's not like the movies," she said maybe harsher than she wanted to. She sucked on her lip — a pretty darned luscious lip, too — and sighed. "Sorry. People always think they know what it is like and it isn't. It's probably like any other kind of coven."

"Oh, no problem. Like I said, it's your thing. No judgments here." But even saying "no judgments" sort of sounded like a judgment to me. "Can we just rewind? I'd love to help you out with whatever you and your, uh, practitioners need."

"Yes, thank you. I have a list." She pulled it out of the pocket of her dress and unfolded it. I offered to take it but she declined.

"It's written in Creole. I'll have to translate."

She read it out loud and I bagged up some common herbs and some of my more exotic. When I rang her up she looked at me steadily. "Maybe you should come to one of our meetings and you can see for yourself."

I donked again, looking at her. She was *really* gorgeous. *Wake up, Jeff!* "Yeah, that would be awesome."

She handed me a card with her name — Nadège Toussaint — and her Instagram handle and phone number on it. "We're meeting tonight. Seven o'clock. Come and see. I'll text you the address."

"Oh...yeah." I grabbed a business card and scribbled my cell on it. "Please do."

She took the bag, gave me a smile that I could probably live on, and left the shop.

I was still staring at the card when Luis showed up.

"Jeff, my man. What are you doing?"

How long had I been staring at that card? "Dude, fine."

"So we'll see you today actually working?"

"Brah." I looked away a little sheepishly. I did ditch them yesterday for surfing, but a man's gotta do what a man's gotta do. "I'm all in today. No playing hooky. Looks like the inventory is all caught up. There are just a few things I want to order." I handed him my list. Some of the ingredients I'd need for wolfsbane.

He looked it over. "Weird," he muttered. "Hey, it's your shop." He wandered around the counter to hit the computer.

"Hey, Luis. What do you know about any local covens?"

He didn't bother looking up from the keyboard. "Not much. I don't deal with the witches."

"There was just this gorgeous woman in today—"

"Jeff Chase is back," he said with a wide smile.

"Yeah," I chuckled. "Anyway, she's with a Voodoo coven..."

He looked up at that. "Voodoo? Dude, that's out there, isn't it?"

I shrugged. "Not any more than any other kind of coven."

"That sounds dark to me."

"Naw, I'm sure it's just like the others." But was it? Well, I was gonna find out tonight.

☾☾☾

CAM ARRIVED, SMOOCHED Luis just to say hello, and everything was back to business. People came in to shop; ladies in short dresses and flip flops, guys looking for the other kind of herb but bought some pipes anyway, the usual customers who were glad to see me again.

And all the while, my mind was only half on it. I tried to whiff any scent of wolf. I secretly sniffed the customers, snuck outside now and again, and hung in the window, nosing the screen.

"Hey, Jeff," said Cam, startling me.

"Yeah?"

"I don't have a price on this."

It was a little ceramic plate made by a local artist. I had a few pieces like that in the shop. Gave it character. "You'll have to look it up."

"It's for this gentleman." He thumbed behind him.

I glanced his way as I headed for the counter. When I caught the guy's eye, I stopped dead. There was something about his eyes. Something familiar, different...

He stepped toward me and finally stopped like inches from me. We were almost nose to nose and his eyes were just staring into mine. Ordinarily, someone in my personal space freaked me, but this time... I held my breath. Because I smelled...wolf.

CHAPTER THREE

❧

WE JUST STOOD there staring. I wanted to say something. I wanted to ask a million questions, but for some reason—like I was under a spell—I couldn't. He was tall, with wild dark hair but styled that way. He was tan and wore some designer black, silk T-shirt and jeans. I was not into dudes at *all* but if I were, I'd be into *him*, because he just exuded this magnetism and strength. I could tell that Luis *and* Cam were both staring at him with a little too much interest.

"Did...did you get that price, Luis?" I asked over my shoulder, never losing eye contact.

"What? Oh yeah. It's, uh...forty-eight bucks."

We all seemed to gaze at him expectantly.

"I'll take it," he said, finally. "Are you the manager here?" he asked me.

"Yeah. And owner. Jeff. Jeff Chase." I tried to smile but I don't think it came out that way.

He handed his credit card over to Luis while we still locked eyes. "Have you owned this store long, Mr. Chase?"

"Uh...yeah. For something like six years. I created this place."

"I've never seen you here before."

"I've been away. Almost half a year."

One side of his mouth smiled. "That explains it." He didn't clarify that but just signed the card reader and took his bag.

"See you around," he said, before he finally turned away and left the shop.

"He was totally into you," breathed Cam. "If you were gay, you would have dropped trou right there."

That woke me from my stupor. "Cam, dude!" I shook my head. "I would *not*."

"You totally would have."

He and Luis laughed. I spun, grabbing the register receipt. The name at the top read, Jesse Vargar. Ignoring their, "Where are you goings?" I hit the door and ran.

I looked to the left and the right, didn't see him. I put my nose to work instead. There! That way.

The sidewalks were crowded with people. In March, it was still a little foggy along the coast in the mornings, but that would burn off. It was supposed to be warm today in HB, and already the cyclists with the fat tires were out, the dudes in shorts and sunglasses, the babes in short shorts—bless them—all heading toward the shore. But for once, I didn't care about any of that. I needed to find the guy that smelled like dark/musk/earth.

Up ahead, he was walking, just moving through the people in long even strides. My blood was screaming in my head. I wanted to shift so badly. I kept opening and closing my hands as they morphed just the tiniest bit from nail to claw and back again. It hurt but felt good too, like stretching an aching muscle.

The scent was like a pathway floating above the sidewalk. If it had a color I'd call it green, like a mist. Like a snaking, trailing organic cloud.

I finally caught up to him, about to reach for his shoulder when he spun, grabbed my wrist, and held it away from him. We stared again.

Breathlessly, I said, "You gotta tell me."

He looked me up and down and let me go. "I don't have to tell you anything."

"Come on, man. I know why you came to my shop."

"Do you?" He lifted the bag. "I like artistic knick-knacks."

I wanted to swat it out of his hand, let it shatter on the ground. "Sure you do," I gritted out.

He bared his teeth, not in a smile. He had canines but they weren't particularly long. Mine began to grow involuntarily. I covered my mouth with my hand. When he saw that, he seemed to sneer in disgust. And then he just turned and walked away.

I stood there. I wanted to go after him…but couldn't. I *hated* that look he gave me. Like I was the worst. The stupidest. And I felt like it.

I let him go. I had no choice. And when I looked down at my arm, the one he'd grabbed, the wrist was all dark and bruised.

☾☾☾

I GOT BACK to the shop, rubbing my wrist. Cam and Luis gave me a hard time, joking that that guy had turned me gay. I laughed with them, but it didn't reach my head. Because that guy was a werewolf…but also more than that. What kind of werewolf *was* he? He'd had me in a thrall, like I was unable to look away or follow him or…anything. I had thought a werewolf was a werewolf was a werewolf. I guessed that wasn't true.

And all *I* had was his name.

I slipped behind the counter and got on the computer. I made sure my boys were doing other stuff — making tea, straightening shelves, restocking — while I Googled werewolves.

Same old stuff I'd seen before. I was getting nowhere. I stared into the distance and got an idea. Were there any occult shops in town? A place that might have books and people that knew stuff? I Googled that and found one. Starlight Occult Shop. It was only two blocks away.

I flew out the door before anyone could ask me.

I found it next to a smoothie place, just one of those micro shops like a shoebox, its façade covered in dark wood, with a metal sign with the name Starlight Occult Shop cut out of it and blue light behind. In the window was a display of Ouija boards, a fake raven, a plastic skull, an array of crystals, and some old books that reminded me of the Booke of the Hidden…which kind of creeped me out.

I went in and was immediately accosted by the strong scent of patchouli. It was what I expected; crystals and crystal balls, candles, incense, black light posters, silver daggers and even some axes, jewelry, dragon and fairy statuettes, various kinds of tarot cards in a glass case, and lots of books in a regiment of bookcases. I headed straight for the books and started running my finger down the spines, looking for supernatural beasts when I almost ran into a fairy-like girl in a midriff peasant blouse. The pale skin of her stomach shone with a bright ring in her navel, and she wore her blonde hair parted in the middle, straight, and down past her bare shoulders. Her low-rise jeans were embroidered with vines and flowers, and her tattoos of Celtic designs were just peeking above the waistband.

"My name is Bliss. Can I help you?"

"Hey, Bliss." I turned on the charm. No harm in it, and it usually got me extra service. "How's it going? You know, I'm looking for some real particular information. Looking for stuff about—" And then I suddenly realized how stupid that would sound. I mean, it didn't look like a dusty library of really old books. Just all the new stuff that probably didn't have any better info than the internet. "Uh…about…m-mythical creatures…and stuff."

I winced. *Lame, Jeff. Very lame. Good one.*

She flitted away and gave a Vanna White wave toward a row of books. "Here's what we have on mythical creatures. Are you interested in unicorns? We have a whole section over here."

"Actually…Bliss…" I got in close, talking softly. "I'm really only looking for stuff about…werewolves. That kind of thing."

She frowned. Her eyebrows were very light, almost non-existent. "I don't think we have any on them specifically. Let me ask Lauren."

"No, you don't have to do that…"

"LAUR-en!" she cried, as if the store were twice the size. "Lauren! Hi, this guy wants to see books on werewolves."

My face burned. I knew it was red with embarrassment but I made myself turn around.

Lauren seemed slightly Hispanic and she was probably about my age. Her brown hair was pulled back in a loose ponytail with a lavender scrunchie, and she wore a simple tie-dyed T-shirt and jeans, with some Celtic knot earrings. She looked like the kind of sensible person I needed to confide in, but she also looked like a person who would — rightfully — laugh me out of the store.

My palms began to sweat and I rubbed them down my shorts. "Uh...you know what? Never mind. I'll just browse a little." And get the hell out of there as soon as I could.

Bliss wandered blissfully away, but Lauren cocked her head at me. I turned away from her scrutiny, face still blazing, and pretended to look interested in the books. How long did I need to hang there before I could make my escape? I had just about decided that enough was enough when I spun around and there she was.

She was still cocking her head at me. Quietly, she said, "Are you all right?"

"Yeah! Totally fine."

"Are you really interested in werewolves? It's an odd thing to —"

"You know, just...it was something I...I..." It was past time to leave. I glanced toward the exit and was about to jam when she caught my arm. She looked down at the bruises and I yanked my arm away.

"You're that guy who owns the tea shop on Main, aren't you?"

Caught. Should I be rude and just run? Nope, cause she knew where I worked. Shit. "Um...yeah. I'm...Jeff."

"Hi, Jeff. I'm Lauren Castro. This is my shop. I send a lot of business your way."

"No kidding? Well...thanks."

"No problem. I should have introduced myself a long time ago. I bet we get a lot of cross-traffic."

I was still sweating but not as bad. I wiped the back of my neck, and secretly rubbed it off on my shorts. "I bet we do. Covens and all."

"Oh, yes. I deal with a lot of covens. I have some Wicca books."

"Got any on Voodoo?"

"I do. From what country?"

"Uh…" Was there a difference?

She made her way over to the next aisle and down to a bookshelf. I had no choice but to follow her. If I ran out of the store now, she'd only remember me as that douchey guy who owned a tea shop.

"You see," she went on, "there are different types of Voodoo depending on the country of origin. West African countries, the Caribbean, Haiti…"

"The last one. Haiti."

"Ah." She took down a book with a skull on the cover. "This one deals with the culture and history. It talks about the rituals too."

I took it from her and turned a few pages, looking at the table of contents: *What is Vodou? How to make a mojo bag; Aphrodisiac Incense…* "That seems to cover a lot."

"It's a pretty good general book on the subject. But…you wanted one on werewolves."

There went those hot cheeks again. I clutched the book. "Yeah, I just…I was watching some movies and then someone, a friend of mine, mentioned all these legends and I kind of wanted to know more…"

She looked out to her shop with its glittering wares and strange items. "More than the internet you mean? I don't have any for sale, but I do have some research books I keep in the back. I've been working on my Master's thesis in cultural anthropology, specializing in totems and tribal mythologies."

Maybe she could be my Girl-Who-Knew-All-the-Answers. I perked up. "I'd love to see some of your research books." I turned on the Jeff charm and my high wattage smile. A smile on a blue-eyed blond guy never seemed to fail.

Now it was her turn to blush. "Come on back, then."

The back of the shop was like any other, including my own. Lots of shelves, boxes, general chaos, a watercooler, microwave, bathroom, table and chairs all crammed into a tiny space. But it also had some shelves filled with the kind of books my ex's coven had; old, leather-bound monstrosities. The kind you'd find in some rich guy's library, or museum.

She suddenly turned to me. "Are you serious? Do you really want to look it up? I mean, you seem kind of…nervous."

"Nervous? I'm not nervous," I said, totally unchill and nervous.

She raised her brows but didn't look at me. "I own this occult shop and I believe in a lot of things, but not everything I sell. Yes, I'm pagan, and I have practiced a personal form of Wicca, but not with a coven. And…I mean, let's face it, some of this stuff is a little off-kilter and over the top. But I do find it interesting, and I'm always discovering more as I go in search of the next thing I need in the shop…or for my research."

I gestured toward her books. They did remind me a lot of Doc's. "So you like to research?"

"Yes, I think it's fascinating. Most of it is pure mythology and you can tell by the culture and the historical setting just where some of these myths came from, but I have to say, some of these texts, though old, are pretty…well. Detailed. As if the people experienced it. Well, they obviously experienced *something*. Just what, I'm not sure."

I decided to be straight with her. Not *that* straight, but upfront. "Since you're almost a master in this, the legends…I'd be genuinely interested in knowing more. I'm not writing a book or anything, but it seems pretty interesting."

She nodded. It didn't seem to faze her, my not giving her a good excuse. I guess she'd seen a lot. Maybe not as much as I had. But owning a shop like this must bring them in. And great! Now I was one of *them*.

Except that she seemed as if she enjoyed sharing. I mean, I got it. It was like a really great day of surfing. You like to tell your friends about it, relive it, tell the tales. But not everyone is a surfer.

Looking over her books, she took down an old one. Looked like it was falling apart. She held it together long enough to place it on the small table. There were ribbons as markers, and she carefully thumbed through those pages before she found the right ribbon.

"This is a part about lycanthropy. It's written in French, from the eighteenth century. It's about a village that was terrorized by what they believed was a werewolf and in fact, the king of France sent hunters to kill it. It's a well-known case, the Beast of Gévaudan. I can translate but I'm a bit rusty."

She slid into one of the chairs and pulled the open book toward her. She followed the text with her finger. I sat in the other chair. I touched the paper and could feel the indentations of the lettering on the printed pages. She read haltingly, changing words as she translated, shaking her head a bit in frustration:

"In the summer of 1754, the young maid, Janne Boulet, was killed most foully near the village of Les Hubacs near the town of Langogne, in the eastern part of Gévaudan... Anyway, it goes on to tell the details of the many attacks."

"I know about all that, attacks and stuff." Truth was, I didn't want to dwell. I had had a taste of that, and it was like a stone in the pit of my stomach. I never wanted to feel that again. "What I was interested in knowing was, what *kind* of werewolves there are. I mean, are there kinds that sort of enthrall others? Like a vampire is supposed to do?"

She was looking at me strangely. And I was thinking, *Now you've done it, Jeff.* But she didn't kick me out or start laughing. She just studied me. Not that she would, in her wildest dreams think *I* was a werewolf. I was just a guy who liked werewolf movies for all she knew.

I started picking at my nail under the table.

She turned the pages, looking for the passage she wanted. "There are all kinds. In Haiti, for instance, since you're interested in Haitian Voodoo, there's *jé-rouges,* 'red eyes' and *loup-garou.* They're actually men, Voodoo sorcerers who cover themselves with a wolfskin and magically change. They're akin to Skinwalkers. They can become these creatures but as soon as they remove the skin, they are back to normal. But while they are transformed, they drink the blood of their victims to weaken them, and at night they are known to steal children. They still believe this in Haiti, in fact, and even recently they've hunted these 'werewolves' down and lynched them."

My hand went to my neck and then I dropped it in my lap. I cleared my suddenly tight throat. "They do?"

"Yeah, but mostly these child-stealers are actually selling these kids into slavery. They're not werewolves. So more power to the hangman, I say."

"So even today they believe this? About werewolves? Why don't they believe these are slavers?"

"The belief is so ingrained in the culture. It's a tough thing." She flipped some pages, carefully. "But I remember a passage somewhere here...Let me see...yes. This is it. It's interesting because I had never heard about it before until I stumbled on it. Like you said, I only thought it was a vampire thing, at least in books and movies. But this says," she tapped the page, "that the head of a pack can act very much like that, being mesmerizing. Especially one who was raised as a werewolf from childhood."

"Wait. Someone bit a kid?" Then I calmed it down again. *Jeff, this is supposed to be mythology. Don't scare the lady into thinking you're a 9-1-1 call.*

"That's what it says. And if that child grows up to become a leader of his own pack — we don't say 'alpha' anymore, because we now know there is no such things as alpha males — he seems to have some sort of thrall over them."

"No alphas? I thought that was a, you know, scientific thing."

She shook her head, and the ponytail whipped back and forth. "A scientist named Rudolph Schenkel studied wolves captive in a zoo in the late 40s, never researching wild wolf behavior, and the notion stuck. For decades. But more recent work has revealed that wolves live in families with two parents and cubs...with an assortment of siblings. There's no fight for dominance of the pack from younger cubs. It's just cubs growing up, finding other wandering wolves, and forming new packs. No weird lupin social order. A male seeks out a female to mate with, that's all."

But how did that shake out with werewolves?

"Anyway," she went on, "with werewolves it has to be different." I froze. Did she read my mind? Did I say it out loud?

"These werewolf leaders can make new werewolves by biting people, right?" she went on. "Not the same as forming a pack from their own children, though I suppose that might also work. These that have been werewolves since they were children and who bite others, can mesmerize and make others do their will. Not just by exerting the usual kind of violent power, but this other, ineffable one. A...supernatural one. It's weird, isn't it?"

"It sure was," I muttered, staring at the page. When I realized what I'd said, I slowly looked up. She was looking at me intently, but didn't say anything.

"What about the *First* Werewolf?" I asked, because that was the dude that bit *me*. And I wanted to know if it would mess me up even more than normal...whatever "normal" was these days.

"The first one? Like, the first *ever* to turn into a werewolf? That would be Lycoan the King of Arcadia. The poet Ovid tells about this first mention of a werewolf in western culture. As the story goes, Zeus, the king of the gods, is invited to dinner by King Lycoan and Lycoan serves him human flesh, just to brag about how powerful he is. But Zeus is not impressed and is, in fact, pretty pissed off at Lycoan's lack of empathy—which is a lot coming from Zeus. Anyway, Zeus throws a thunderbolt and changes Lycoan into a wolfbeast with a taste for human flesh. So that's the oldest mention."

"Lycoan. Like 'Lycan', someone who suffers from lycanthropy?"

"That's the root of the word. A lot of the Greek words we use are based on characters from mythology. Like echo...and narcissist."

"I seem to remember that from school. So Lycoan was the First Werewolf."

"If you believe the mythology." She gently closed the book, picked it up by holding it to her chest, and returned it to the bookshelf. "Of course, every culture has its own version. Skinwalkers can be found in Navajo culture, for instance, but the

Greeks wrote it down first, I guess." She turned. "Was that the kind of thing you were looking for?"

"Yeah. Thanks. I mean, really. Thank you. You know a lot. You didn't have to show me your books. Looks like a serious collection."

Suddenly she smiled. "You should see my house." Then she blushed again, thinking she was giving me the come on. I didn't mind.

I smiled back. "I'll bet."

She shut me down with, "Out of curiosity, why are you so intent on finding out about werewolves? Do you...believe in them?"

It took me a second to look all amazed and offended. "Seriously? *No!* Of course not. Werewolves?" I forced a laugh.

She shrugged. "It's just that I've interviewed a few people for my thesis. Some scholars who think that lycanthropy might be a real thing, in a sense. Not exactly people turning into a wolf, that is, but that the person *thinks* they can. They call that 'werewolf syndrome', or clinical lycanthropy. So it's not *so* unusual to run into people who believe in it. And don't forget about the wolfboys in the freakshows, who have hypertrichosis, abnormal hair growth, so they *look* like what we expect a wolfman to look like."

I didn't know what to say to that. She was giving me an in, but there was no way I was biting. I stood there like an idiot, just staring instead. Until I woke myself, and fingered the book I was still holding. "Boy, you've really done your research."

"Of course." She leaned against a bookshelf, just looking at me until she blushed again and looked down at her feet. "I'm sorry. I went off on it, didn't I? I guess I just really love my subject matter."

I guess I would really make her day if I told her. But this just wasn't her day.

"So I'll, uh, get this book on Voodoo."

Subject successfully changed. She smiled. "Sure. Anything else?"

We walked through the doorway and into the shop again toward the register. Bliss was hanging crystals on a small tree branch mounted on a pedestal. "Hey, Lauren." She picked up a box and opened it, shoving it toward us. "We just got these silver pendants in. What shall I do with them?"

I should have been prepared in a place like that. I'd seen the jewelry as I came in. But when my eyes caught the glint of the silver I jerked back, nearly running into Lauren. I spun around, making sure I hadn't stepped on her. "I'm sorry! Are you okay?"

"No problem." But that eyeing-narrowing thing she was doing was more overt.

Thanks for the silver in my face, Bliss!

She rang me up—with a discount—and I gave her a business card and told her she could get the company discount in my shop, too. That drew a smile and she handed over the book in a thin paper bag. "I'll definitely check it out. I haven't seen you around recently."

"Oh, I was out of town for about six months. Dealing with some...issues. Back now, though." I offered a low wattage smile, and she took it well.

I leaned into her, talking low. "Do you know anything about a local Voodoo coven?"

Her eyes flicked to the bag with an "I get it now" look to them. "I have *heard* of them, but I don't personally know any of them."

"Do you think it's straight up? You know. Not bad magic or anything like that?"

She shrugged. "I don't know. Sorry. That's not my area of expertise. But that book should help you to understand what they're practicing."

"It's just that...I'm going over tonight to sit in on a meeting."

"How exciting for you." She looked genuinely intrigued. "But if things get too weird for you, you shouldn't be afraid to just leave. Be polite, of course, but don't stay if you're uncomfortable."

"That's good advice." I nodded, thinking. I wasn't scared or anything. My wolf helped me with that. There wasn't much I was afraid of these days, having been faced with angry gods, zombies, demons, and a host of other monsters—just a slice of what I'd already seen. But I was just a little worried about *what* I'd see tonight.

I huffed a laugh. "Okay. Thanks. You've been more than helpful."

She looked like she wanted to say something, but pressed her lips together and stayed quiet instead. I waved my good-byes and left.

Clutching the bag, I knew I had some homework to do. Should I call the coven in Maine? No, I couldn't depend on them anymore. I was my own wolf, uh, man now. That's why I left Maine, right? To learn to be on my own again? I thought about my wolfsbane stash and how many more days it would last before I needed to make more. Life was different now. Very different.

But even as I walked back to Main Street, there was a wisp in the air, just the tail-end of wolf. Could it be that I was being followed?

I looked back, but no one seemed to be paying attention to me.

Yeah. This new life was gonna be fun.

🌙🌙🌙

I GOT BACK to the shop and had to explain where I had been. So I told them about the occult shop.

"Hey," said Luis. "Maybe we should get together with them to do a joint sale or something. Coupons you can use in both shops. Get some of that crossover business." Ever the entrepreneur.

"That's not a bad idea," I told him. "I should talk to them again and maybe do a little display with their business cards, and they could do one of ours in their shop."

"We already get our share of weirdos coming in here," said Cam.

"They aren't 'weirdos', Cameron," said Marlene, striding in. "They are our clientele." She said it like "CLEE-n-tell." "It's the weird ones who keep coming back."

"Marlene," I said sternly. "I thought I told you to take a couple of weeks off."

"Yes, I heard you. I just wanted to make sure my boys were all right." She took my face in one of her hands, squinching up my cheeks. She looked over the top of her reading glasses at me. "Are you okay? You look a little peaked. Are you sure you were okay to travel back home?"

I slid out of her pretty tight grip, glancing at my boys. "Yeah, Marlene, I'm fine."

"Hey," said Luis, coming over. "I thought you were just trying to get Kylie back."

"I was—"

"But he discovered a blood problem," said Marlene, unhelpfully.

"What?" He put down the tea cannister he had been filling. He grabbed my arm and looked me up and down. "Dude, are you okay?" He noticed the bruises on my wrist.

"I'm fine," I said, snatching my arm back. Damn, I felt awful lying to them. But then again, I had to lie to them. There was no way I could tell them the truth about me. "I got some great medical care and some meds and I'm fully recovered. I just...didn't want to mention it."

"I'm sorry, Jeff," said Marlene. "I thought you'd told them."

"The fewer people who knew the better. But I'm fine now. So...go back to what you were doing." I liked attention, but not this kind. Luis watched me like I was made out of glass or something, and Cam was still standing there with his mouth open. "I'm...gonna...check something," I said, and left out the back door. But as soon as I'd gone, I realized that they must think I was trying to hide some big bad disease from them. Shit. Well, I guess I was. A bad case of real live lycanthropy.

☾☾☾

I WAS IN the Tequila Tiki, a place with an odd mash-up of Mexican food and Hawaiian a few doors down from mine, eating a bloody teriyaki burger and having a brew. I sat at the bar where Dave, the bartender, made sure I was taken care of without a lot of chit-chat. That's what I liked about Dave. He was all work. Though he did give me the eye at the burger order. He was used to the vegetarian Jeff. He still didn't say anything.

I thumbed through the Voodoo book and scanned the pages. Pretty interesting stuff and very different from the Maine coven way of doing things. I was a little excited about tonight, but cautious. Lauren had told me to leave if it was too weird for me. But she didn't know what weird could be. I certainly did.

The TV above the bar was playing the local news when I saw it. I jolted from my stool and leaned against the bar. "Dave! Turn it up."

He looked at me only a moment before he reached for the remote and upped the volume. The local news anchor lady was sitting at her desk and over her right shoulder a little box was showing a video. On the crawl below her were the words "Wolf Spotted in Huntington Beach."

"A Huntington Beach man shot this footage last night of what appears to be a blond wolf," she was saying.

Oh shit. And there I was for all to see, blond WereJeff sniffing around the dark streets of HB, trotting to and fro. It was surreal. I'd never seen myself wolfed out before. I watched, mesmerized as they played the footage shot on someone's cell phone, looping over and over during her broadcast, a sleek blond wolf—me!—sniffing around, trotting across an alley.

"The local SPCA speculated that it could be a hybrid of a dog and a wolf, perhaps even a pet," she went on. "They are on the lookout for it now. Authorities are warning people that if you see it to stay away. A wild animal should never be approached. If you do see it, call the police."

Great. Just great. I was wanted by the police now. I had to be more careful. I couldn't be seen again or I'd end up euthanized. "Jesus."

The newscast when on to other things—a body was found on the beach not too far from the pier—but I'd already tuned out, stunned. I wanted to hide. My wolf instinct was to find someplace dark and stay there till the danger was over. But it would never be over. As long as I was a werewolf, the danger was here to stay.

Now, more than ever, I wanted to get to this Voodoo coven tonight. Maybe they could help me. If I told them. But could I? They lynched werewolves in their part of the world, didn't they? I'd have to find a way to convince them I was no threat.

I needed them.

CHAPTER FOUR

꩜

NADÈGE HAD TEXTED me earlier in the day with the address. I was excited to see their coven, but truth to tell, I was more excited to see her again.

I drove up into the tree-lined neighborhoods of small beach houses next to McMansions, their modern counterparts. I was glad to see that the house I was looking for was one of the original little houses from the forties, a one-story gray clapboard, trying to look like a mini cape cod, complete with pilings and heavy rope draped between them for a fence.

I parked a few doors down, and walked up to it. I opened the little gate, and there were shells along the walkway, old school.

I knocked and after a moment, Nadège answered the door, wafting her strong perfume toward me. And there was that flawless face again. "You came."

"I said I would." I put my hand to my heart. "Jeff Chase keeps his word."

"Then come in."

She opened the door wider and I stepped in and just as quickly jerked to a halt. It was a normal house on the outside, but inside it was totally different. It was like walking into a foreign land. The walls were painted dark blue and red with long gauzy drapery with sequins, hanging in the corners. Gave it a sort of sparkly, otherworldly look to the room, almost like a big tent. There was a sort of altar against the main wall that had countless candle drips all over it from past different colored candles. It was set up now with black candles, a Virgin Mary statue, bowls of dark liquid, a stick of sandalwood incense burning next to crosses, miniature coffins, dried gourds, a bell, and more religious icons.

"Whoa." I'd barely cracked that Voodoo book. My mind had been consumed with werewolves instead. And then I realized how rude my reaction probably sounded. "Hey, I'm sorry. I just didn't expect...this." And then I looked around. All the furniture had been pushed back against the walls, and there were no other people here. "I thought you said you were meeting your coven or whatever tonight."

"My congregation. They're coming at eight. I wanted to give you time to get used to it, for me to explain things before they arrived."

I breathed a little easier. "You're a wise woman. I guess my reaction wouldn't have endeared me."

"No, but it was expected."

Ouch. I guess that said it all. "I'm sorry. I'm just a...uninitiated. The equivalent of a *pinche gringo*."

She cocked her head. "I don't understand."

"Um...'effing white boy'? Whatever that is in Haitian."

She laughed. It was nice. Her body doing it was nice. "You were open to coming. That's points for you. Would you like some wine?"

"Please."

"Feel free to look around. But...don't touch."

I held up my hands as she left the room. I blew out a breath and passed my hand up through my hair. Damn! This was some serious shit. *What have you gotten yourself into, old Jeff?* I got closer to the altar and looked at it. I hadn't noticed the knife before, but it made me flinch. Yup. Silver. I hope I wasn't going to have to touch any silver tonight. I just didn't know what would happen if I did...or if I *could*.

I looked around at the art on the walls, all in colorful frames. Lots of mirrors, too. Everything was colorful, really. The soft purple sofas were strewn with wraps and shawls in bright colors. They were piled with equally colorfully-patterned pillows. Even the rugs on the floor. It should have hurt my eyes, but I kind of liked it. It had personality, that was for sure. She also had sculptures of what looked like African figures, some painted with tiny colorful dots of paint. There were even mini-altars on the walls in frames. It reminded me a lot of Mexican art for different festivals, like Día de los Muertos, only without the sugar skulls.

"You like my home?" She came back with two stemmed glasses of red wine, and handed me one.

I took a sip. "Yeah. I really do. It's very...colorful."

"I find most Americans don't use this much color."

"But we should. It's very joyful."

She slid onto her sofa in one elegant move. Hesitating, I sat beside her, giving her some breathing room. "I'm glad you think of it that way. It *is* joyful. It reminds me of home and all the celebrations. The color of the jungle flowers. The clothes of the people."

I just continued to look around and slurp my wine. She watched me, and I kept thinking that if I was going to ask her out—and I was—I needed to up my game at home and get some furniture, nice stuff. Colorful stuff. Ikea, here I come.

She cupped the bowl of her wine glass between long fingers. She wore several jeweled rings on both hands. "I wanted time to explain my practices to you."

"It's not a coven then. It's more of a religion, right? I know people view Wicca that way."

"It isn't so much a religion than it is a collection of practices that embody our beliefs. We don't really call it 'Voodoo', but *sèvi Lwa*, serving the Lwa."

"What is a l'WAH?"

"Lwa are *mystères*, the invisibles, spirits responsible for all sorts of aspects of life...and relationships. They stand between mortals and the Creator, *Bondye*."

"But, uh, there's a Virgin Mary and other Christian stuff on your altar..."

"Most Haitians are Catholic—that is their *religion*—but they practice *sèvi Lwa* as their ancestors did. It is ancestral magic passed down from the Voodoo priesthood of West Africa. I know only the Haitian rituals and beliefs, because it varies from culture to culture as needed. But we believe in the Creator, Bondye—the Good God—who doesn't interfere with our lives."

"So…it's not a coven?"

"Not as such. These are family practices. But magic, too."

"Then it's your family coming tonight?"

"My adopted family. Haitian-Americans. What family I have left after the earthquake are still in Haiti. As a *Vodouisant*, I found a family of people to practice it with."

"A what was it you called it?"

"Voh-DOO-wee-ZAHN," she pronounced for me.

"This all sounds more complicated than I thought. I bought a book today…but I didn't get much of a chance to look at it."

She smiled, sipping her wine. It made her lips moist and I was getting that feeling again. She was really sexy and like I said, it's been a while…

She leaned toward me. My heart sped up. "Books are fine in one sense, but these practices are an *oral* tradition passed down from one generation to the next. And frankly, most of the books about Voodoo are written by white people who think there is only one kind."

"This book I got was written by someone named Mambo something."

She smiled again. I so wanted to kiss her. She was all that.

"A 'Mambo' is a title, like a priestess."

"Oh." I rubbed the back of my neck. I was *not* nervous. "I flubbed that right away."

"Don't be so hard on yourself. This is a different experience than you are used to."

I drank a little wine and then set the glass on a varnished side table. "You'd be surprised what I'm used to," I said quietly. "Okay, then. What's going to happen tonight?"

"We will be doing magic. It is specialized, and only those expert in it should perform it."

She explained it all in general terms. Clearly, she wanted me to absorb it, to understand what I was going to see. But as the hour was getting closer, I began to wonder if I belonged here. It really wasn't like the Maine coven. This was, for all intents and purposes, Nadège's faith. Did an outsider like me have any business here?

But if there was a chance that they could do real magic, I figured they were my best hope for a little help.

At eight sharp, there was a rapping at the front door. I shot to my feet and began straightening my clothes and hair. Three ladies, dark-skinned, all colorfully dressed, each of different body types, two with bandanas, or as Nadège had explained earlier, *gele* wrapped around their hair that must have been piled up on their heads. They wore beaded necklaces — lots of them — and bangle bracelets and big earrings. They greeted Nadège joyfully like a long-lost sister — maybe she was in a way — and noisily made their way in.

Until they saw me.

All came to a stop, the noise, the bustle, the talking. It was as if they were the wine and I was the cork.

I gave a little wave. "Hi, everyone."

I saw it in their eyes. *Who is this white boy? That blond nobody?*

Nadège stepped beside me, placing her hands on my shoulders. And I realized she didn't really know me at all. I ran a tea shop. Didn't mean I wasn't a serial killer, burying the bodies in the backroom. She only knew where I worked, my phone number, and my name. That isn't a lot.

"This is Jeff Chase. He owns The Organic Leaf on Main Street. He wanted to come, to see how we serve the Lwa."

They turned their collective eyes on her like she was crazy.

And you know, I didn't really know her either. Maybe I was going to be the sacrifice tonight. All I knew was that she was beautiful and I had wanted to get to know her, like so many other women before her. I realized that in my little world of seduction and release, I didn't know a lot about my hookups. That was before Kylie, my ex. And…during, I guess, to be truthful.

I mean, she could be a serial killer, too. Serial sacrificer? Although…if she tried it, she'd get quite a surprise.

A rather short, plump lady came right up into my face. "Who do you think you are?" Her accent was heavy too. Not as melodious as it was out of Nadège.

"I, uh...I..." I looked toward Nadège. "Help?"

"I told you," she said. "He's Jeff and he came to learn. So back off, Widelene."

"You invite this surfer boy in here?"

"I invite anyone that my ancestors wish to welcome."

A tall woman with a *gele* wrapped high, with braids coming out of the top, pushed her way in front of me. I might have taken a step back. Yeah, big bad werewolf. "And what do you know about him?"

"This is Tamara, Jeff. She is our mother hen."

Tamara lifted her chin, a little proudly, I thought. "That's right. I must look after my girls, like Nadège, who sometimes don't know any better."

"Jesula," said Widelene, gesturing toward me. "Are you going to permit this?"

Jesula seemed more like Nadège, in both figure and temperament. She was pretty too, but older. She wasn't sneering at me, at least. "If Nadège says he's okay, who am I to doubt her?"

"Listen," I cut in. "I was just curious. If it's going to bother you my staying, I can leave. It's no sweat."

"You see that?" said Jesula.

"Come, come, come," hissed Widelene. She ushered the women into the other room, just past the doorway. I could hear them but they were speaking Haitian, though I did hear the occasional English word interspersed, like "idiot" and "sneaky." I didn't really need to speak Haitian to figure out I wasn't welcomed.

"Nadège, I should just go," I called to her. I backed toward the door.

She glanced at me and rushed back through the doorway. "No! You stay." She grabbed my hand and pulled me toward the sofa where she pushed me down.

Actually, I *was* getting a little scared. These other women looked mean, and they were staring daggers at Nadège. But she held firm. "This is my house and I am mambo here. It's getting late. We need to get on with it."

Her hands were at her hips and she wasn't taking any shit. If I were the others, I would have shut up too...just like they were doing.

There was some muttering but they wandered back in where Nadège moved the rest of the furniture out of the way, leaving a space before the altar.

The women took off their shoes and set them aside. Nadège dimmed the lights as Widelene lit the candles on the altar. I felt my palms sweat and my breathing came faster. This was way more than just going to church, something I hadn't done in years.

Barefoot, they all sat on the rugs before the altar, crossed themselves, and bowed their heads. Nadège started speaking in a sing song kind of voice. She told me earlier that this was the *Priyè Ginen*, reciting the history of her ancestor's culture. Then they started in on some Catholic prayers, all in French. And they were intense about it, heads down, prayerful hands to their mouths. It was a call and response thing. I could almost understand what they were saying, but not quite. I mean, I wasn't Catholic but I knew the Lord's Prayer and just the barest of French from high school.

By then, Nadège had gotten up and stood in front of the altar. She took up that gourd with the beads on it and rattled it and then picked up a brass bell and rang that. Jesula grabbed a drum in her lap and started beating a rhythm.

Something weird was going on. I felt all these sounds in my chest, as if it were all amplified, like some big-ass speakers were pounding us. I noticed Nadège picked a different kind of rattle and was really going to town shaking it, and they were chanting faster and faster, rocking back and forth. She'd told me about this part, moving into a different phase of the ceremony, repeating something over and over—*zo-ali mache*. She said it meant, "The bones are walking." It was about repeating the history of the ancestors, but now that I knew what the words were, it was giving me the creeps.

They were singing now, and the drumming and the rattling and the smell of the incense and the candle wax was making me sort of light-headed. Even though I was sitting down, I found myself clutching the sofa cushions, just tightening my hands on them, afraid I'd fall over.

Suddenly everyone was standing. The drumming kept coming, and the singing and chanting. They had their eyes closed and began to dance. It was wild. I kind of felt the need to dance too. But I held back. Didn't want to interfere. It was really powerful. I knew I was witnessing something pretty old, maybe far older than that Wiccan stuff back in Maine. This was visceral. There was no other way to see it.

"*Anonse o zanj nan dlo...*" sang Nadège. She said it meant, "Announce the angels in the mirror," telling us the Lwa were coming.

Nadège had warned me it might happen, that the spirit of the Lwa could possess one of them and they'd become a *chwal*, a horse for the Lwa to ride in on. It was Tamara. She was suddenly dancing wildly, all over the place. Her eyes had rolled back in her head.

I couldn't help it. I got to my feet. The fight or flight instinct was getting stronger in me. And I wanted to run. I wanted desperately to wolf out and run from there. Hair sprouted on the backs of my hands and the nails grew to claws. It took all of my willpower to shove them back down, but the blond hair on my hands were stubbornly staying.

Tamara was yammering in a foreign tongue, definitely not French. The others gathered around her. Jesula was still drumming, only softly. They leaned in, eager to hear what she had to say.

She seemed to switch to French, only a different kind. Haitian? Tamara, her eyeballs all white, turned toward the room and raised her hands. "*Jé-rouges!*"

Wait. Wasn't *jé-rouges* what Lauren told me about? A Haitian red-eyed werewolf?

Something was happening in the circle. There was smoke and for a second, I thought maybe one of the candles had fallen over and started a fire on her rug. But it wasn't.

Something was coalescing in the middle of us. It swirled a lot like smoke, was transparent like smoke, but obviously *wasn't*. Slowly, it took shape into the ghostly form of a wolf.

I cowered back. Yeah, even after all I'd seen in Moody Bog, all the creatures and gods I'd faced. This scared the shit out of me.

The ghostly wolf snapped its jaws toward each of us.

And then it looked at me.

"*La bête!*" screamed Tamara. "*Bèt la se nan mitan nou! San an! Yo te mouri!*"

The beast, she shouted. The blood! It kills!

CHAPTER FIVE

℄

SUDDENLY, TAMARA DROPPED to the floor, moaning and the ghostly wolf disappeared, leaving the merest wisp of smoke. The others gathered around her, soothing her, smoothing her hair back from her face.

I was panting and my heart was beating a million miles a minute.

She knew. The spirit or Lwa knew at least. I remembered just enough high school French to know she was talking about the beast, *la bête* — me. And blood. It knew I was Wolf.

I shook my hands out behind my back, shaking loose the hair from the back of them. I flicked a glance at my hands and they were normal again, thank God.

I guess the Lwa had left her. The others were helping her to sit up.

Nadège was looking worried; at Tamara and at me. She had seen the ghost wolf too. They all had.

The women gently lifted Tamara to a sitting position until she slowly came back to her senses. They spoke in French quietly for a time. I caught snatches of words I knew, but that was all. I couldn't understand it.

The three huddled together as Nadège slipped away, looking at them from across the room. She was hugging herself. I wanted to put my arms around her too, but I knew that was too forward. And maybe she was afraid of me now.

"Hey," I said real quiet. She looked up at me with wide eyes. "Maybe I should go."

"I'm sorry about this."

"No, don't apologize. It was really interesting. And…a little freaky, with that…that ghostly thing. I'm sorry I upset your guests."

She wasn't scared anymore. She was mad. "Don't you apologize for bigots. That's what they are! I have some talking to them to do."

"But what about..." I swallowed. "What about that ghost thing? That..." I couldn't bring myself to say it. To say "wolf".

Impatiently it seemed, she pushed that aside. "Our little congregation has a great deal of magical sensitivity. We...we see spirits sometimes. Don't let it worry you."

"But she kept saying—"

"It means nothing. What happens is sometimes in metaphors. We have to be able to interpret the messages."

That sure seemed coincidental to me. I glanced toward Tamara being attended to by the ladies. "Is she going to be all right?"

Nadège looked back. "Yes. It does happen sometimes. The spirits want to talk to us. You don't have to worry."

Didn't I?

I headed for the door and Nadège followed me outside. We stood on her walkway and I felt better breathing the fresh air instead of the incense. "I'm sorry they made you feel unwelcomed. And I'm sorry also because I expected it. I hoped they wouldn't be so blatant, but I suppose that was a false hope."

"It put me in the deep end for sure. But I'm not complaining," I was quick to add. I didn't like that downcast look she got. "Um...look, this might be bad timing, but you can make it up to me. I'd really like to take you out. Or as a thank you for inviting me tonight... Well. Not just a thank you. I'd just really like to take you out."

The anger and uncertainty melted away from her and a smile formed at the edge of her luscious mouth. "I'd really like to go out with you, too."

"Awesome. Are you doing anything tomorrow night?"

"Not a thing."

"Then...how about I pick you up here at seven?"

"All right. I...I'll see you then." She leaned into me and kissed me on the cheek. It was amazing how a kiss could change a guy's attitude. I felt a lot better now. I snatched a peek back at the group of ladies through the open door. Tamara still seemed out of it. But Jesula and Widelene were staring hard at me... and did I ever hear it loud and clear.

$$\mathfrak{C}\mathfrak{C}\mathfrak{C}$$

THEY HAD POWERS. They tapped into magic, and I needed that. I hoped I could persuade the coven...uh, *congregation* to help. That there were good wolves and bad wolves. I wondered how *that* would go down. They didn't seem the types to be persuaded by a pretty face.

I hoped Nadège could help with that...and maybe a little bit more. I touched the place on my cheek where she'd kissed me. Yeah, she could help a lot.

All the talk of beasts and wolves sort of gave me the itch. Even as that lady accused me of being *jé-rouges*, I really wanted to wolf out. It was like a tonic. Like something calming and addicting at the same time. I knew it was risky now. But it just didn't matter. I had to do it. I couldn't go too long or I'd get all uncomfortable, like I'd burst through my skin. And it wasn't as if wolfing out at home in a small apartment was going to be enough.

I found a quiet street down by the beach, where I could park the truck under a big tree so I was in the shadow. I carefully took off my clothes. I was used to doing it in tight spaces to change from my wetsuit, so I laid my clothes out beside me on the seat, and got out. The air was cold on my skin, but as I stood there this immense feeling of relief flooded me because I was finally doing what now came naturally. It's hard to define the sensation. You just sort of — pushed — your body into its other form, like pushing through all the layers of yourself, all your fears, your attitudes, and just got down to the most basic part of you, the most primitive part.

Yeah, it was painful. Muscles shifting, bones transitioning, stretching...but it was also like a good work-out; it ached but in a satisfying kind of way.

I allowed myself to feel it all, slowing down the process. I felt the hair sprouting, getting longer, thicker, cocooning me in warmth and musk. My ears grew, stretched, and suddenly my hearing became more acute. My nose and mouth shifted together into a long snout, and I was now aware of *everything* — smells identifying every creature hiding in the dark, the scent of every finished dinner lingering on the breeze, every scent of every person that had passed by that spot today.

I was on all fours and hadn't even realized it. I shook out my coat, lifted my snout. I wanted to howl, and if I hadn't taken my wolfsbane, man I would have. But I was still cautious. Couldn't call attention to myself. So I let it lie. Instead, I sniffed the wind, the salty air, the particles of life all around me swirling through my snout. So alive! So...*me*, now.

I leapt forward. My pads ran on the cold sidewalk. It was dark but still early. A weeknight but people were still around. Lovers walking along the beach, a homeless guy making his way with his loaded shopping cart of his worldly goods rattling along the sidewalk, and me, loping, staying in the shadows. I looked both ways this time before crossing the strand, making sure no one was around, keeping my nose alert. When I reached the cool sand, I trotted quickly. No one was along the beach north of the pier, so I shot under the dark shadows of its long expanse and ran full pelt on the beach, on the hard sand along the tide line as far from the street lights dotting the strand as I could go. I booked it, just loving the wind through my fur, the salt in the air, the damp in my nose. I didn't care in that instance if these Voodoo ladies thought I was *loup-garou* or whatever. I was WereJeff on my own, in the night, being the wolf I was.

I might have danced a little as the moon peeked out from behind the clouds. I yipped at the waves. I even wondered if I could surf as a wolf. That would be awesome! Two worlds colliding. I was giddy with it and yipped some more, my wolf version of a laugh.

If I saw someone along the strand, I flattened myself near the surf. My blond fur sort of blended in with the foam, and when they were farther away, I'd run in the opposite direction back toward the pier.

As I approached the pier again, my nose was suddenly on alert.

I smelled it. Blood.

Shit. There was a *lot* of blood somewhere. A seal? But no. That was a distinct odor I remembered well. It was human blood. My hackles rose as I slowly approached. Under the shadows, I sniffed. It was here, close by. And then I saw the lump nearest the pilings. I tip-toed as best I could on my paws. A body, lying face up. That smell was strong. Another good reason for the wolfsbane, or I would have been all over that, *eating* it. And the thought made my stomach turn, even as a wolf. Without the wolfsbane, the blood would make me want to kill.

It wasn't only the blood that put me on alert. I smelled wolf, all around it. And there! Lots of paw prints. And with a spike of horror, I finally looked at the derelict man that lay there. He was the dude I saw earlier. His shopping cart was overturned, and all his stuff strewn out along the beach. His clothes stunk from sweat and urine, and hung in layers of rags around him.

But his face! It was wide-eyed in terror. And his neck. It was torn open, like it had been ripped apart by tooth and claw.

CHAPTER SIX

❄

SHIT! I HAD to get out of there. I backed away, all the competing smells overwhelming my senses.

My ears turned first before I swiveled my head. Someone was shouting and they were running toward me, waving their arms. I whined and leapt back and then shot in the other direction. I scrambled up the sidewalk, skidding on the loose sand, and ran down an alley, temporarily forgetting where I'd put my truck. I should have just gone home in the first place, parked it at a familiar location. But I'd left my keys and stuff in it and I had to get back to it.

I made a meandering route through a bunch of quiet neighborhoods. No one had followed me. I easily outran them. But I was panting from more than the run. They saw me. They saw a blond wolf standing over a dead dude. *Fuck!*

I spotted the truck up ahead and I couldn't wait to shift. My fur fell off all around me like a cascade of falling leaves as my bones and muscles contorted in mid-run. I stumbled a little as my spine pulled me upright and my forelegs suddenly became arms and were lifted off the road. My legs stretched, became man legs, and I was sprinting, naked, back to my truck. I yanked open the door and slid in, slamming the door. Hunching over the steering wheel, I just sat there, breathing hard and fast. *Shit, shit, SHIT!* Dammit, it wasn't me! It was that asshole's pack. But *I* was gonna get blamed for it.

I had to find that guy. What was his name again? Jesse Vargar. "Yeah," I grumbled, digging my keys out of my pile of clothes, didn't even bother dressing before I started her up and slammed it into gear. "I'm gonna find you, Vargar, and when I do, your pack leader ass is mine."

I drove home fast, threw it into park, and killed the engine. I slipped on my shorts but bundled the rest of my clothes under my arm and hurried, barefoot, over the asphalt and up the steps to my apartment. Slamming the door, I leaned against it, panting.

"Goddammit!" I bet that motherfucker *knew* I'd get blamed somehow. Did he know *I* was the blond wolf? And *how* did he know? His weird pack leader mojo?

I heaved my clothes toward the bed, but now I was cold. I slipped on a T-shirt and my sweats and got out my phone. I Googled his name, including Huntington Beach, and look at that? His address.

Just to be sure, I looked him up on Facebook. There was his ugly mug with a little wolf in the corner. Cute, asshole, but it only confirmed he lived in HB. How many Jesse Vargars could there be? Besides, I'd know by the smell of the place if it was him or not. I was tempted to shift and go over there, but now for sure they'd be out looking for me with guns and shit. That *sucked*, man.

No choice. I had to take the truck.

I went in my sweats with only my keys, wallet, and phone. Didn't need my shoes since I was going to shift when I got there.

He was way over the other side of town off of Palm. I found the street and the house on a dead-end. It was a big Mediterranean job with a huge driveway and cypress trees. I decided to park at least a few streets over so I could wolf out safely over there. After I stowed my stuff, I shifted.

I hid behind the truck, just sniffing things out. When the coast was clear, I headed out. It had only just happened. It hadn't hit the news yet. So he wouldn't be expecting me. And yet, somehow, I felt he probably was.

I kept to the shadows, stayed by trees and kept it slow. I could smell every damn dog who pissed on every tree trunk, every bush, every road sign post. That one was a Pekinese. And that one some kind of poodle. It was weird knowing.

I stood across the street, staring at the house. Could he smell me from here? Could I smell him? I tried to, but the breeze was blowing in the opposite direction. I only had that brief window of opportunity.

I trotted across the street and slipped toward his back gate. There was no way I could climb that as a wolf, so I briefly shifted back to a man, grabbed the top of the fence, and hurled myself over as quietly as possible. Good thing it was cold or I might have hurt myself, if you know what I mean. I quickly shifted back, warm in my fur again. I sniffed around near the foundations, up the wall and into the air. There! *I caught you, you son of a bitch. Got your scent.*

Funny. I didn't smell any other wolf scent. Just his. There were some stale scents of others, but they were all human, and definitely not recent. Single? Divorced? Unhappy, I hoped.

I kept it stealthy going around the corner in the backyard, where a turquoise pool shimmered under the backyard light. How was I gonna get in? There was almost an entire back wall of sliding glass doors. Somebody had some money.

I didn't sense anyone else there. Just him. I backed up as far as I could against the edge of the pool and gave myself a running start, hurling with my shoulder right into one of those glass doors. In a tremendous crash of breaking glass all around me like a glittering snowfall, I was suddenly standing in a dining room.

The smell was different coming from upstairs. He shifted. I could tell. Positioning myself by the stairwell, hiding in the shadows, I heard him rush down the steps on all fours.

He was a *big* motherfucker. Dark, with gray edges and fully fluffed out, like some kind of arctic wolf. Yellow eyes with evil in them, and his lips snarled back, revealing his fangs. I gave him a smiley too. I was so angry. It all came out in my snarling growl.

I readied myself. *Come on!*

He leapt. I sprang forward and we clashed in midair. My jaws were open, trying to find something to bite down on. I was going for the throat, but then thought better of it. I didn't really want to kill him. Not at first. I wanted to wound him, to show him I wasn't weak.

I clamped down on one of his forelegs, breaking skin.

He yelped, but then turned on me, nipping my shoulder. He could have gone deeper but he was showing me his control. It only made me madder.

I grabbed his ear, trying to rip it. He smacked my jaws aside with a powerful paw. And then we rolled on the floor. If we hadn't been wolfed we'd have been bloody from the glass, but as it was, our fur protected us. There was still blood, because I wasn't kidding with my bites, but not as much as there could have been had I been serious.

My nose filled with the heady scent of blood, of werewolf blood, which was distinctly different, and the taste of his musky fur, which was also unlike anything else.

We jumped back from each other, panting, sizing up the other. Our snarls echoed in the small space and up to the high ceilings.

All at once, he took a step back and shifted. He stood there, a naked guy with dark hair on his chest and torso, the hair on his head all tossled. Blood on his ear and on his arm. His intense eyes bored into mine.

Okay. I could do this man to man, if that's the way he wanted it.

I shifted and faced him.

"Blond," was the first thing he said. "You're a fucking *blond* wolf. Who *does* that?"

"Hey, asshole. That's the least of what I'm here to do."

"You broke my door."

"Shut up! You killed that guy. I know you're trying to frame me."

He just stared at me coolly, looking me over like he was trying to figure me out. He rubbed at his arm. I knew it would heal in a few seconds. "Where are you from anyway? You smell all wrong."

"*You* smell all wrong!" I said like a third-grader, stabbing a finger at him. And then he tried that mesmerizing thing on me. I got a little woozy, stumbled a bit. I put a hand to my head. How was he doing that?

His stare was intense, dark brows crunched over his eyes. I felt an overwhelming urge to back down, to leave, to just get out. *No, I don't want to leave. I want to kick his ass.* I shook my head, shook it hard, and looked up at him. And just like that I felt that urge fading away. It tried to come back, but I pushed at it, made it go, gave him my own intense glare right back at him.

Then *he* stumbled, a shocked look on his face.

"You can cut that crap out, too," I said triumphantly.

"How did you do that?" he muttered. "Where's your pack?"

"I don't have a pack. I came home looking for one. And it turns out it's *you*. That's a disappointment."

I suddenly realized we were two dudes standing in the mess of his dining room, shattered glass all over the floor, and us naked. It was starting to get uncomfortable.

He turned his back on me, went into his dark living room, grabbed something. It was a couple of throws. He tossed me one and I wrapped it around my waist. He draped the other around his own. "You might as well come in." He turned his back again and sauntered into the living room, turning on a single lamp.

I didn't feel in danger anymore. I felt a little let down, truth be told. My hot blood was cooling and it all seemed anti-climactic. I wanted to tear at him, make him bleed again for what he'd done to that homeless guy. And that was completely not the Jeff I used to be, Mister Mellow. Now I was Mister Blood. That was something I didn't want to wrestle with at the moment.

Reluctantly, I followed him. He was pouring drinks from a bar in the corner. "Bourbon okay?" he said, like we were friends or something.

"Yeah."

He walked over to me in his knitted "sarong" and handed me a glass. I took it and sat on the nearest chair, making sure I was closest to the dining room in case I had to make a hasty exit.

I sipped. It was smooth stuff. Only the best for the rich asshole.

He was still standing and still looking at me.

"Take a picture, it'll last longer," I growled.

"No, your scent will last longer."

Uh oh. Now you see, that was the kind of stuff I needed to know. That was clearly a werewolf thing to sniff a guy to remember him, though I guess I had done it naturally already. But that's something I could have learned from a pack. His pack. But I had no intention of ever belonging to his stupid pack.

"Whatever," I snorted, taking another sip. "So...you were bit as a kid?"

Again with the look like I was the stupidest person in the world.

"Hey, you know what? There's stuff I don't know, okay? I just read somewhere that a werewolf that has that power that you have — *used* to have over me — has it because he's been a werewolf since he was a kid. So stuff you attitude."

Vargar sipped, looking at me over the rim of his glass. "Where are you from?"

"Hey, asshole, *I'm* asking the questions."

"No," he said, eyes suddenly blazing. "I am."

But his eyes had no power over me. That had vanished. I held the glass away from me straight-armed, and I slowly tipped it to pour his expensive bourbon on his carpet in one stream. Then I dropped the glass.

He was pissed I'd done that.

But he also looked worried.

"Why are you not affected by that?"

"I don't even know what the fuck *that* is. Your weird stare thing won't work on me anymore."

"It's supposed to work. Where are you *from*?"

"I'm from right here in Huntington Beach!" But I knew what he meant. "All right. Okay. I, uh...got bit in Maine. I was there for six months."

"Who bit you?"

"The First Werewolf."

"No. That's impossible."

"I've learned in the last year that there are very few things that are impossible. It was the First Werewolf, and I killed him."

He slowly sat on the edge of his sofa, drink forgotten. He was doing that staring thing.

"So like I said, *I'm* asking the questions. Why did you kill that homeless guy? He wasn't hurting anything. Unless it was to frame me."

He frowned. "I don't know what you're talking about."

"Dude. I don't like being lied to."

"I'm not lying."

"There were wolf prints all around him. I smelled them!"

"Not my work."

"I don't believe you."

"Fine. Now answer me a question."

I folded my arms. "Maybe. Maybe not."

"What do you mean by the 'First Werewolf'?"

I shot to my feet and began to pace. "What do you mean 'what do I mean'? The first fucking werewolf. The first ever. He was there, he bit me. End of story. Until I killed him." He didn't need to know the details. That I hadn't actually killed him. That I couldn't finish the job. It was my ex who had to kill him because he came out of that cursed Booke of hers.

It was like he didn't know what to say. Maybe he could tell I wasn't lying. I didn't know how the pack leader thing worked. Technically, *I* was an Alpha, or, according to Lauren, a "pack leader" since there were no "alphas" and since I had made a werewolf out of one of the coven. Accidentally. I could still feel him sometimes, even though he was far away back in Maine. It was better this way. They had said it would fade with time and it seemed to be doing that. They had told me—as far as they knew—that I was becoming a lone wolf, and if I didn't get a pack soon, I'd remain one. And I didn't know if that was a good or a bad thing. I felt the call to belong to a pack. Kylie's friends had served as one all those months ago, but when I left Maine, it was like tearing off a scab. I felt an ache to belong. But I would be damned if I joined

Vargar's pack. That was no longer on the plate. I wouldn't take orders from him.

"I don't know if that was all bullshit or what," he said.

"And I don't give a damn if you believe me or not. But I'll tell you this. I won't let you or your damn pack kill anyone ever again. Not on my watch."

"We didn't kill him. How long do you think we'd last if we went around on killing sprees every night? We'd end up on the nightly news." He gave a smug smile at that.

"How did I know somebody filmed me!" I was so mad that that had happened. But come to think of it, if Vargar's wolves *had* killed on a regular basis, that *would* have been on the news. So what gives?

"You don't use wolfsbane," I said. "I can't smell it on you."

That sneer was back, the one I wanted to smack off his stupid face. "No. Only weaklings use wolfsbane. It isn't natural."

"Your 'natural' shit means that you kill."

"No, our 'natural *shit*' is about control. And you don't have any, Mister Blond Asswolf."

I opened my mouth but stopped. They controlled their urges by practice? And what about maintaining your humanity? I couldn't seem to do that without the wolfsbane. Shit. More stuff I needed to know. I licked my lips. I still tasted blood. "You...you don't need to use wolfsbane?"

"And we don't kill. Yeah. How do you think wolfpacks survived all these thousands of years without being wiped out?"

I think my mouth was hanging open...before I closed it and stared at the floor, at the carpet I ruined with the bourbon.

I needed to learn that control. Not that the wolfsbane was a problem, but...there was the strong urge to go without it. And I couldn't. One day I might get into a situation where I couldn't get any of it. *Then* what would I do? I knew I couldn't control it by myself. And *they* knew how. Or so he said.

"There were wolf tracks all around the dead guy. And his throat was torn out."

He looked away from me, pinching his lips between his fingers. "I don't know about that. I...I don't think it was my pack."

"Maybe you'd better find out. By the way, I don't necessarily believe you had nothing to do with it."

He scowled and turned a nasty look toward me.

"Is there another pack around here?"

He shook his head. "Another wouldn't dare come into our territory."

So that meant there *were* other ones. Maybe close by. It made sense but it still felt good to confirm it.

"Look." I took a deep breath. "I don't know half the stuff I need to know. The werewolf that made me was not a man anymore. He had been a wolf so long he wasn't human, didn't even know he could shift. There was no one to tell me things."

I didn't want to ask. My pride wouldn't let me, so I left it there. Anxiously, I watched him. His face lost its scowl and it all passed through his eyes, all his emotions, his thoughts. I could almost smell them.

He spoke at last. "You're a pack leader, but an incomplete one. You don't smell quite right to me. I don't know what it is. You might be telling the truth, you might not, but...you don't smell right to me." He stared off into the corner of the living room. "But if you want my help, you'd have to trust me."

"I don't know if I do."

"Maybe in time."

"I'd have to know if you killed that guy. Or if your pack did. I couldn't trust you until I was sure."

"Meanwhile, you'll be hunted."

"Yeah," I bit out.

"They'll get dogs. They'll find your scent."

"They won't find a wolf."

"They will eventually. You'll slip up."

"I won't."

He sat back, looking all smug. "We *can* help you with that."

"Is that a fact?"

"You'd have to trust me."

I shook my head and gritted my teeth. We were getting nowhere. I couldn't trust him. Not yet. Maybe not ever.

There was a shift in the wind. I could smell wolf on it. His pack sensed his danger. They were coming.

I tore off the throw and shifted, shaking out my fur.

He looked me over under his lidded eyes but he didn't move from the sofa and stayed human. I snarled a little, blew out a huff of breath, and turned my back on him. I trotted along the edge of the dining room, avoiding the glass, and rushed out of the doorway.

Once I climbed over the fence as a human and wolfed out again on the other side, I lifted my leg on his gate. Take that, asshole.

CHAPTER SEVEN

❦

I SAT IN my truck again. I'd pulled on my sweats and my shirt and sat staring ahead at nothing. Could I trust him? If I was to learn the control I needed, I'd have to. But the dead guy... I scrubbed my face with my palms. This was a crapload of problems to overcome. Meanwhile, his pack couldn't be trusted if some of them were out there killing.

I started up the truck and headed for home. It just now occurred to me that tomorrow night, I had a date with a beautiful woman. Granted, a woman whose Voodoo coven didn't exactly like me and my wolfy ways.

"One thing at a time, Jeff," I muttered, pulling into my parking space again. "One thing at a time."

The next day, it was Luis' turn to open up shop, so I got myself over to Ikea in Costa Mesa and did some whirlwind shopping. Got a sofa, a bed frame (always being optimistic), some rugs and pillows, and few other things to make the place look a little more grown-up. I got it all loaded in the truck and hauled it home. Cam helped me get it upstairs and I was busy for the next few hours putting it all together. When I was done, it didn't look half-bad. Almost like I knew what I was doing.

Cam came up later and gave it the once over. "Yeah, dude. It looks good."

"I was hoping you'd say that. I got a date tonight."

He laughed. "Oh, so *that's* what all the hurry was about."

"Yeah. It looked a bit rugged before."

"So who's the lucky lady?" he asked as we both descended the stairs.

"That woman from the Voodoo coven."

"Whoa. You mean it went that good last night?"

"Well…" We got to the backdoor and entered the shop. "To tell you the truth, it was kind of weird. Freaked me out."

"What freaked you out?" asked Luis.

"Jeff's dating that Voodoo lady."

"No way."

"You saw her, right?"

"You sure it wasn't Starey McStarey Eyes, that dude from yesterday?"

"What? No! Why would you say that?"

"Cause I saw him hanging around this morning."

That is not cool, Vargar. I rushed to the door, yanked it open, and stood on the sidewalk, looking both ways. Didn't see him *or* smell him.

"I said that was this morning," said Luis suddenly behind me. "Dude's got under your skin."

"No, he hasn't." I scowled, then I thought what this looked like. When I turned to Luis, I blanked my face and shrugged. "It's, uh, personal."

I came back into the shop and saw the lunch Luis brought for us all. "I got you your veggie wrap," he said cautiously.

I stared at it. "Oh, dude. That's cool of you, but… When I had my blood problems, the doc said it was partly because of my veggie diet. I'm on red meat now."

They both stared at me. Yeah, I used to be Mr. Bean Sprout. I knew this would be a shock. I shrugged again. "Weird, I know."

Luis shook his head, mouth hanging open. "It's all weird, dude. What's going on with you?"

I sort of laughed it away. "Just some changes. Um…you know?" Nope. Wasn't gonna tell them. They'd totally freak then. I needed my boys here. "I'm still the same old Jeff inside."

They exchanged glances.

"So I'll just…head over to the Tequila Tiki. You guys want anything? Some Maui fries? Kona taco?"

They shook their heads. I got out of there fast and hurried down the sidewalk, ducking into the dark bar. The windowed walls along the sidewalk were rolled wide open. There was a long bar across the whole front so patrons could sit on high stools and watch the world go by, and be both inside *and* outside. It was great in the summer and fall. I opted for the interior bar and ordered an Angus burger from Dave. He got me a beer without my asking and I settled in. He was slicing oranges and putting them in their containers when I sipped and asked, "Dude, if you had a big secret about yourself, would you tell your friends? I mean a *really* big-ass secret that could really tear them up?"

He flicked his gaze up at me once before returning them to his work. "I suppose that would depend on the secret and the people I was telling, if they could take it or not. And if I really needed to tell them or if it were just vanity that I *wanted* to tell them."

"That's deep, Dave," I said, raising the bottle to my lips. Did I *need* to tell them or just *wanted* to? I wasn't dangerous. Hell, if I were, I wouldn't even be at my shop anymore. I'd have stayed in the woods of Maine and just took my chances, living as a hermit or something. So did I *need* to tell them?

Someone plopped on the barstool next to me and I looked up.

"Hi. I noticed you were in here; thought I'd say hello."

Lauren from the occult shop. She looked a little less leery of me, a little spritelier.

"I'll take an iced tea and a crab salad," she told Dave.

"Hey. How's the research going?" I toyed with my beer mat.

"It's going okay. How was your Voodoo meeting?"

Dave started eyeing us, and I took her arm and maneuvered her to a table. "We'll be over here when our order comes up," I told him.

We settled in and I answered her inquiring eyes. "Sorry. I just didn't need Dave to know all my business." I hunkered down over my beer, arms on the table around it protectively. "It was kind of weird. One of the ladies got possessed."

"Really?" Her eyes were suddenly wide with wonder.

"Yeah. And...and there was this manifestation."

"A manifestation?"

"Some kind of smoke rose and formed into a...a wolf. And she was going on in French about *jé-rouges* and *loup-garou* and *la bête*. It freaked me out."

She rested her chin on her hand and just stared at me, eyes flicking from chin, to nose, to eyes, like she was trying to figure me out. Probably trying to tell if I were lying or not. "That is very unusual. I wish I'd seen it."

"No, you don't. It was—"

Dave arrived, laying my plate in front of me, and Lauren's salad in front of her.

I watched him leave before I leaned forward again. "You don't wish you'd seen it. It was terrifying. The lady's eyes were rolled back and she was speaking in this other voice and...I mean, I don't know. If she was faking, she was doing a good job. And how did they do that smoke thing?"

She stabbed at her salad, moving pieces around. "Well...to be a devil's advocate here, they knew you were coming. They could have set something up. Staged it."

Decision time. I pushed my plate aside. "I'm gonna be straight with you, Lauren. You don't know me, so you don't owe me any kind of politeness. But I'm going to be honest with you. I was out of town for the last six months. In Maine. And I saw some things that I never would have believed. Stuff my ex's coven could do. The things that...that came through a...a... portal. Creatures. Demons." I shook my head. Whenever I thought it might have been a dream or hallucination, I just remembered it, and it all flooded back, the sensations, the smells, the...the deaths. "Stuff I can't explain or ever want to see again. Now I can get you in touch with Dr. Fred Boone who lives in Moody Bog. He's the head of that coven and he knows a lot. Has tons of books like you have in your backroom. This shit is real. It's terrifying and it's real."

I waited. I couldn't measure by her face or her eyes what she thought of that. Slowly, she raised her fork to her mouth and crunched down on lettuce, chewed while looking at me steadily.

Finally, she put the fork down, dabbed at the corner of her mouth with a napkin, and rested her wrists on the table. "I have no doubt that you saw something that scared you. But...might there have been another explanation for the things you saw? I mean this Dr. Boone. Was he...part of a hospital...or...sanitarium...?"

There was one way to prove it to her, but there was no way I was going to do that. I sighed. "No, I was not institutionalized when I was there. Doc Boone was not my doctor. He is a retired country doctor that happens to be interested in the occult. I saw things. I interacted, fought them. Stuff that will get you a PhD, not just a Master's. It's okay if you don't believe me. If I weren't there, *I* wouldn't believe me. But I thought if there was ever a person I could trust it would be you."

"Hmm." She looked down at her salad but didn't go for the fork. "And...you need to trust me...why?"

Lauren was sort of a plain Jane. Like cast-in-a-movie-as-the-scientist plain, always wearing her hair in a pony tail, no make-up, not a sparkling personality. And the rest of her was not curvy at all. Mentally—and I hadn't even realized I was doing it—I was assigning her a point tally. And then I psychically slapped my hand. *Dude, you do not rate females who are going to help you!*

"Because...there are things out there. And...I have a feeling I'm going to continue to encounter them. And I'll need someone's help, because I can't do it on my own."

She continued gazing at me, slowly eating her salad. "I have studied this stuff for a while," she said at last between bites. "And I must admit, the things you are saying intrigue me. I've never seen actual magic or a manifestation like you said you saw."

"Or demons. Because you'd remember if you had."

"Or demons."

"Unless someone cast a forget-me spell on you." I measured her closely and frowned. She was this big researcher, but she's never seen demons or other creatures? How hard *was* it? I mean, once you knew, you saw them everywhere. "Is it possible you know about this stuff but just don't remember?"

She looked at me blankly. *Strangely* blankly, and I remembered that look. I grabbed her wrist and bolted from the table. "Dave, keep our stuff on ice, okay?"

"Even your burger?"

I ran out, dragging Lauren behind me. What she must have thought, I don't know. She wasn't resisting, but that might have meant she was scared. Didn't matter. We got to her shop and I stood outside it. I finally let her go and searched all over her doorway. I didn't see anything there, until I looked up at her steel sign. It stuck out from the wooden façade about five inches, enough room for a transformer and the neon light to shine through the cut-outs of her signage. And shit. There it was.

I climbed up the wall, using extended claws to get a grip on the wood, reached up, and grabbed the charm bag that had been tacked up there behind the transformer. When I brought it down I showed it to her.

"Have you ever seen this before?"

Her face was all kinds of odd. She blinked and shook her head, like she was coming out of anesthesia. She took the bag in her hand and turned it over and over. "What is this? Some kind of trick?"

"It's a forget-me spell. Someone put it here. What are you remembering?"

"I'm...I'm..." She clutched her head and leaned against the wall.

"It's okay. Some of these can be pretty powerful."

She suddenly looked up at me, clear-eyed and...angry. "He did this to me. He can't *do* this to me!"

She grabbed the door, yanked it open, and stomped inside. What else could I do but follow?

Bliss was at the counter, polishing her nails with some pink lacquer. She didn't even look up. "That was a fast lunch," she muttered.

But Lauren stomped right to the counter and grabbed the phone, punching in a number.

"You have a lot of explaining to do," she shouted into the phone when they picked up on the other end. All I could hear was a man's voice. "No, you listen to me. I found your little charm pouch...Yeah. *That*. I'm coming over tonight and I will get the rest of my things. All of them."

Then she slammed down the receiver.

I stood sheepishly by the door. I knew better than to get in the way of a woman's fury.

She whipped toward me, clutching the charm pouch. "An ex-husband. Who's a bastard. And yeah, I remember now. All sorts of things I personally researched. I had *researched*! Goddammit." She shook her head.

Neither of us said anything for a time until she took a deep breath and blew it out. "I want to thank you. You seem to know what you're talking about."

"You're welcome. It's just that I encountered one of these before."

She stood there, the anger draining away, getting replaced with...well. I don't know.

She lifted the charm pouch. "What do I do with this?"

"You burn it. I'm sure you'll want to study it first. But the magic is mostly in the incantation. So I've been told."

She kept looking at the pouch, turning it over and over in her hands.

I honest-to-goodness shuffled my feet. "Do you...do you want to go back to the Tequila Tiki? We could, uh, finish our lunch?" She didn't respond and I nodded. "Or, I could pick it up for you, bring it back here."

"That's okay, Jeff. Thanks anyway. I lost my appetite." She dug into her pockets and started pulling out bills.

"Hey, no, let me take care of it."

"I can't let you — "

"It's okay. Dave's a friend. I'll, uh, see you around." I turned to leave, then paused. "If you need any help — you know, with your ex — I'd be happy to go with you. Moral support, some muscle?"

She looked me over. I had muscles now without even working out. It was a wolf thing.

"Thanks. Not this time. But...thanks."

I gave her a conciliatory smile, slipped out the door, and headed back to the bar. I was hungry now, but also kind of concerned for Lauren. It seemed like there was paranormal activity everywhere you looked. And with a wince, I also realized there were dudes being douches all around, too. *I guess it takes one to know one.*

☾☾☾

LATER THAT EVENING, I headed over to Nadège's place. A date. I hadn't been on one of those for ages. But I planned on taking her to a nice dinner and see if she'd be interested in heading back to mine. You know, just for a drink or…who was I kidding?

I wasn't nervous, just excited. New adventure, new woman. Got a little of the creeps walking up to her door from the last time, but once I was knocking, I was in smooth Jeff mode.

She opened the door and there was that stunning body and face that struck me dumb the first time I saw her. Another short dress showing off those long legs, with delicate sandals on her feet, displaying toe rings…in gold, thank goodness. Her skin shimmered in the street lights, bare shoulders, long legs. And I didn't miss that sensuous smile either, with lips wetted with gloss.

"Are you ready to go?" she said, throwing a wrap over her shoulders. She took a small bag with her and I was struck dumb again, because even the way she moved was like some luscious dance.

I snatched a glimpse of her living room before she shut the door behind her. The furniture was all back in place and it looked like any normal living room…with an altar on the wall where a fireplace should be, but still.

"Where are you taking me?"

I opened the car door for her. "Have you ever been to Deek's? It has a great ocean view from the dining room."

'Sounds perfect."

I liked how she said it like "paw-fect". I got in beside her.

She apologized again for her Voodoo ladies and I stopped her right there. "You can't keep apologizing for others. They'll come around. Assuming you'll be seeing me."

She smiled again, her eyes crinkling to amused slits. "We'll see."

No pressure, Jeffy.

We arrived to the restaurant, were seated at our table with that ocean view, and settled in with cocktails. I tried to find out a little about her life back in Haiti, but she didn't seem to want to talk about it.

So I launched into a bit about my life; how I had lived with my dad part time and my mom part time when I was a kid, how I went to college, got my place, and opened my business. Told her how important surfing was to me (and she smiled a lot at that). Kind of skipped over the women in my life, including my ex, except when she asked me why I had been in Maine for six months.

"Oh...well. Um...to tell you the truth, my girlfriend had broken up with me and I went there to try to convince her to come back."

"For six months? That's dedication." She poked a bit at her salad before looking up at me through her long eyelashes, those lustrous brown eyes. "But...you did not convince her? If you had a girlfriend, I wouldn't be here."

"No, nope. I didn't. I...had some other business there. That's why I stayed so long. She got together with someone else, so that was over. In fact, I stuck around a little to help her out with this problem. All solved. And then I came home. And that is the exciting life of Jeff Chase."

By then our entrees had arrived. I had the Cajun Ahi, while she got the Miso Grilled Salmon.

"Most men seem to like their beef," she said, looking over the dish in front of me. Though it was true that I liked my meat beefy and rare these days, I never lost my taste for fish.

"It's the beach, dude. Gotta have the fish."

"Why do you call everyone 'dude'. You said this earlier."

"Well…like I said. It's a California thing. Everything's a dude. I even say it to my truck."

She laughed, and it was like singing. Everything she did was music or dance, so elegant and dainty. I couldn't help but comment on it. "I can't believe how smoothly you move, like a dancer. Do you dance?"

"Why thank you. My mother always said that there was no need to be herky-jerky when a fluid movement would do." She demonstrated by moving her hand in front of her face and bringing it outward, elbow first in one smooth gesture. "And I do like to dance. I used to love the Hustle."

"Ha! The Hustle? You must have been a baby at the time. Well then. Maybe if you can put up with me for a few more hours, I can take you somewhere we can dance."

"I would like that. You don't seem so hard to…'put up with.'"

The old Jeff charm was coming back to me.

When she talked between bites, she started opening up about Haiti, at least in general terms, wistfully, it seemed. She didn't actually tell me what her job was, but I got the impression it had something to do with fashion. It must have been lucrative because that house she lived in wouldn't have been cheap, either to own or to rent. I wasn't a fashion dude, so most of what she said just skimmed over my head, especially because I was more intrigued with looking at her than really listening that closely, watching her lips.

I told her about how I started my shop, about the guys. I knew she was already interested in the place because of the herbs she could get for her Voodoo stuff, which gave me the perfect in to talk about last night.

"So…that whole manifestation thing that happened at the coven meeting…" I began awkwardly. The glitter seemed to dim in her eyes. "Had that ever happened before?"

She sipped her wine and looked out the window to the sea, resting her chin on her hand. "Not too often, no."

"It, uh, seemed very specific." I licked my lips. "And I was reading how werewolves are sort of big in your culture."

She turned to me then, and her eyes narrowed. She looked angry. "And you think every Haitian believes in them? In something so obviously pedestrian?" She leaned in and stabbed her finger into the table for emphasis. "That is old superstition. Those fools back in Haiti lynch men who are child-stealers, slavers. And they deserve it! But some of us know better. We know there is no such thing as werewolves, only predatory men."

I sat back, blinking. *Make a note, Jeff. Don't bring up that shit again.* It was a sore point, apparently. "Yeah. Okay. Got it."

Her mood shifted again and she lowered her eyes. "I'm so sorry. I just get very…emotional where some things are concerned. I hate stereotypes. Just as all white people are not backwoods hillbillies, not all Haitian people are superstitious."

"I didn't mean to offend you."

"You didn't. You asked a legitimate question. Especially after what we all witnessed the other night." She looked off into the dark ocean again. "When the Lwa come, we don't always like the message they send to us. I heard about the deaths by the pier. And there was that part wolf part dog on the news. The Lwa was warning us. Perhaps this was the beast, the wolf they were talking about. Or perhaps it was only a metaphor, the meaning of which we haven't yet discovered."

My heart stopped. Like it really stopped and my breath caught. When it started again it was going a hundred miles an hour. She saw me on TV too. WereJeff. And she was blaming the murder of that guy on me. Wait. She said deaths, plural. I was almost about to ask, but thought better of it.

"I've upset you," she said, curiously.

I wiped my mouth with my napkin in one big swipe. "Naw, I'm just…thinking about it all. Who are these ladies that came over to your place last night?"

"They are Haitian-Americans. They aren't related to me, but they are related to each other. They're sisters. I found them in a chatroom and we've been celebrating our *sèvi Lwa* together for about a month, since I came to Huntington Beach."

"Oh, so you haven't been here very long."

"No. As I said, I came here from the Valley."

"And how long have you been in the U.S.?"

Our server came and left the check.

"You said something about dancing," she said, sliding out of her chair. "I just need to wash my hands." She smiled and sauntered through the restaurant to the ladies' room. I watched her go, all sensuous moves and elegant curves. I blew out a breath. *Aw, man.* No question. I wanted to get her back to my place. I adjusted myself under the table, and grabbed my wallet.

☾☾☾

WE TOOK SHEILA, my truck, over to a little dance club. It was a real informal place. Part restaurant and bar, it had a dancefloor on the roof with an awesome DJ. But it was crowded. We walked to the front of the line passing all those people, and the bouncer — a surfer buddy of mine — opened the velvet rope just for us. "How's it rippin', Brosef?" He glanced lingeringly at Nadège with an eyebrow raise.

"Boglius, brah." I gave him a shaka as we walked through. I preened. I could tell Nadège was impressed as we made our way up the stairs to the dancing.

As soon as we got through the door, the music blared. Major Lazer & DJ Snake laid down the beat I could feel in my chest. I took Nadège's hand and pulled her immediately to the dancing and she was going with it, neck and shoulders moving with hips following. I did my best white boy moves — I was pretty good on the dance floor if I do say so myself — and I lead my lady through it. She was a natural at following with her own flourishes. It was thrilling being able to take her by the waist…maybe even a little lower…and holding her hand as we did our steps. I felt like the old Jeff was back and the wolf could stuff it for now.

We danced for a few sets, but then Nadège dragged me off to get away from the loudness of the music and to take a little air.

We went outside and leaned over the railing to look out over the city and the ocean beyond. "That was hot in there," I said. I meant more than the music and the temperature. She had a sheen of sweat on her skin, and it made her look even more appealing. *She* was hot. "You move as gracefully on the dancefloor as you do…just anywhere."

"Thank you. And you do very well yourself."

I smiled at her and she cocked her head, gazing at me, her lids shading her eyes. So it was the most natural thing in the world to lean in and touch my lips gently to hers. She kissed back, and though I wanted to take more, it wasn't necessary just then. When I drew back, her smile was growing.

I hooked my finger with hers and swung her hand a little. "Can I get you something to drink?"

"Water, please."

"You got it."

Reluctantly, I let her go and made my way back inside in search of some water bottles. Threading my way through the bodies, I was almost to the bar when I smelled it.

There was a wolf here.

I pricked up my ears, careful to not *actually* prick them up, and I raised my face, letting the notes of the scent flow into my nose.

I pushed through the crowd, said my absent "excuse mes" to people, and pissed off ladies as I elbowed and shoved. I could smell the wolf just on the faint waft of the ceiling fans and air conditioning. It was easy to sense, easy to follow and I knew it wasn't a latent scent because it was warm and alive, because it came off the living person in this room. I knew that instinctually.

I kept moving, turning my face this way and that, resisting the strong urge to morph my face into one with a proper snout so I could fill my nose and mouth with scent.

I kept looking. Where is the guy? There was something about the scent that was really drawing me. It was different from the wolf scents I'd smelled before. It was something earthy, not like Jesse Vargar's scent, which was also kind of earthy but in a different, musky way. This one was lighter, more…intense, like incense or spices or something.

They were right here, right in the circle of people I was among. I turned on my heel, staring at everyone. And suddenly...I whirled around.

A girl, standing on the outer edge of the people, was looking at me. She had soft blonde hair to her shoulders, and wide, green eyes. She had on a lowcut satiny blouse, sleeveless, with an eye-popping cleavage and shapely hips in their skinny jeans. And she was staring at me with glossy lips parted.

I approached her, wedging my way through the people and she was coming at me at the same time.

"Is it you?" I said.

"You, too?" she said breathlessly.

I was not in control anymore. I just took her hand and pulled her in, my heart pounding. I could feel her own racing pulse under my fingertips. I drew her in tight and planted my mouth on hers and she responded, arms snaking around me, body pressed against my sudden hard-on, and we both stood there in the middle of strangers — strangers even to each other — and kissed and kissed, deepening it, living in each other's breath and soft play of tongues, not caring about anything else, writhing against each other...until some dude tapped me sharply on the shoulder.

"What are you doing with my girlfriend?" he bellowed.

CHAPTER EIGHT

I STARED AT him dazedly...until it all came into sharp focus. I pushed her back and looked at her. She was staring back at me, just as puzzled.

"Dude," I began, pushing my hand through my hair. "I...I..."

It was like in slow motion. I saw him take a swing, but it moved sluggishly like he was underwater. Was it wolf sense? I easily shifted back out of the way. And without even thinking about it, I grabbed the back of his neck, kicked at the back of his knees, and pinned him down, cheek flat against a table, knocking over the drinks and scaring all the people sitting there. They jumped to their feet, shouting, and it wasn't till a moment passed that I realized what I'd done. I let him up and put my hands in the air. *Whoa.*

"Dude, I'm sorry. I didn't know she was your girlfriend — "

"I'm *not* his girlfriend!" said the pretty wolf lady.

The guy slowly rose, his face red with anger and embarrassment. A beer mat was stuck to his face for a second until it fell away. He glared at her then at me. He wasn't wolf. I didn't smell it on him.

"I'm sorry," I said stupidly. I didn't know what else to say.

"You can have the bitch," he snarled, and hurried out of there.

I watched him go before I turned to the people at the table. "I'm sorry. Can I replace your drinks?"

They all declined. Looked like they just wanted me to get the hell away from them, so I backed off.

When I turned, the wolf girl was hurrying through the crowd in the other direction. I took off after her.

"Wait!" I grabbed her hand but she shook me off. I held up my hands again, showing I didn't mean any harm. "Can we just...talk?"

"I don't know you."

"I know. And I don't know you, but..." I gestured between us. "We're the same," I whispered.

She was breathing hard. And I have to say, that even though this was intense, I couldn't help but appreciate what it was doing to her chest. *Slow down, Jeffy.* I took a deep breath. "I...I never met another one. Not a girl, I mean. Can we please talk?"

She looked around anxiously. She seemed to decide, grabbed my hand — it felt good there — and yanked me outside. She didn't stop when we hit the sidewalk. She kept going till we moved over the sand and to the surf line.

Then she slowed and dropped my hand. She scraped her hair over one ear and looked me over in the dim light from the restaurants back on the strand. "Who are you?" she said tentatively.

"I'm Jeff. Jeff Chase. I live in HB. Have a tea and spice shop called The Organic Leaf, on Main." It just all came tumbling out. I guess I wanted her to know that I was okay, that I wasn't some random...um, wolf.

She looked me over shyly. "I'm Lindsay. Carter. I...I live in HB too."

Damn, I *really* liked kissing her. It was pure animal. And...I guess we were.

"Do you belong to that pack?" I asked.

She shook her head. "I don't belong to any pack. All this is new to me. I...I s-smelled you in the room up there."

"Yeah. I smelled you too." I couldn't help it. I smiled. "Gives new meaning to 'Smell you later.'"

She smiled a little. But then I realized what she said. I moved closer. She seemed to let me, only cautiously. She sort of held her hand out warning me from coming too close. "What you said. Were you *just* bitten? Recently?"

She winced at it, but slowly nodded. Oh man. *Be careful, Jeff.* "Do you know...who it was?"

She shook her head again. Her eyes glossed with tears. "I didn't know they could be like you. Normal and everything. I thought *he* was. Until he turned."

"Oh God, yeah. I'm normal as heck. Except for this...werewolf problem. I surf and everything."

"You surf too? I was afraid I wouldn't be able to anymore."

"No, it's great. Maybe even better. You can smell the ocean, the wind. It's awesome."

"But what about..." She started walking, sandals kicking at the cold sand. "What about having those cravings? The b-blood?"

"I take wolfsbane. It controls all that. Jesus, didn't the turd who bit you tell you all that?" She shook her head. "Well...would you...would you like to come to my shop and get some doses? No charge. I consider it a public service."

She smiled again and glanced at me. "That would be nice. But maybe we could walk a while first. I feel like ants are all over me."

"When was the last time you shifted?"

"Just the one time, a few days ago."

"Oh, you gotta do it more often. If you don't, you'll go crazy."

She wiped at her nose. "But I'm afraid."

"I'll do it with you, if you want. That way it'll be okay. I can keep an eye on you."

"You'd do that?"

"Hells yeah. When I first shifted, I had a lot of help from a lot of people who knew how to help me."

"Your pack."

"No, I don't have a pack. They were my friends. Just normal people."

She sniffed and lifted her hair in a frustrated gesture. "I don't have a pack or friends I can rely on. I'm messed up."

"No, you're not. You're dealing with something that not a lot of people know about. And it's...like a disease but you can't Google it."

"No kidding. Everything I read is bullshit."

"I know. But I can help you. I can. Without…any strings attached." *Well, Jeff, you are certainly growing up.* Because I sure wanted to kiss her again and get tons of strings.

But when she glanced at me again with gratitude in her eyes, I felt bad about how I was looking at her. But I meant it. Someone was there for me. It was time to pay it forward.

She stuffed her hair behind her ear again. "What were you saying about a pack?"

Man, I didn't want to raise it, but she had to be told. "There actually is another pack here. I met their leader. But I don't know if I'm interested in joining them. I just…" I shook my head. It wasn't fair to influence her one way or the other. "The pack knows things I don't. I've been a werewolf since October of last year. And I'm still trying to figure things out. I learned to make wolfsbane to keep me from needing the blood or getting vicious. But the leader of the pack told me they don't use it. They just learn control."

"But that homeless guy was killed by a wolf. I heard it on the news. They said it could have been a dog but I knew it was a wolf. That wasn't you, was it?"

"No, ma'am. Not me."

"They showed that blond wolf on the news again…"

"Oh. Well, *that* is me…but I didn't kill anyone."

She stopped and stared. "You're a *blond* wolf?"

I tried to shrug it off, laughed a little. "Yeah, that's me. Surfer wolf."

She put her hand to her mouth and laughed. Then we laughed together, and it was good letting it out. She was looking at me steadily, not afraid to approach me. "That was a pretty wolf."

"Thank you."

"I'm sort of brown when I…when I…"

"Shift."

"When I shift. I'm a little brown wolf." She shook her head. "It's weird admitting it."

"Let's get to my shop and I'll give you some wolfsbane. Then we can talk some more."

She nodded, and we walked back to the club where we got into my truck and drove it back to Main. I parked it and opened the back door to my shop, turning off the alarms. I switched on a light and went to the desk in the backroom. I unlocked it and took out the growler I kept in it. I figured out that one dose was about two tablespoons, so I just kept it all in one bottle instead of lots of little ones like Seraphina used to make for me. But I had another growler in my apartment. I handed this one to her. "You just take two tablespoons daily of this. It tastes terrible but it really relaxes the urges. Swear to God."

She took it, looking it over, before she smiled. "A *growler*. Seriously?"

I laughed. "Dude, I *know*. It's poetic."

Her whole face looked brighter. "You don't know how much this means to me."

"Yes, I do. I was there. I know."

She hugged the glass jug to her chest.

Her smile was amazing and having quite the effect on me. "Do you want any coffee...or a beer?"

"I'll take a beer," she said, looking happier already.

I locked up the place, secured the alarm, and led her up the outside stairs. I opened my door for her and I was surprised again at how nice the place looked.

"Oh, this is so cute," she said, clearly pleased. I congratulated myself at my choices...that the nice sales lady helped me pick out.

"Thanks. It's not much, but the commute is great."

She smiled warmly. She really did have a nice smile. "Sit down. I've got Corona. That okay?"

"Anything is fine." She settled in, setting the growler on the coffee table.

I popped the caps off of two and handed her a bottle. Then I clinked mine to hers. "Here's to a new lease on life."

She clinked back and touched the bottle to her lips. She set it down on her thigh and nodded. "It *is* a new lease on life."

"It is. Don't you feel stronger?"

"Yeah. I do. I used to have a scar on my leg from being tossed from my board to the rocks, and it's gone."

I sat next to her and set my beer aside. "I know. I had some too. And they're all gone. And it's a rush, like hitting the waves just right. And wolfing out..."

"'Wolfing out'?"

"That's what I call it. *Shifting*, as the lingo goes," I said, giving it air quotes. "It's a rush. Like no other."

"I was afraid to. After knowing what I was. I thought it meant I would kill someone."

"With control, we can learn to ween off the wolfsbane. Or so I've been told."

"But for now..." She stared at the growler.

"Do you want to take some now?"

She sighed with such a heaving of relief. "Yes, if you don't mind."

"I don't." I went to the bathroom and grabbed the plastic cup that I used to measure it out. I cleaned it in the kitchen and handed it to her. "Be my guest."

She unscrewed the growler cap and carefully tipped some in.

"All the way to the top," I told her. "Now brace yourself, because it really is awful. And you can't add flavoring because it will make it inert. I was told that right off the bat. Get your beer ready."

She screwed up her face at it, paused, and then knocked it back. "Oh!" she winced, sticking out her tongue. "Oh my God, that *is* awful."

"Drink the beer," I urged.

She tilted it up, waving her other hand and swallowed several gulps. When she lowered it she was back to normal. "And that's it?"

"That's it. Once a day." I screwed the cap back on her growler.

"I can't believe it. It's gonna be okay, isn't it."

"It is." I sat back with her, us just sitting, drinking our beers. She put hers down and I put mine down...and she turned to me.

"Do you want to shift?" I asked.

"You mean…now? Like…now?"

"Right now. Right here. It's okay. I'll shift too."

She stood up. But now she was shy again, because we both knew we had to strip. So I turned my back first and started taking off my shirt. Of course, I did it fast because I could shift in the wink of an eye now. But I remembered that it was hard at first and gave her time. I looked over my furry shoulder and she had changed already. And she was a little brown wolf like she said, cute as hell. I yipped at her, and she rose up on her back paws, paddling the air. I walked around her, sniffing like crazy, and she — kind of shyly — sniffed at me. And once she realized it was okay, she jumped in the air and ran around the room, getting down on her front paws like a dog asking to play.

I chased her, and she ran in circles. She was so funny I wanted to howl, but I knew the guy next door wouldn't like it.

She ran up to me and we snuffled noses. Then I don't know what happened next. One minute we were wolves and the next minute we were two naked people, kissing and touching. We managed to get ourselves to the couch, and when she lay back, I dug my face into her neck, covering her breasts with both hands, rubbing my hardness against her. She opened her thighs and wrapped them around my waist, pulling me in. That's all the urging this boy needed.

I was kissing her, and she was writhing beneath me, and I was thrusting and moaning. Her hands were all over me, squeezing my butt and moving with me. "Yes," she kept murmuring. My nose was filled with musky wolf and woman, and I bent my head again to nuzzle her breasts, nibbling a nipple between my lips. But things were moving quick and I didn't want to finish before her. I reached down in between us and moved my thumb in just the right places. She started raising her hips at me.

Control, Jeff. Don't pop too soon. You can do this. But man, it had been a *long* time.

Just as I thought I couldn't hold on anymore, she seemed to stiffen and gasped out loud. I could feel her inside and I couldn't stop. I breathed hard and finished and hadn't even realized I didn't use a condom. That was bad. But I wasn't really capable of thinking beyond that. Everything went a little hazy as I settled down, trying not to crush her, even as she threw her arms around me and held me close.

She breathed harshly at my ear. "Don't worry," she whispered. "I'm on the pill."

I nodded, touching my lips to whatever my face was closest to. Mostly her neck and chest.

"And I'm twenty-five," she added, with a giggle. "I know that I look barely legal."

Shit. I never even thought of that. I was so out of practice.

I lay beside her on the couch, trying not to fall off the edge, and running my hands over every luscious inch of her…and there was a lot of luscious inches…when an alarm suddenly went off in my head. I sat up so sharply I *did* fall off the couch.

"Shit! Nadège!" I croaked.

CHAPTER NINE

❦

"LINDSAY, I'M SO sorry." I jumped up off the floor and grabbed for my pants that I had left somewhere. I found it on the other side of the coffee table, pulled my phone out of my trouser pocket, and started jabbing at it. "I totally forgot that I was with someone at the club."

"So was I," she said, hand to her head. "But I guess it doesn't matter." Still, she scrambled up and went for her own pants, and I was momentarily mesmerized by the sight. The phone clicked, and Nadège came on.

"Jeff! Where are you? I looked all over — "

"Babe, I am so, so sorry. A friend called me with an emergency and I had to go. I totally forgot about...well, *you*. It's unforgiveable. Can I call you tomorrow? I'll make it up. I will."

There was silence on the line for quite a long pause. "Okay. I'll let you *try*."

"Oh, thank you. You're an angel. But I've gotta go. Bye!" I clicked off and lowered the phone to my thigh with a huge exhale. Well, that wasn't the first time I'd lied to one girl while I had another on the hook. It felt kind of bad this time, though.

Lindsay hadn't had to call anyone. She was looking at her phone forlornly before she sighed and tucked it away again. Her expression probably mirrored my own. What were *we* gonna do?

"Was that your girlfriend?" she asked.

"No. I just met her. This was our first date."

"Yeah, mine too. But I didn't even want to go. I just wanted to do something normal, you know? All the time I was worrying I'd...I'd shift and kill him. I guess, since he saw us kissing and all, there won't be a second date. Doesn't matter. I wasn't really into him."

That sort of hung in the air between us. Was she into me? Or was I just convenient? I've never been in that position before.

We didn't say anything more after that, the implication being that we didn't owe them anything. That was certainly the old Jeff. The new Jeff seemed to have a bit of a conscience about it all. Hey, welcome to the twenty-first century at last, dude.

But...then again, the old Jeff was noticing what a luscious naked female he had standing in front of him, smelling of sex and the most delicious scent of female wolf. It was like an aphrodisiac. I walked toward her. "We don't have to do anything about them right now, though," I said.

She met me in the middle and placed her bare skin right up against mine, looking up at me. "No we don't. You have a bed somewhere, don't you?"

"Yeah. It's in the other room."

She ran her hand down me from my neck, down my torso, and landing just where I was beginning to perk up again. "Then let's go."

I followed her in.

☾☾☾

THE NEXT MORNING, I was tuckered out. We'd done it two more times. That was my limit these days. *You're slowing down, Jeffy.*

I rolled over and looked at her, those wide eyes and glowing cheeks, a tangle of hair hiding one eye. She offered a lazy smile. But then the smile seemed to fade. "What was last night?" she asked. "Some werewolf kind of thing?"

I laid back, my hands laced behind my head. "I don't know. I just don't know enough about being a werewolf myself. I'm afraid I won't be much help to you."

That smile was back, got wickeder the more she looked at me. "Oh, I wouldn't say that."

"Girl, you wore me out. And..." I sat up, trying not to think about a round four. Even though I wanted to. "We really have to figure this out. I mean...we can't just attack each other in public. We gotta find out what's going on."

She pulled the sheets up to cover her chest. Darn it. "You're right. I've never done anything like that before."

She fell silent and I tried not to look at her when I asked, "Do...do you want to tell me about it? The guy who...who bit you?"

"It was just another date with some guy I met at a bar. We were walking along the beach. It was dark. And he'd been acting a little off all night. But I didn't know what it meant. When he turned into a wolf—shifted, I mean—I screamed. He jumped me to hold me down, maybe shut me up. I was terrified. Then he bit my arm." She rubbed at her left arm, but of course, there was no scar there. It had healed right away.

"Then he...ran off. I never saw him again. That was a week ago. I was scared but I felt sick and I dragged myself home. And that's when I changed. That scared me, too. I stayed home from work. I didn't know what to do. I thought I was going crazy. Stuff like this doesn't happen in the real world."

"I'm afraid it's all too real. God, what an asshole, biting you and leaving you like that. What was his name?"

"Jacob something. I can't remember his last name."

"Where was this? That you met him?"

"Crabworks. It's the bar I work at. He picked me up after my shift was over. I waitress there."

"Damn. Have you been back to work?"

She shook her head. Her eyes were getting glazed again. "I may not even have a job."

"Call 'em up. Tell them you had a medical emergency. Beg for your job. If they're cool, they'll let you keep it."

"Maybe. I will call them, though. Jeff, is it going to be okay?"

"Listen, babe, I'll make sure it'll be okay. I'm gonna do some more research on all this and I'll keep you updated. Text me your number."

She did and I looked at it on my phone. But then she looked up at me as so many other women had when I told them I'd call them. I remembered that look. Was I gonna ghost her? That's what it looked like she thought. "Dude, Lindsay, I'm gonna call you. I will. I mean...we may not...you know...do *this* again, but I will keep track of you. I swear, werewolf to werewolf."

"You don't want to do *this* again?" And she gestured between us.

She looked pretty fetching with her hair tosseled like that, with sleep-weary lids hanging low and slanted in her gaze. I lifted my hand to push her hair out of her eye and slid it over her ear. "It's not off the table. As long as it's mutual, and you don't feel obligated. Cause you're not."

She lowered her face for a moment. "Thanks, Jeff. I appreciate your honesty."

I appreciate it too, I murmured to myself. *I guess.*

She got up and showered, while I slipped on my shorts and made coffee. It didn't take her long and she came out dressed in the same outfit from last night. She still looked damned good in the morning. I offered her a mug. "How do you take it?"

"A little milk."

I gave her the half gallon and she poured some in. "I can make us some breakfast. I'm sure you're feeling the need for more red meat these days."

"Yeah. It's kind of bad since I was cutting down."

"I was a vegetarian."

She slumped her shoulders. "Oh man."

"Yeah. Kind of a surprise for my boys."

"Your boys?"

"My crew. Downstairs in my tea shop."

She sipped the coffee. "Oh. How did you explain it?"

"I told them I had this blood disorder and the doc said I had to go on more red meat. For the iron."

She nodded. "That's a good idea. I might have to use that one."

"So…breakfast?"

"No, thanks. I should get going." She put down the mug and got her purse, pulling the strap over her shoulder and clutching it. She looked around, a little reluctant to leave.

"I'll call you today. I swear I will."

She nodded again, grabbed the growler of wolfsbane, and turned toward the door. I escorted her before I realized I'd driven her here. "Can I drive you home?"

"No, thanks. I only live a couple of blocks away."

"You sure?"

"Yeah." She paused at the top of the stairs and turned back to me. "You've been really nice about all this. A real gentleman."

A real gentleman wouldn't have banged her. *Baby steps, Jeff.*

She reached up and kissed my cheek. I gave her a half-hearted smile as she slowly descended the stairs.

When I closed the door, I was determined to kick the ass of this *Jacob.* Wherever *he* was.

☾☾☾

I GOT CLEANED up, and realized Luis was opening today. I called him on my cell as I was getting into my truck. "I got some stuff to take care of this morning. Can you handle it on your own, bro?"

"Yeah, but what about last night with the Voodoo chick?"

"I'll, uh, catch you up on that later."

I tossed the phone into the gearshift well, and started driving toward Vargar's place. I pulled up in front this time and rang the doorbell like a civilized human...or...werehuman. Shit. Whatever.

He was there and opened the door, standing in the doorway like he was expecting me. He probably smelled me. I pushed him aside and made my way through.

"Come in, why don't you," he said with a sneer.

"Your pack are assholes, you know that?"

"Some are."

"Maybe they're only following your lead. Do you have a Jacob in your pack?"

He narrowed his eyes. "What's he done?"

"He's making werewolves. Didn't you know, oh high and mighty alpha-hole?"

"What!"

"I met this girl last night. She said he bit her and left her all alone with it. Didn't explain shit. And I found her and helped her out."

"Fuck." He raked his hand through his hair and paced like a wolf in a cage.

"I think I'd like to have a little chat with him."

He looked at me then. I didn't realize my voice had gone wolfy. Probably my eyes too, because he made calming gestures with his hands. "Just chill, okay."

"I'm not gonna chill. You didn't see the terror in her eyes at what she was. She didn't know if she had gone insane or not. That was some fucked up shit your boy did there."

"I know, okay! I'll take care of it."

"No, *I'll* take care of it. What's the asshole's full name?"

"Listen to me. Listen." And then he tried that hypno shit on me again. I shook my head free of it.

"Cut that out! She fell into *my* lap. I'll take care of her. If you can't control your pack, maybe I should do it for you."

He partially shifted, just his eyes, his muzzle and his shoulders, hackles raised. "*I* will," he said all wolfed. Sounded so weird half human and half wolf like that.

I wanted to, but I knew it wouldn't do any good to get into a fight right now. I pointed a finger at his muzzle. Wanted to poke it. "You *do* that!"

I turned my back on him and stomped out the door. I got into my truck, started her up, and drove around the corner. Then I snuck it back near the end of his street, and sat there against the curb, watching to see what he was going to do. Soon, the garage door opened and he backed out his black SUV, a badass Cadillac ST5. He screeched the tires backing into the cul-de-sac curve, then tore rubber getting out of there. I whipped Sheila around to follow him.

It occurred to me as I watched him weave in and out of traffic, that this Jacob could have been responsible for killing that homeless guy. And maybe that other body that I heard about on the beach. Looks like Vargar had himself a regular lone wolf on the rampage. I was going to have some words with the douche. And maybe some fangs and claws while I was at it.

I followed him north, almost to Fountain Valley where he pulled into a hardware store parking lot. I parked way in the back and slammed my truck door as I wandered in after him.

I came just in time to see him drag some red-faced guy by his plaid flannel shirt toward the back door. Vargar slammed the panic bar and leaned on the door with his hip. They both disappeared outside.

I moved forward, sloughing off a guy with a nametag who wanted to know if he could help me. Dude, I *knew* what could help me. I slammed open the door and the two looked up at me like deer in the headlights. "Is this asshole named Jacob?"

Vargar snarled. "Get out of here, Chase. This is none of your concern."

"Oh, I think it is. Are you? Are you Jacob?"

"Who the hell are you?" said Flannel Shirt. And looky there, a nametag that said *Jacob — the Ass-faced Wolf.*

"I'm the guy that's going to kick your sorry ass."

Vargar's eyes wolfed and his teeth elongated to sharp canines. "Back off!" he snarled again in a human/wolf voice.

"I don't think so." I half-changed, showing my teeth. My arms and hands morphed with hair and long claws. "I'm going to show this fuckwit that he can't treat a lady like that."

Jacob had as guilty a look on his face as there was. He instantly shifted, doffed his clothes, and leapt into the pampas grass and ice plant-covered slope.

"Ah *hell* no, bruh," I growled, before I shifted out of my own clothes in broad daylight and took off after him.

CHAPTER TEN

❦

I SCRAMBLED ON all fours up the slope. I had his smell in my nose now. No way I'd lose him, no matter where he went. I just saw his tail disappearing through a whole in a chain link fence along the top and I dove after him.

He was booking down a backstreet along a concrete wash and I was gaining on him. He looked back once, whined, and poured on the steam. *Not gonna do you any good, man. Your ass is mine.*

I was almost on his tail and leapt. We growled and barked and we rolled over and over one another right in the middle of the street. He tried to get out from under me, but I bit and shook his paw in my jaws. He rolled to his back, showing me his belly, an obvious display of submission. I wanted to rip my claws down that torso, open him up, rip his entrails... Whoa. Shit. Did I forget to take my wolfsbane today? No, I did, but the wild side was obviously just below the surface.

I backed off. He whined a lot and tentatively rolled back but stayed on his belly, tilting his head way over, still in submission mode. He was a coward as well as a dick. But how was I gonna question him as a wolf? I looked around. It was kind of public, so I jerked my head meaning for him to follow me. I wondered if wolves communicated in other ways that I didn't know about, but he got the idea and slowly trotted in front of me, tail between his legs and head down.

I made him go back through the fence and I followed him down the slope. Vargar was still there, though he had been pacing and his hands kept shifting back and forth from paws to hands. He looked up at us when we appeared sliding down the ice plant.

I grabbed Jacob's ruff with my teeth and shoved him toward his clothes. He shifted at once, rubbing the arm I bit, and bent to reach for his stuff. I shifted and slowly grabbed my jeans.

"Okay, dickwad. You get to explain to your fearless leader here why you bit a girl, changed her, and just left her to figure it all out for herself."

I slid my pants on as Vargar looked daggers at him, arms folded over his chest. He was vibrating with anger. "Yeah. I'd like to know too. Talk."

He hopped around, getting his leg in his pants and zipping up. He shrugged into his flannel shirt and stuffed his hands in his pockets. "I don't know. I just...she was kind of being a snooty bitch —"

"And that's a lie right there," I cut in, "because she is *not* a snooty bitch. Tell us another, asshole."

Jacob looked toward Vargar but the leader wasn't backing down. He was doing that eye thing with the guy and Jacob was getting all nervous.

"I don't know. I just felt...I felt reckless. I felt like I wanted to break out, to do something real wolfy."

I lunged at him and he shrank back. "Did you kill that guy on the beach?"

"What guy? What are you talking about?"

"You're not even a very good liar."

He pleaded with Vargar. "I didn't kill no one. This guy's trying to pin something on me."

"Did you?" said Vargar, eyes deadly.

He shook his head.

"And what did I say about wanting to act out? I told all the pack they needed to control it or come to me. Did you forget that?"

"It was a rush, Jesse. Like doing coke. It was a total rush. *You* must know how it feels."

"Ask him how many times he's done it? Ask him if he killed anyone else, going too far?"

Vargar growled deep in his throat and stood over Jacob. He seemed somehow bigger, looming over him without even shifting.

But what Jacob said was filtering back to me. Yeah, how about that? Werewolves weren't born, were they? Weren't they made? How many did Jesse Vargar make against their will?

"It's only in extreme circumstances," said Vargar between clenched teeth. "You *know* the rules, Jacob!"

He looked desperately at Vargar and then at me. He was gonna bolt again and I edged toward the door of the store, blocking him.

But Vargar grabbed his arm and squeezed. Jacob bent his body down, obviously in pain.

"You don't take it into your own hands, Jacob. You know the rules. You broke with the pack."

"No! I didn't. Don't throw me out, Jesse. I can't handle it."

"Who said anything about throwing you out?"

Jacob's face went gray. If they weren't going to throw him out, then...

I got up behind Vargar. "What are you saying, man? What are you gonna do?"

"This is not your business, Chase."

"Dude, when are you gonna learn? Any supernatural shit in this town *is* my business. So what are your plans, bro? Do you kill him? Shoot him with a silver bullet? What's the plan, because I'm not letting that shit go down."

"Back off, Chase," he husked, in that half-human/half-wolf voice.

"Not gonna happen." And I grew just my snout with its rows of sharp teeth, snapping them a few times to let them both know I meant it.

Jacob shrank back again. It was clear he was afraid of me, but he feared Vargar more.

"Code of silence, huh?" I paced. "Look. There's a new wolf in town, and I'm keeping my eye on you and your dumbshit pack. I'll sniff them out one by one and there are a few tricks I've learned to keep track of them. If I find out any of them have killed...I'll be back. You won't know when, but I'll be back. And take care of it the WereJeff way."

I gave them the once over, and then turned my back on them. Yeah, they could have jumped me, but I knew they wouldn't. And I wasn't afraid of them.

When I drove back to my shop, I was thinking hard. There was a lot on my plate. Nadège; Lindsay; dealing with shifting and not getting caught; whoever murdered that homeless guy...and wasn't there another murder too? I had to look that up.

I parked in the back of my shop and sat there. First thing I did was take out my phone and looked up local homicides. Yup. There was that other one, with a photo of cops and a covered body. But wait. What was that in the background?

I pinched the picture bigger, as big as it would go. Wasn't that a bunch of those Crackpots? I mean Cutbacks? Yeah, those surf gang boys, and they had big dogs on a short leashes; Rottweilers. What if it hadn't been a wolf? What if it was one of those dumbshit Cutback Boys? Those *were* big paw prints... Great. One more thing on my plate.

But first things first. I had to find out why Lindsay and I went all *Body Heat* on each other. It was like some weird love spell. I could call the Maine coven...but as I weighed the phone in my hand, I knew I just didn't want to call on them. Oh, I know they told me I could — once your coven always your coven — but I still felt the need to cut the apron strings, so to speak. I needed my own coven here. Nadège? No, since her people had a werewolf aversion with a hanging rope.

I touched my neck. That meant...Lauren? Could I trust her? And worse. Do I *burden* her? But wasn't she a werewolf nut, kind of a groupie? Loving research was not the same thing, I supposed. But if anyone would know, she would.

I got out of the truck, pushed my hair back into place, and walked around to the sidewalk. I'd go to her shop, see if I could talk to her about it.

Starlight Occult was just around the next corner. I passed through the door, and there was Bliss behind the counter. Her hair was done up in blonde corn rows today. She was reading a book on Tarot and slowly looked up. "Hey."

"Hey, Bliss. Lauren around?"

"She's in the back. Want me to call her?"

"No, that's okay—"

"Hey, LAU-REN!" she bellowed. "JEFF CHASE IS HERE LOOKING FOR YOU!"

I gave her a firing pistol with my fingers. "Thanks."

Before I could get to the back room, Lauren came out. She looked a little disheveled, with dark bags under her eyes.

I must have looked surprised because she shrugged. "Yeah, I know I look terrible. Bliss already told me."

"She's a subtle one, that Bliss." Then I remembered about the forget-me charm bag and her ex-husband. "Hey, if it's a bad time..."

"No, no." She flopped her hands into the air and let them slap her thighs. "Everything's just peachy."

"Ordinarily, I'd recommend some ginger tea. But maybe it calls for a dose of old-fashioned caffeine. Can I buy you a cup at the Mermaid Café?"

She nodded like she'd given up and I escorted her out the door and up the street to our local coffee hangout. The Mermaid had a logo that looked suspiciously like Starbucks' but with an angrier and more determined mermaid, along with a merman to help her attitude. We ordered our brews in ceramic cups and sat with them at a window table. We settled in and I let her brood for a second or two. "I'm sorry about your troubles."

"No troubles. I just gave my ex what-for, told him never to bother me again or risk a court order, and got my stuff back. So that's done for good, I hope."

"Doing a forget-me spell was just chicken shit, if you don't mind my saying."

"I don't mind." She leaned in over her cup. "But I wouldn't mind knowing where you learned about that."

"Oh...well. Didn't I tell you that before?" I was getting my women mixed up. I'd told that to Nadège, but not to Lauren. Or did I? Jesus, I had three on the hook. Sort of. Lauren was just a friend. "I told you how I got to know the local coven and they taught us some tricks. Well, not *tricks*, really. Real magic. Um...like charm pouches. So I believe in some supernatural things."

"So you said before. The stuff that would get me several PhD's, you mean?"

"Y-yeah. Like that."

"Even with all my research it does seem really hard to believe in the real sense."

"It's pretty real. Which brings me to why I came to your shop today." Jeez, how was I going to approach this? I didn't really want to tell her about me. I didn't want to be a guinea pig for her, for one. And for another, I just didn't want to tell a lot of people. It was on a strictly need-to-know basis, as far as I was concerned. "So I had more...werewolf questions."

"You seem pretty obsessed with them."

"Not as much as you are."

"Point." She sipped her coffee. She took it with a lot of cream *and* a lot of sugar. I don't know why, but it struck me as kind of cute, like a little kid would take it to mask the coffee taste. "Go on," she said.

"Okay. So. Two werewolves—one a man, the other a woman. And they didn't know each other. They meet and suddenly sparks fly. They can't control their instincts and they...you know. Do it. Almost right then and there. No control whatsoever."

"Mate, you mean?" She cocked her head, a little like Lindsay did, I thought. "Are you writing a novel or something?"

I shrugged. Okay. "Maybe..."

"Can't you just make up whatever you want if you're writing fiction?"

"I like it to have a basis in fact. So what do you think that is?"

"In the animal kingdom, there's the rut, when the female is in heat."

"In heat? Like a *dog*?"

She gave me a "what kind of idiot is this" look. "*Fiction*, right?"

"But you know this stuff, don't you? What else could cause that? Among werewolves."

She sighed and drank a little. Still holding the cup by the handle, she gestured with her other hand. "There aren't a lot of details available on the mating habits of werewolves. There isn't that sort of David Attenborough kind of documentary information out there. All the info I've ever seen is how they're made, what kills them, and some information on pack behavior, but that's all. I mean, it's complete speculation as to whether they exist or not, and I lean more toward the non-existing side."

"Oh." My expert, though thorough, was still a skeptic.

"But," she said with a sigh, "I seem to remember some obscure reference to mating pairs finding each other. Maybe it's that."

Gulp. "*Mating* pair?"

"There's more than one way to make a werewolf."

Shit. I didn't want a…a *litter* just yet in my life. "So…are they like *destined* for each other? Without free will?"

"Not that I know of. No texts seem to mention that."

I sat back and blew out a breath. I mean, Lindsay was really sweet and all. But I didn't know if she was someone I wanted to spend my life with. Just…maybe hook up with now and again.

"Pretty sure they can only conceive another werewolf when they're wolves. Mating. Mating as wolves."

"Dude, no. That's just…wrong. Isn't that like…" I looked around to make sure no one was close enough to overhear us. "Bestiality?"

"You're *really* into this, aren't you."

I pulled it back. Didn't want her thinking I was a freak or anything. "What? No! I just…I'm in this writing group…" It kind of amazed me the kind of lies I could come up with on the fly. It was easy. It didn't make me feel any better. Because I was going to be telling a whopper to Nadège later. But I guess I've been doing it for years. Not cool, Jeff.

"Well, thanks…" I said lamely, turning my mug on the table. We fell silent and I looked up at her through my hair. "You…want to talk about your ex? I'm all ears."

She started tearing her napkin into thin strips. "Just a poor choice on my part. Married three years. He was never there. He had secrets. And the occult wasn't supposed to be one of them. Figures since he walked into my shop. That's how we met. But I never knew he was into that stuff, not like that. A forget-me spell. I'm still astounded."

"You don't believe in the occult?"

"I do. Some of it. The rest is just old superstition. I've been to places where I've seen charm pouches, gris-gris bags...all kinds of spells actually work. But why did *he* do that to *me*?"

"Do you want me to beat him up for you?"

She laughed, then took a moment to look me over. "No," she said, still smiling. "It's a nice thought, though, and I appreciate your offering, but no."

"Um...do you surf? I could take you out sometime. Get your mind off things. Teach you, maybe."

She laughed and tucked her hair behind her ear. "I've never surfed."

"Oh, dude! You have to! You'd love the freedom."

"I don't know. I don't have a board."

"I've got two. You let me know and we'll take off sometime. Play hooky from work. Weekdays are better anyway, since the hodads aren't there."

"'Hodads'?"

"Surfing groupies that don't surf. They can get annoying."

"You don't seem like a surfer."

"What? Are you kidding me?"

"No, I just mean you seem too sm—" She suddenly closed her lips. "Uh..."

I sat back. "I seem too smart? Dude, you've got the wrong idea about surfers. I went to college with a degree and everything. Just because I'm an Aggro doesn't mean I'm stupid."

"'Aggro'?"

"Aggressive surfer."

"I'm sorry. I didn't mean it that way... But I guess..." She winced. "I sort of did. And I'm...sorry."

"That hurt, no lie. A lot of guys out there are professionals in all kinds of fields. Silicon Valley computer geeks, accountants, engineers. You don't have to be a bum to surf."

"I am sorry."

"Well...that just means I have to make a fool of you out there to make up for it."

"Jeff!"

"Nerp. You've done it now. We'll go this week."

"It's March. It's still a bit cold out there, don't you think?"

"I'll dig up a wet suit for you. You have to go now since you dissed me and my tribe."

She laughed. She was looking less ragged. "Okay, okay! Thursday?"

"You're on!"

I told her to meet me at my place early, like six am on Thursday, and we finished our coffees, said our good-byes, and each retreated to our respective shops.

☾☾☾

"JEFF!" SAID LUIS for maybe not the first time.

I snapped my head up. "Sorry. I was zoning on the internet."

"Yeah, I see that. Are you ever gonna spill about your date?"

"Yeah," said Cam. "The Voodoo lady? Was it...magical?"

"Uh..." The truth? Not the truth? "It was...a mess. We were at the rooftop dance club and getting down with it, and when we took a break, I went to the bar to get her some water and I met this girl..."

Luis' mouth dropped open. "You did *not*. Dude!"

I felt my face redden. Yeah, every time I thought about it, I felt like the douche I was. But to be fair, it was part of the wolf thing. "I...I got caught up and the next thing I knew I was taking her home and I forgot about Nadège..."

"Oh man!" Cam laughed and laughed.

"I know. I was a total douche and I apologized to Nadège."

"You *told* her?" said Luis.

"Are you crazy? No! I told her one of you had an accident and I had to take you to the hospital."

Luis looked at Cam and they both burst out laughing. "You never let us down, man," said Luis.

"Yeah." *I never let you down.* But I felt I let myself down and even worse that we were all laughing about it. What the hell happened to me in Maine? Besides the wolfing, I guess I did some growing up. Caught the woke train or something. I was determined not to be that Jeff anymore. WereJeff was going to stand for something else beside the picture in the dictionary next to "douchebag".

Took care of business earlier by calling Nadège and squaring with her. I was going to cook her dinner tonight. That meant I had to wash the sheets. You know…just in case.

But I also had to check out those Cutback Boys, maybe check the crime sheets to see if they were on the police radar.

I turned back to the computer and called up HB police blotter. Yeah, going back a few weeks, there they were. There were some guys named Joe Webster, Sean Brill, and Ben "Darkhorse" Richardson. They had been caught vandalizing cars. The week before another identified with the gang had broken into some shops close by mine. "Idiots," I murmured, scrolling through. Nothing worse than that, though there was a fight but the case was dismissed. Real winners, those dudes.

How was I going to find them? My nose had been full of seawater when I met them, so I couldn't sniff them out. But I had their names so I could check out where they lived.

Maybe a little sleuthing today was in order.

"So I've got more errands to run," I told my crew, coming out from the office. "But Cam, my man. Are you interested in a free car straight outta Maine?"

His eyes widened. "Are you serious?"

"As a funeral. I don't want Sheila to get jealous. I only needed it to get home from the east coast. If you want it…" I dug in my pocket, pulled out the keys, and tossed them to him.

He caught it and stared into his hand. "Dude, I don't know how to thank you."

"Extra shifts to take over mine for a while?"

"You got it!"

I'd sign it over to him later. Right now, I had some sheets to wash, food to buy, and some surfer idiots to find.

CHAPTER ELEVEN

❦

I SAT ON the sand, scanning the beach, the waves (nothing special today), and didn't see the gang. There were some surfers out there but since the waves were trash, there was a lot of decking it.

I was having no luck. But when the surfers came into shore, I decided to ask them. I dusted the sand off my legs and strolled out there. It looked like one or two guys recognized me from my own surfing, and gave me friendly waves. I approached one of them first.

"Total shorepound, isn't it," I said.

Blond-tips guy bobbed his head. "Totally. You're not even giving it a try today?"

"Naw. Just checking it out. Hey, can I ask you something?"

"Sure." He tucked his board under his arm, and began heading toward the parking lot.

"Did you ever run into some losers calling themselves the Cutback Boys?"

He gave me the side eye. "Those guys? You don't belong to them, do you?"

"No way. The beach is for everyone in my book."

He looked relieved. He used his key fob to beep his trunk open, took out a towel, and ruffled it over his hair. "That's good. Because they are primo assholes. They show up here and try to pull their shit. Like this hasn't been an open beach like forever."

"Did they ever get violent?"

He unzipped the top of his wetsuit and let it flop around him, like a peeled banana. "Dude, I saw them beat up these young guys. Way younger than them, the fucking cowards. Me and some of my friends chased them off. They are losers with a capital L."

"Do you think they are capable of killing someone? I mean...they have dogs."

"I saw their dogs once. They each have them. That was some bullshit, man. I wish the cops would do something about them but they're never around when the Cutbacks do their shit."

"Yeah." I looked around as he wrapped the towel around his waist and peeled off the rest of his wetsuit. "Do you know if they show up on certain days or...?"

"Most weekdays." He swiveled his head to look around. "I'm surprised they aren't here today. But they usually show up early."

"Okay. Well bro, thanks for talking with me."

"Hey, no prob. I've seen you out there. You're righteous."

"Thanks. If you're ever in the market for herbs or tea, I own the Organic Leaf on Main."

"Oh? *Organic* leaf?" He mimed toking on a doobie.

"Sorry, not that kind of leaf. Tea."

"Oh. Not a tea drinker, brah."

We bumped fists. Early weekdays, huh? I'd check it out tomorrow. But as for tonight, I had to come up with some dinner ideas. Nadège was coming over and I wanted my place spic and span.

☾☾☾

THE TUNA WAS marinating in a tropical blend of fruit and juices, a recipe I got from the Tequila Tiki, and I was setting the table when the doorbell rang. Glancing at my watch I wondered if it was slow. I shook it. Maybe she was just an early bird.

When I opened the door, it wasn't Nadège. It was Widelene, the hefty woman from Nadège's Voodoo ladies.

"Uh..."

"You inviting me in, white boy?"

"Not if you don't stop calling me that. My *name* is Jeff."

"*Jeff*, then."

I stepped aside and let her pass through. What the hell was this? The proscribed warning me off? Could this get any more cliché?

She walked around the one-room place, inspecting things, and lastly the fish, of which she seemed to reluctantly approve.

"To what do I owe the pleasure?" I tried not to sound snarky about it, but seriously? What *was* this? I checked my watch again. Nadège was supposed to be here in half an hour. "And, uh, how did you get my address?"

She finally turned to me. She wore another colorfully-patterned cloth wrapped around her hair. And her long dress was also colorfully-patterned but didn't match the *gele*. "The bones tell me." She said it like "da bohns". With her accent and knowing their Voodoo stuff, it kind of gave me a chill.

"Bones? Like…real bones?"

"Bones." She mimed rolling them between her palms and casting them. I didn't know I was in the bone listings.

"Um…okay. So why are you here? Is this your obligatory telling me to stay away from Nadège? So noted. Thanks for stopping by." I gestured back toward the door.

"I'm here to warn you. You don't know what you are getting mixed up in."

"The Voodoo. I get it. I was just curious about it and now…my curiosity is satisfied. Good enough?"

"No, it is *not* good enough." She stomped toward me and I took a step back. She pointed a finger into my face. "You. Don't. Know."

"Then *what*?" I ran my hand through my hair and stepped away from her. "Jeez, I just wanted to have a date with a pretty lady. She seems really nice. I'm not a threat to her or you."

"The wolf," she said and that stopped me. Shit. Could she *see* the wolf in me?

"The wolf," she said again, "is near. You bring bad things to this place. You should leave it alone, leave *us* alone."

"Okay, I get it. Big bad white boy. Got it. Does Nadège know you're here?"

"You don't understand..."

"And neither do I," said Nadège, standing in the doorway.

Uh oh. I crept backwards, trying to get out of the line of fire. I didn't think this was going to be pretty.

Nadège stomped into the room and got right up to Widelene. And then they started yelling in Haitian. Widelene seemed earnest but Nadège wasn't having it. I got that they didn't like me. Maybe Nadège was going to be more trouble than she was worth. The Voodoo ladies were out anyway in terms of helping me, what with their hatred for the wolf. I'd have to get my supernatural coven help elsewhere. Maybe Lauren? Maybe somewhere else?

The argument seemed to culminate and then die down as they stopped yelling and had a stare-off for a few moments instead. Then Widelene threw back her head and stalked toward the door. She sort of knocked into me as she went, but then I felt something pressed into my hand. She gave me one more look before she passed through the doorway, and when I looked down, there was a small charm bag in my palm. Or, I guess, it was a gris-gris bag. I was about to show it to Nadège when I suddenly stopped.

Why had she given it to me? She could have just planted it somewhere in my place. Why did she want me to know about it? So it could do *more* harm? Was that how it worked? Damn, I didn't know as much as I thought.

When I turned to Nadège I held it behind my back. Was this bad Voodoo or good Voodoo? I tried to remember what Widelene had really said to me. Was she warning me *off*...or just warning me?

"I'm so sorry about her," said Nadège.

What was I going to do with the thing? I stuffed it in my pocket and took her arms. "Don't worry about it. I don't."

"I can't believe she came here. What did she say to you?"

"Oh, you know. The usual. 'She doesn't need you...blah, blah, blah.'"

"The nerve of her!"

"Look, let's not let it spoil our evening. Would you like some wine? Something stronger?"

She blew a breath out and loosened her shoulders. "No, wine will do."

I poured some for both of us and gestured that she should sit down on my new sofa. She glanced around the room. "This is very nice," she said and took a sip.

"Thank you. It's cozy enough for me."

"How is your friend?"

I blanked for what seemed like a whole minute before I realized she was asking about the guy that I had lied to her about. "He's fine! Fine. He's out of the hospital."

"But a traffic accident? I thought he'd be there longer."

"He just got a scrape on the head. They wanted to make sure it wasn't a concussion. You know." Boy, the lies just rolled out of me.

"I'm glad."

"And I am so sorry for running out on you without even a call. The truth of it is, I just forgot about anything else." At least that *was* the truth.

"That's okay. This was your friend."

"Yeah." I dunked my face in the wine and sipped, hoping we could move on.

"I like your apartment. It seems like you."

"Thanks. It's sort of minimalist, but I'm not here much."

"Your shop. You spend a lot of time there. How long have you been interested in spices and teas?"

"Since my dad asked me if I wanted to run a shop. It wasn't a burning desire, but after I got it running, I found I liked it."

"So...you said your father paid for it."

Yup, privilege up to my neck. "He worried about me. I was pretty aimless. Just surfing. That's all I seemed to want to do. That and..." And girls. "I mean, I dug into my studies, sure. Liberal arts...but I had no plan. So...he gave me one." I shrugged. "Then I got really interested in the spices and tea, the history of them, where they came from, what they could be used for. I became an expert. I'm...I'm proud of that. And grateful to the old man for making me do it. But don't tell *him* that." I smiled. She smiled back, though it didn't quite reach her eyes.

I put my glass down. "Look, I know what this sounds like, what it *is*. A rich guy gives his son all the privileges, buys his way into a business, a place of his own rent-free, a jumpstart on life. Poor little rich boy. And no, I probably couldn't have made anything of myself on my own. But there it is. I got into it, and now it's pass or fail for me these days, because daddy felt he's done his job and doesn't want to hear me whine. And that's fine. I'm doing it. I'm keeping the business going and growing and *I* did that. With the help of my crew. So I'm good with it."

"You don't have to apologize to me for it."

"I'm kind of feeling these days that I do. I know how it looks from the outside."

She put her glass down. A faraway look bloomed in her eyes. "I had to leave Haiti," she began softly. "There was nothing left for me there after the earthquake. And it was chaos. Family dead, no water, no power. I was privileged, too. My father had money and connections, and I used them to come to the United States. I'm…I'm a clothing designer. And I took advantage of the charity the world offered to move forward. Everyone wanted to help the destitute but amazing Haitian woman who designed her own clothing line. I grabbed the attention. Would I have gotten that attention if there had not been a disaster in my wake?" She shrugged. "Probably not. Even with my connections. But here I am." She frowned. "I don't apologize for it either. There are few enough opportunities out there for people like me. And I don't apologize for taking them."

"And you shouldn't."

"I don't."

We sort of sat back, not looking at each other, eating our own guilt at the paths we took. I didn't blame her. Not one bit. But I still felt a little guilty at my own. Because I knew I had a huge leg up.

I rose suddenly. "I think I'll cook dinner."

There was no hiding from the kitchen. It was all out in the open in my place. It got much easier as I cooked and she offered to tear salad greens. We were starting to have a better time of it. And then she gushed at my dinner. Afterward, we moved back to the sofa and began to get cozy.

I moved slowly, my arm across the sofa back kind of slid toward her shoulder, and my finger began a slow, casual stroke of her skin. When that seemed all right, I scooted a bit closer. Her smile and languid eyes signaled that maybe it was time to try a little kiss. I leaned in. Our lips met. She was beautiful. So sensual. She kissed like she'd devour me. I was really getting turned on. She wore a heavy layer of perfume which I didn't ordinarily mind, but I wanted to smell *her*, smell the *woman*. It didn't stop me though.

My hands found their way to her waist and I drew her in, and we were getting into it. She *was*, I was certain of it. Until she suddenly kind of squirmed. I was attuned to the signals, trying to be a woke dude, and when I drew back her expression was getting me concerned. Especially when she stood up.

She seemed confused. "Jeff...I'm sorry. I...I just...I can't stay. It was lovely."

"I'm sorry." I couldn't help but follow her as she grabbed her sweater and punched her arms into it. "Was it something I did?"

"No, no it wasn't."

"It's okay to tell me. You don't have to be polite. If it was something I did...read the wrong signals...it's entirely on me."

"No," she said, rushing to the door. "It isn't you. I just have to go. I'll call you."

She was suddenly out the door like lightning. I hit the doorjamb and looked out, but she was already down the stairs and in her car. I slumped against the door with a tragic case of blueballs.

"Well...shit." I ran over all we had done, all I had said — not much as we were kissing — trying to remember if she didn't seem into it. I didn't cop any feels. I'd remember that. I felt bad. I felt guilty, even though I don't think I'd done anything. "Dammit."

After moping around my apartment — and maybe a splash of cold water — I decided to trudge over to the Tequila Tiki and drown my sorrows with Dave the bartender.

I started with tequila shots, then moved on to beer. I think I was on my third bottle when Dave came over and wiped down the bar next to me. It hadn't needed wiping. "What is it?" I said, definitely *not* slurring.

"I haven't seen you down like this in a while. What's up?"

I turned my back to the bar and scanned the nearly empty place. It was Wednesday night in March. It just wasn't all that busy this time of year on weekdays. "What is it these days, Dave? I used to be a chick magnet. Now I can't even..." I rolled some words around in my head. "Close the deal," I ended up with.

He cleared away my empty bottle. I noticed he didn't offer me another. "Even you, Jeff, can have a dry spell."

First Kylie and now Nadège. Though...my ex had had a real good reason. Nadège just seemed to get scared off. "I thought the date was going well, and then she just ran out liked a scared rabbit."

"First date?"

"No, second. A better second and then just...poof!"

"Maybe she had a bad experience before."

I swiveled my barstool toward him. "Oh man. You may be right. She told me about how hard things were in Haiti after the earthquake. She was traumatized. God knows what actually happened to her."

"Damn. That's harsh."

"Yeah." I hated to admit it, but that made me feel better. Not that she had suffered, but that it hadn't been *my* fault that made her skip out on me. I leaned on the bar. "Oh man." I shook my head. So okay, it was feeling fuzzy. "Thanks, Dave. I think I better go home now."

"You didn't drive, did you?"

"No, I hoofed it. Time to stagger home."

"You be careful out there."

I dragged out some bills from my pocket and put them on the bar. "'Night!" I did stagger a little so I took my time walking home. The streets were nearly empty. It was late on a weeknight. Hardly anyone was on Main at this hour. All the shops were closed. So were the restaurants. Only the bars were still open, and they were emptying out. I could be forgiven for thinking that the shadow ahead of me was just from an awning. I was too out of it to even smell anything, until it was right on me.

The shadow loomed up. Bright eyes, snarling snout, rows of teeth. I fell back, completely unprepared for the wolf baring down on me.

CHAPTER TWELVE

☾

I RAISED MY arm to fend off the jaws. I didn't even shift. Like I suddenly forgot how. I just saw the teeth and jaws. My ears were filled with snarling and barking.

And then all at once it was gone.

I was lying on the sidewalk up on my elbows, looking around. Did I imagine that? I wasn't *that* drunk. Was I?

I peeled myself from the pavement, trying not to think about what I might have been lying on, and pulled myself upright. I sniffed. No, I smelled it. Wolf mixed with…something. It had been right here. But I was in no shape to shift. Was it Jesse Vargar? It wasn't familiar. One of his pack? I had to be more careful. I had to be on my guard from now on. No more self-indulgence at bars. I could get into real trouble if I couldn't properly shift and watch out for myself…or people with phones taking videos.

I leaned against the taco shack doorway for a minute, getting my bearings, before I ducked down an alley to take the shortcut home. I should have gone after them, but it seems that alcohol made it hard to smell scents…as well as hard to shift. That was something to remember. I couldn't do this kind of thing anymore. I couldn't just drink and toke like I used to. It interfered too much with my abilities. With my way to protect myself. Time to grow up, I guess. What a wake-up call.

I got back to my place and there was a figure standing at the bottom of my steps. I immediately crouched in attack mode. My snout grew, my claws, and my ears, but that was all. But that was enough. And then they turned into the light of the street lamp several yards away. Lindsay!

It took me longer to shift back, but once I had, I walked toward her.

She snapped her head up. Her eyes had wolfed for a minute, seeing into the dark, and then they went back to normal. I bet she didn't even know she'd done it.

"Lindsay. What are you doing here?"

She seemed to snap out of it. She looked around with brighter eyes. "Oh. I'm so sorry. I should have called first. I just didn't even think."

"It's okay." It was tough trying to sober up but I managed it. I trudged up the stairs, holding on to the railing for dear life. She followed and I succeeded in getting the door unlocked. She went inside and I went directly to the fridge and pulled out some Gatorade. I drank it from the bottle, downing nearly all of it before I set it down. Wiping my mouth with my hand, I turned to her.

"I'm just a little…I had a bit too much to drink," I explained, but it didn't look like I needed to. She got that faraway look on her face again. "Lindsay, are you okay?"

"I don't know. I…do you ever…like, lose time?"

"Only after a bender." I finished off the rest of the Gatorade and set the bottle in the recycling bin. "I guess you aren't talking about that." I carefully touched her shoulder—since she seemed jumpy and I didn't want to lose a hand—and directed her to the sofa. She sat, fidgeting with her fingers.

"Do you mean stuff like forgetting things? Like…maybe wolfing out and not knowing it?"

"Yeah," she said, her voice shaky.

I thought about it. "I can't say I've ever done that."

"It's happening to me. Is that…normal?"

Damned if *I* knew. Wait. Could that have been her sneaking around and attacking me? I couldn't tell. My nose wasn't working right now.

But I was getting that weird feeling again, that loss of control. And a hard-on to cut steel. I backed away from her on the sofa. Damn, that was weird. I mean, she was beautiful, but I hadn't felt anything one way or the other about her…until this moment.

"I have to tell you honestly...I just don't know. Maybe...maybe we should contact Jesse Vargar and ask him. He's the leader of the pack around town."

"I'm kind of scared to contact him. You think it will be okay?" She scooted closer to me. I don't know if it was a conscious thing, but she was looking at me with dreamy eyes and parted lips. Shit. But then she kind of wrinkled her nose and shrank back. For whatever reason, it made me feel marginally better.

I was working on my poker face, cause I didn't trust Vargar...or myself at this point. But maybe this was her best hope. And maybe he could tell me about this weird attraction. "Sure. We can go *now*."

"It's one in the morning."

But that didn't seem to bother *her* when she was looking for *me*. "Wolves are on a different schedule than normal people. Let's go." Maybe I could pawn her off on him. No, that wasn't a good idea, since I really *didn't* trust him. But dammit, he knew things I didn't.

I was still a little too toasted to drive, so we got into her car and I gave her directions. We parked across the street from his place and got out. The house was dark, but as I slowly sobered, I could smell him out. Yeah, he was there.

Instead of creeping around to his backyard, we went to the front door like civilized werewolves and rang the bell. I sensed a change in the house. And I knew he smelled me too.

The porchlight came on and the door swung open. He was bare-chested and wore sweat pants. I couldn't help but glance at Lindsay because I smelled/sensed something different in her. She was digging on this guy. And I didn't know how I felt about that.

"Chase. Do you know what time it is?"

I pushed my way through. "I'm not a freakin' cuckoo clock," I muttered.

Lindsay followed me in, ducking her head and looking away from Vargar.

He closed the door and turned to face us, crossing his arms over his chest. "What is this?"

"This is Lindsay, the werewolf that Jacob bit."

At least Vargar had the grace to lose the attitude and look more concerned. "Oh. Hey. I'm sorry."

She shrugged. It wasn't as if anyone could reverse it.

"She needs to know stuff. Stuff I don't know."

He smirked at that.

"Don't make me punch you, cause I really, really want to."

His smirk fell away. "What do you want?"

"First off, she says she's losing time, maybe wolfing when she doesn't know. Uh...sleep-wolfing?"

He frowned and moved toward the bar. He poured himself whiskey, and turned, asking with an eyebrow lift if we wanted anything. I shook my head. I needed to be sober, especially around him. Lindsay didn't seem to notice.

"I've heard of the time loss thing before," he said, sitting in a recliner. "Sometimes new wolves do it."

She was sitting on the sofa's edge. "What can be done about it?"

Vargar sipped. "I don't remember. I'll have to look it up."

I leaned back on the sofa. "We'll wait."

"Jesus, I'm not doing it now. I'll...I'll give you a call tomorrow."

"And what did you do about Jacob?" I asked.

Lindsay started looking all kinds of uncomfortable.

"I've disciplined him."

"And what does that mean?"

"It means pack business."

"And just what is that?"

His voice got wolfy and he grew enough snout for a full snarl with sharp teeth and yellow eyes. "It means *pack*. Business." He made a lunge toward me just to try startle me, but I wasn't startled. He got right in my face, but something changed in his eyes.

"You don't scare me, Vargar. In fact, I have a feeling that...*I* scare *you* a little."

Ding, ding, ding! On the nose. His snout shrank back and his eyes unwolfed and he glared at me with some surprise. Yeah, he didn't know what to do with an unpacked wolf. Lone wolf. Maybe that made me dangerous.

I stood. And then I realized I still had a hard-on. Dammit. I turned to Lindsay. "Will you excuse us for a minute?"

There was no private place except upstairs. I caught a glimpse of his backdoor sliders that I had crashed. They were covered in plywood.

I smiled and grabbed his arm—which he tried to shake off—and tromped up the stairs with him two at a time. We made it to the landing, where the walls were full of family photos. He finally shook me free and stepped back. "Touch me again and I'll—"

"Shut up. I have something to ask." Faced with it, I started getting embarrassed. I kind of turned away. "So...if a werewolf meets a female werewolf...do they sometimes, like, lose control?"

"Fight, you mean?"

"No, not fight. Definitely not fight."

It took him a second but then he cottoned on, looking back down the stairs. "You and Lindsay?" he whispered.

"Yeah." I ran my hand through my hair. "I mean it was sudden and unstoppable. We barely got home."

"I've heard of that too. Sounds like mating pair activity."

"No! No. You see, I can't have a...a...mate. I'm not mate material. I don't want more werewolves in the world and I sure as hell don't want it forced on me. What can I do to—" I gestured down to my problem.

His eyes glanced and I saw the smile creep onto his face.

"Okay, all right," I said.

"Wait," he said as I turned to leave. "Besides cold showers, stay away from her."

"I *did*, but then she came to me..." I blew out a breath. "She might have tried to attack me earlier this evening when she was sleep-wolfing."

"What?"

"I told you, things were totally out of control."

"That's why I told you to come to me—"

"And I'm here."

He ran a hand down his face. "Jesus." He paced on the carpeted landing. "I've only heard of some of this stuff. I never experienced it. There's someone...someone we can talk to, but I don't know if she'll talk to me right now."

"You're a real charmer, aren't you?"

"Hey! *You* came to *me* for help."

"All right. Okay. I'm sorry, man. You're just..." I held up my hands in surrender. He knew what buttons to press for sure.

"Let me...let me work on it. And...and I'll get back to you."

I sighed. "Okay. Whatever works. What do we tell Lindsay?"

"She can always shackle herself at night. A collar and a chain."

"Jesus, really?"

"It's old school but it will work."

I didn't suppose there was a twenty-four-hour hardware store around. "All right. Uh...thanks." As I turned, my eyes swept over what was obviously his wedding photo. And then I spotted the bride.

"*Lauren?*"

"How...how do you know Lauren?"

I squared on him. I let my canines grow a bit. "What kind of bastard leaves forget-me charms on their ex's shop?"

His jaw dropped and his eyes widened. It would have been funny if I hadn't wanted to punch him so badly. "How did—"

"I used to have a coven and I learned stuff. *You* will *not* talk to her. *I'll* talk to her." But then I couldn't believe it. "Is that why she knows so much about werewolves? Christ."

"No. NO. She doesn't know about me."

"Are you shitting me? How could she not?"

"I kept it secret. It was one of the things that...well. Secrets aren't good in a marriage, I guess."

"Oh, you think?" *Steady, Jeff. You were no angel.* "I can't believe this. She doesn't know? And she's *studying* it?"

"That's how we met. She doesn't know about any of the pack."

"You're an idiot. I'm glad she divorced you."

"I loved her, okay! And why am I talking to you about this? Are you dating her? *And* this Lindsay chick?"

"No! I'm not dating either of them. Shit." That just made life ten times more difficult. "All right, look. I'm gonna go now. I'll tell Lindsay about the...the chains." I didn't know what else to say. I couldn't believe any of this. All I wanted to do was find a pack and belong somewhere. Well, isn't that a laugh.

I didn't look back as I barreled down the stairs. Lindsay looked like she woke up and I grabbed her hand. "Let's go."

She dragged her feet and looked back up the stairs. "What did he say?"

"I'll tell you in the car."

It wasn't the most comfortable drive home. I've never had to tell a woman that we needed to chain her up. Maybe I was missing something before, but this wasn't what I expected. And she seemed really antsy, especially when I tried to get close to her. She wriggled away as quickly as she could, barely let me out of the car before she squealed her tires getting away.

What? Did I smell or something?

CHAPTER THIRTEEN

☾

SOMEONE WAS KNOCKING on my door. I opened bleary eyes and stared at the clock. Six am. What the hell?

I began to close my eyes again when I suddenly jerked upright with a start. Shit. Lauren. I told her to be here at six.

I scrambled out of bed, kicked my trousers that I had left on the floor out of the way, and tugged on some sweats. I held up the loose waistband as I opened the door. "Hey, Lauren."

"Hey...Jeff." She looked me over. "You...did tell me six in the morning, right?"

"I did. I just had a rough night and forgot to set my alarm. Give me two seconds."

She walked in tentatively with a towel slung over her shoulder. All I could think of when I looked at her now was that she was Vargar's ex-wife. Fuck.

I didn't even have any coffee to offer her, but I closed the door on my bedroom and threw myself into the closet, looking for that extra wetsuit. I should have gotten it all ready the night before, should have dug the other board out of the storage room downstairs. But like most normal stuff these days, I forgot all about it.

I flapped the wetsuit. It stunk. I hoped she'd be okay with it. I dragged it to my bathroom and sprayed deodorant down the neck, hoping it might help. Then I got on my swim trunks, grabbed a towel, and ran a comb through my hair. It remained delightfully bed-tossed, but I hoped she'd overlook it.

"Hey," I said, striding from the bedroom. "Wetsuit's got a little stank in it. It's been a while since someone used it."

She took it with a bit of a wince.

"We won't be doing anything fancy today. Just paddling out, getting a feel for the board and so on. You might try standing up on it."

"I want to," she said, chin tilted up.

"All right then."

I led her downstairs where I got both boards from the storage room. My ex had tried surfing a few times, but didn't love it, so the wetsuit and the board had remained in mothballs, but I was glad to let them get out today.

Boards situated in the back of the truck, I started her up, and drove down to the beach. I found parking near the spot I liked—because after all, it was six am—and we got out. I helped her on with her wetsuit. She tied her hair back in a pony tail with a scrunchie, and she waited with a nervous smile.

"Dude, relax. We won't do anything that will be too rough your first time out. I'll wax your board so it has some gripping power for your feet and we'll get started."

"I always thought waxing the board was like waxing furniture. You know, for the whole thing to keep it looking good."

I laughed. "That's a sweet thought, but no. It's to leave a surface for your feet to grip onto, especially when it's all wet. Now had I been on the ball, I would have scraped off the old wax and got it all pretty for you. That's why you're gonna use *my* board."

"Oh, no, I shouldn't. Won't it be too big?"

"They're the same size. Don't worry. It won't hurt my feelings."

I showed her how to carry it and we headed out to the foggy surf. We were under a marine layer and yeah, it was cold. The wet suit helped.

We got in the water—letting her get used to it—leashed ourselves, and paddled out.

She seemed to have good form paddling and I was sure to praise her for it. I knew she was nervous maybe scared but she was doing it like a trouper. We did a few waves lying on the deck and she seemed to take to it. Next, I had her get up on her knees and hold on or not. The waves were small today, so nothing scary.

I was just loving being out there. The salt on my lips and in my nose, the way the blue-gray water looked, swelling and lowering, the shore stretching out before us… Man, there's nothing like it.

I kept asking her if she wanted to stand, but she wasn't ready. Finally, I stood. "See, Lauren. Just up from your knees. Put your arms out for balance. The board loves you, wants to cradle you. It also wants to love the waves and take you with it. Love the board, dude." I glanced behind me. "Here comes the wave. It's a baby one. If you want to try it, just hold on with your toes."

"Cowabunga," she muttered, but she was slowly rising from her knees, sort of scared to let go with her hands, but doing it anyway.

"You're getting there. Don't be afraid. Don't be afraid to fall off, too. It's a rite of passage. We all fall off our boards. Even I do. Like, all the time."

She got up shakily and I reached out and took her hand.

"Oh my God! I'm doing it!"

"You *are* doing it! You're a surfer chick!"

She stiffened, but she bent her knees like I told her, let the board do the work, and rode it like a champ…before she lost her balance and fell in, taking me with her.

I popped up, whipped my wet hair away from my face, and looked around for her. She popped up too, coughing a little, but she had a wide grin on her face.

"You did it, girl."

"I did!"

"Shall we do it again?"

She nodded, up for it.

We were out there a full hour, and she rode the waves and didn't fall after that first time. Finally, I let her come in.

"You must have really good balance," I told her as we trudged to the shore.

She dropped my board and lay down on her back on it. "I'm exhausted."

"It uses muscles you may not be used to using, that's for sure."

I sat on the board and looked out to sea. There were a few surfers out there. I waved to some of the guys I knew.

A shadow passed over me and I looked up.

"You're on our beach. I warned you about that."

Ben "Darkhorse" Richardson. Long dark hair, square jaw, and a shitty attitude. He had a Rottweiler on a chain, holding it tight. The dog eyed us suspiciously.

"And I told you, dude, that this isn't your beach."

I heard a click and the guy actually pulled a switchblade on me.

"Jeff," said Lauren in a strained voice. She leapt off her board.

I stared at the blade and laughed. "Seriously? Did you watch *West Side Story* too much as a child?"

"You think this is a joke? This is the Cutback Boys' beach. And if I have to, I'll carve that into your skull."

"We don't want any trouble," squeaked Lauren. "Jeff! Come *on!*"

I made sure I faced away from Lauren so she couldn't see. But I shifted part of my face; my eyes, my snout, my teeth and gave him a growl.

His face opened in surprise and fear. Mouth falling open, he took a step back. I expected his dog to growl but it didn't much like the wolf either and whined and backed up, tail between its legs.

I shifted my face back to normal and was going to grab him and give him a swift kick in the butt when something soared passed me.

A bare foot slammed him in the face and he fell backward, his blade flying in the other direction. And suddenly there was Lauren, like a ninja, beating the absolute crap out of him, while the dog cowered, trying not to look me in the eye.

I stood there for a full few seconds just watching her make him cry, before I pulled her off of him. "Dude, Lauren. That was righteous."

She was breathing hard and her pupils were blown. She had been really into it.

Cutback Bro leapt to his feet, arms over his head, and ran. The dog, suddenly bereft of his master, turned tail and went after him, dragging his leash through the sand. I let them go.

Lauren calmed down and straightened her wetsuit. "I took some classes a while back. I wanted to be prepared."

"You were. I am truly impressed."

She offered a smile, though she was trying to look serious. "Well...I don't believe in violence..."

I laughed outright at that. "Seriously?"

She wrung out her pony tail. "Yes, seriously. I might have gone overboard a little..."

"A little?"

And suddenly she was mad at me. "Yes! I didn't mean to go all feral on him. I got scared and just acted out of instinct. So you can stop making fun of me now." She grabbed her board and stomped over the sand toward the parking lot.

"Whoa!" I grabbed *my* board with the idea to run after her. But I caught a glimpse of Cutrate Boy's knife stuck in the sand and I grabbed it, folding the blade away. "Lauren! Wait, Lauren!"

She put the board in the back of the truck kind of roughly and stood there, arms crossed over her chest. "I'm sorry. I wasn't making fun of you. I wouldn't dare now." She glared. "No, I mean it, I'm sorry. You were just...awesome. I mean, seriously awesome. And the guy had that mean-looking dog... You should be proud of yourself."

That put a chink in her armor. She dropped her arms to her side and shook out her hands. "I think I'm a little pepped up with adrenalin right now."

"Yeah. That's okay." I opened the tailgate. "Sit here for a sec and cool down."

She did and breathed. "I've never done anything like that before."

"I believe you. You're okay. Just breathe."

I opened the cab and put the blade in the cupholder and grabbed my water in its aluminum bottle. "Here. Take a drink. It's only water." She calmed and I leaned against the side of the truck. "There I was all prepared to be a hero when you beat me to it."

"I'm sorry."

"Don't be sorry. It's good to be able to protect yourself. Especially working alone in your shop. Everyone should know some self-defense."

"I suppose you know taekwondo."

"Uh...nothing formal. You know, just the stuff guys learn."

She shook her head and rolled her eyes. "The stuff guys learn," she muttered.

It made me tense up. "Your ex never got rough with you, did he?" I felt the hair on the back of my hands start to grow, but I pulled it back.

"No. Jesse wasn't violent."

Confirmed, then. But also that he wasn't violent? He sure did keep it on the downlow.

"He was just your standard asshole." She looked up at me. "I'm lucky that you knew about the charm pouch. I'm still a little mad about that."

"I'll keep an eye out for any more stuff like that."

"I appreciate it. I guess we should head back." She started for the passenger side when I stopped her.

"Whoa, Ninja Lady. We have to get our wetsuits off."

"We do?" Her face was blushing.

"Yeah. The sooner the better." Grabbed her towel and handed it to her and put my towel around my waist after unzipping the wetsuit and peeling it away from my damp skin.

"Normally," I said, goosebumps immediately cropping up from the cold air, "you just go commando under these, but I knew I had company." I slipped off my wet trunks and slid my shorts on under the towel. You get good at it on the beach.

Out of the corner of my eye I could see her struggling to keep the towel around her as she slipped off her two-piece, and got on her shirt and pants. All wet and bedraggled, she didn't seem to look as plain as I thought, though still not very curvy.

I just admired the beach while I waited.

We threw the wetsuits and bathing suits in the truck bed and got in the cab where I cranked up the heat. We drove back to my place and parked in the back.

She looked down at her hands. "Thanks, Jeff. That was a lot of fun. It's good to get out and learn new things."

Before I knew what she was doing, she leaned in and kissed me on the cheek. I was surprised at how much I liked it. I mean, she was no great beauty. She was okay. I never thought of her in any other way but a friend.

Whoa, Jeff. Aren't you supposed to be turning over a new leaf? You've got Lindsay and Nadège. Isn't that enough for now? Actually, it was a lot more than I felt capable of handling. More than enough. And…I just wasn't into Lauren that way. We could be friends. That seemed like a good thing to do. Even a first for me.

Besides, it was only a kiss on the cheek.

I waved my good-byes and trudged up the steps. I needed a shower.

ℭℭℭ

I WAS CLEANING up in my apartment—getting my laundry off the floor, emptying the pockets of my trousers—when I found the gris-gris bag still in the pocket. I studied it. A leather kind of palm-sized bag. I tentatively sniffed it. Smelled bad. It was lumpy and I resisted looking inside but then decided I had to.

I went to the kitchen, got a dinner plate, and dumped out the contents. Just what I thought. There were tiny bones in there. Chicken, I hoped. Some herbs, which I slowly recognized, and some other things; a coin that said "Republique D'Haiti"—a smooth pebble, and a torn piece of parchment with sigils on it. What was I gonna do with this?

My instinct was to throw it out, but then I thought I could take it to Lauren and she could help me figure out what it was, if it was harmful or not. So I dumped it all back in the little bag that I left on the counter.

I was listening to the TV absently, when the news hour started reporting about another murder on the beach last night. The news girl didn't say anything about dogs this time, but they were starting to call them the "Sandman Murders." Catchy. A little disrespectful, maybe. At least they weren't the "Wolf Murders." What was I gonna do about this? I was sure a werewolf was involved. Though it *could* have been the Cutback Boys and their dogs. I preferred to think *that* out of a whole basket of evil possibilities. This was all kinds of messed up. Something had to break soon. Maybe tonight I'd wolf out and investigate, being careful not to get shot myself.

But it was way past time to get back to my place of business. Yeah, the place that made me a living that I've been shirking since I got back.

I got down there before anyone else arrived and looked the shop over, checking out the inventory, the displays my boys had done, liking it all over again. I didn't realize how much I'd missed my own shop after leaving it for nearly half a year.

I actually got a chance to serve some customers, and that was cool. Reconnecting with the clientele, as it were. Old Jeff hadn't lost his spark. Then Lindsay called me, said she'd gotten the hardware we talked about last night. And wasn't it great when Luis walked in at just the moment I said, "You have to make sure the cuffs are strong enough and the chain is short enough..." He gave me a wide-eyed stare, and I turned away. "Um...you know what to do. I gotta go."

When I put my phone in my pocket and turned back to him, he wore a smirk. "It's, uh, not what you think."

He put up his hands. "Hey, bro, it's not up to me to judge. I get up to some fun kinks now and then."

"And I don't want to know about it."

"Same."

Ah well. We were all just one big happy family in the Organic Leaf, after all.

The bell above the door jangled and when Luis said, "Can I help you, ladies?" I heard the shuffle of feet come toward me.

"No," said an unwelcome voice. "We want to talk to that man." A heavy Haitian accent. I knew what I'd find when I turned.

CHAPTER FOURTEEN

❦

AND THERE THEY were, the weird sisters themselves; Widelene, Tamara, and Jesula. "What do you want?" I said none too politely.

"We want to speak to you," said the tallest one, Tamara. They were all still garbed in colorful dresses and *geles*. Tall, medium, and large, like kitchen cannisters.

"Well, I don't want to speak to any of you. Nothing happened on my date with Nadège and she hasn't returned my calls, so you did a real good job on her. Thanks. Bye now."

Jesula glanced back at Luis, who was trying to look like he wasn't listening. "Is there a place we can go to talk?"

"No. I have nothing to say to you."

Widelene got in my face, squishing herself against the counter to lean toward me. "We've got plenty to say to you."

"I don't care. It's over. Thanks for coming by. Now can you not do so ever again?"

Strangely, I suddenly felt compelled to follow them out the door. I started around the counter before I grabbed it and held on. "Stop that! I know you're doing Voodoo on me."

Luis started backing away.

Jesula, always the judicious one, gestured to her other sisters, and smiled at me. "I'm sorry about that. We are used to using our magic to get our way. Won't you please come with us? We truly do have much to discuss with you. A place of your choosing."

I clearly wasn't going to get rid of them easily, so I reluctantly agreed. "The Mermaid Café. Is that neutral enough for you?"

They nodded in agreement and I tip-toed around them getting the door and allowing them out first. I guess I could have slammed and locked it but they'd only be back. I shrugged my apologies to Luis—wondering how I was going to explain this—and led the way to the Mermaid.

We settled into a far corner table. There weren't too many customers in the place. The hipster by the window writing his book that would never be finished, the college-age woman plugged into her phone, swaying to her tunes, and an older black guy, reading his newspaper while eating a muffin and sipping his tea.

We didn't order anything. I felt bad about it, but I wanted to get this over with. "What do you want?" I asked again.

"You're in danger," said Tamara, towering above the others. Even me.

"From what?"

I knew they were worried about the wolf. What they didn't know was that it was me.

Widelene let her voice drop to a soft whisper. "We're concerned about the murders on the beach."

"The Sandman Murders. I'm not a homeless guy. All the victims were homeless, weren't they?"

"It's more than that," said Jesula. "We think we know what it is."

"Don't you mean who?"

"No," she said, her voice also dropping to a whisper. "What."

"You guys are kind of creeping me out. What does this have to do with Nadège?"

"Nothing, you fool!" hissed Widelene. "You aren't seeing her anymore, eh? This is something else."

I was starting to get a vibe from them. Yeah, I had no doubt they were as good as the Maine coven when it came to ferreting out the supernatural. Maybe they *could* help. But maybe I'd also slip up and they'd find out about me. I didn't like the idea of ending up on the hanging end of a rope.

"What do you want from me? I don't know anything about Voodoo and stuff."

Jesula rested her cool hand on mine. Something electric passed between us. She nodded sagely. "You've been touched. You've been very close to strong magic."

I swallowed but didn't say anything.

"You've seen death," she went on. "And great evil. But you came out of it. Your *nanm*, your soul has remained pure."

And just like that I almost lost it. I was a creature, wasn't I? Like a demon because I could understand demon languages, sense demonic spirits. I was something between the worlds of demon and human. I just figured I didn't have a soul anymore.

I felt a little choked up and my eyes stung. I closed them and rubbed at them so I wouldn't cry in front of these ladies. When I got my voice back, I croaked, "Pure?"

"Yes," she said softly. She seemed composed, self-assured, confident. She knew her stuff, right? She knew stuff about the supernatural, about demons and Lwa. This had to be right too. I *hoped* it was right. Hell, I never even *thought* about my…my *soul* before. Not until I assumed I'd lost it.

I swallowed again past that lump in my throat. I just nodded. I couldn't speak without a sob, I was pretty sure of it. I sat back against my chair, trembling and trying to hide it. Jesula kept hold of my hand and squeezed.

"You've been through much, Mr. Chase. But we understand."

Even Widelene wore a kinder expression. "You've known fear. You've known evil. But you've known bravery."

Tamara leaned in. "We want to help. We want to do a séance with you."

That woke me. "Whoa. Séance? What for?"

"The poor devils who died on the beach. We need to call out to them. To help them on to the spirit world. But we also want to ask them who killed them. Their spirits are restless, lost. They don't know they are dead! They must be helped to go on. We believe you can help."

"Oh man." I ran my hand up through my hair. "I don't know about that kind of stuff."

"It can be dangerous, but we will protect you."

"But why me? Why do you need me?"

Tamara laid her hand on my other wrist. "The Lwa trust you. You can be their helper. If you do this, they will owe you."

"And that is very powerful magic," said Jesula.

"How do you know they trust me?" I asked.

Widelene's eyes widened. "The bones," she said, miming throwing them. Like it should be obvious.

A Lwa would owe me? That sounded useful. And I did want to help these dead guys. I wanted to find their killers. I bet it would surprise these Voodoo ladies that it wasn't any werewolves, that is was a bunch of vindictive beach boys...but so what? We could stop them. Isn't that what I wanted?

But a séance. That creeped me out big time.

"Okay," I said carefully. "But I want to bring someone with me."

They all sat back at the same time and gave me those auntie looks. "Who?" said Widelene suspiciously.

"Not Nadège," said Tamara. "She and you..." She shook her head.

"Is this what it's really about? You don't want me to be with her?"

Jesula took a moment to answer, looked like she was parsing what to say that wouldn't sound racist. "You and Nadège...it is bad luck. The stars say no."

"And maybe a trick or two from all of you helped it along?" I sneered. "Never mind. She doesn't seem to want to talk to me."

"It's for the best," said Widelene.

"You know, it's better if we get to decide that on our own without any magical interference."

"That may be true," said Tamara, "but we are used to working in our way."

I was mad. I didn't like this manipulation. Maybe they weren't telling me the truth after all. Maybe they were buttering me up with this talk of pure souls and shit. But...they did seem sincere. And how did they know about the stuff I'd been through?

Though they didn't seem to know I was a wolf.

"Okay. The person I want to bring owns the Starlight Occult Shop just down the street. Lauren Castro. Is she okay? She knows about magical stuff and respects all beliefs."

They exchanged glances with one another and then got into a tight huddle, whispering back and forth. Finally, it appeared to be decided.

Jesula pulled a card from her beaded bag and handed it to me as the others pushed back their chairs and got to their feet. "Come to this address tonight at midnight. Sharp."

"Midnight? Does it have to be—"

"Sharp!" she said and joined the others as they made their way to the door. I didn't even have time to tell them good-bye. They were just gone.

☾☾☾

I THOUGHT IT prudent to get the guys some lattes and returned with them to the shop. Cam was there by then, and clearly, Luis clued him in on what happened.

Cam took the cup gratefully that I offered. "Man, that sounds like some weird shit there, Jeff. What did they want from you?"

"Yeah," said Luis. "They were pretty intense. Were they warning you off of Nadège again?"

"No, not really. Although—" Nope, wasn't going to mention the Voodoo stuff they were pulling on us. Just keep it simple. "They, uh, wanted me to participate in a séance tonight. At midnight."

Cam said, "Cooool," the same time Luis said, "Shit, homey."

They glanced at each other. Cam looked like he was going to talk, but Luis got in front of him. "You don't want to be messing with stuff like that, Jeff. That is some scary shit."

"Luis, dude," said Cam. "A *Voodoo* séance? That has got to be some *wild* shit. You don't want to miss that, Jeff."

Luis spun on his boyfriend. "Cam, it's not something to mess with. And Voodoo? Man...just no."

"Well...I kinda said I'd go..."

"*Madre de Dios,*" he muttered, and dove into his shirt, pulling out necklaces. A crucifix, a saint medal, and an ankh (couldn't be *too* careful, I guess). "You wear these. Promise me."

Thank God they were gold. I took them, looked them over, and then slipped them over my head. "Okay, Luis. I'm all protected now."

"I'm serious. You pay attention. Don't eat or drink anything they offer. You keep alert."

"That's why I'm bringing Lauren Castro with me. The lady from the Starlight Occult Shop?" Though, I supposed I should've asked her first.

CHAPTER FIFTEEN

❧

"A VOODOO SÉANCE?" said Lauren over the phone. "Are you *kidding* me?"

"I know," I said, trying to be cool. "It's totally okay if you don't want to go."

"Don't want to go? Are you crazy? Of *course* I want to go!"

I stared at my phone. I guess I forgot who I was talking to. "When is it?"

"Uh...tonight. At midnight."

"Awesome," she whispered. "Pick me up, or meet you there?"

"I'll...pick you up. At your shop, or..."

"No. Come to my place." She gave me the address and I wrote it down. "This is great!" she gushed. "I hope they don't mind if I take notes. Thanks for asking, Jeff."

"Hey, no problem. I live to serve."

She clicked off and I looked at the phone again before stuffing it in my pocket. I definitely knew some interesting people.

I was kind of antsy all day, thinking about this thing tonight. Finally, some answers. I guess. I mean, if the séance worked and *wouldn't* bring all sorts of dangerous creatures into our midst, that would be great, cause I've already been there, done that. Didn't want to do it again.

I knew I was in for a long night ahead of me. I had a hasty dinner. I didn't much feel like eating. I went online, looking for more mischief from the Cutback Boys, but didn't find anything. And then I kept thinking about Vargar and how could Lauren have married him? And why didn't he tell her about himself when she would have been really interested and could have helped him? And why did she pick such a loser... But then it only made me conscious of how much of a loser I'd been to my ex and…well. I really didn't want to go there.

I thought about what Jesula said about my…my soul and be damned if I didn't well up again. I swiped at my eyes, annoyed at the emotions coming to the surface. I was never the religious type, never seemed to have time for it, but I guess I thought vaguely about souls, that everyone probably had them; the spark inside that made you you. But ever since wolfing and being more creature than man, I started to panic and wondered if I didn't have one anymore. And now that I knew there was a real kind of Hell, maybe there was a real Heaven, too. Could a werewolf go to Heaven? Or were we too much creature?

I suddenly realized I'd been sitting in the dark. Wolf eyes. Didn't need much light. I switched on my desk lamp and leaned back in my chair. There was a lot on my plate these days, and I felt funny about it. Funny that it sort of gave me a thrill…like it was back in Maine. I never used to look for more than an awesome wave or a curvy babe. I used to be a pretty easy-going guy. Now I was getting into fights with other wolves, with Vargar and surf gangs, and I never would have done that before. I'm sure it was the wolf, getting it on with its wild side. Maybe even craved it. Yeah, life was sure different now. I wondered if I would live to a ripe old age as a gray wolf…or if a werewolf's days were numbered. Maybe I'd ask Vargar if I got the chance. Maybe he'd know.

I adjusted Luis' necklaces inside my shirt. Every little bit counted. Finally, it was about time to pick up Lauren. I felt better with her along. I had the feeling she'd know things, if it was going wrong, for instance, then I'd get us out of there. Before I left to pick her up, I grabbed the gris-gris bag out of the kitchen to show her. I hoped she know if it were good magic or bad. Since they invited me to this séance, I couldn't believe they'd give me some cursed thing, but you never knew.

She lived this side of town, up from the beach in a condo. It had one of those fake kiosks at the gate that made you feel as if there was some sort of security guard on duty, but there never was. I found her place—your standard condo, two stories, shared wall, all looking like cape cods with clapboards all painted in a dusky blue with white trim. When I knocked on the door she came right away. She was excited, the nerd in her, I guessed. She wore a skirt and some gauzy blouse and a velvet jacket over that. Her eyes were bright with interest and she got into my truck in the dead quiet street.

The weird sisters lived off of Beach Boulevard and Yorktown. It was a normal neighborhood, with normal houses, some looking Mediterranean and some just California stucco ranch houses. Looked like a tract from the 90s. The street was quiet and dark. There were two street lights and one was burned out. That one was in front of their house. I wondered if they Voodooed it.

We got out, but even slamming the truck doors sounded too loud. It was almost midnight in the suburbs and no one was out or awake. Most of the windows on the street were dark. Some had porchlights glowing dimly, but there were no signs of life.

We went up to the front door. It seemed a little shabby. There were lots of potted plants both on the porch and hanging over it, and a lot of them looked dead. I hoped this wasn't a sign of things to come. There was a plaque that said "Quoiquou". No idea what it meant.

Widelene opened the door and gestured for us to come inside. It was like Nadège's place, walls painted too colorfully for American eyes, with an altar on one wall and numerous mirrors on the other walls, with artwork and sculptures here and there.

Lauren was wide-eyed and buzzed. I could tell.

"This is Lauren Castro. She owns the Starlight Occult Shop not too far from my shop. Lauren this is Widelene, Tamara, and Jesula."

"I'm so pleased to meet you all. Thank you for allowing me to come tonight. I'm a student of the occult. I hope you don't mind if I take notes. May I know your last names so I can use it in my research?"

They gazed at her with widened eyes. That was a lot to spill out in an introduction.

Jesula, the first to recover, smiled. "We are sisters. Quoiquou is the family name." And she spelled it for Lauren who had whipped out a note pad from nowhere.

There was a table in the middle of the room with a black cloth covering it. A candle in the center of the table wasn't yet lit, but the air was already heavy with incense. I glanced at the altar. There was a skull...a human skull...and lots of candles and wax drippings. I guess it wasn't the done thing to clean up after the other candles. A statue of the Virgin Mary, a silver knife, a bell, some gourds with beads on them, and an assortment of other things, including what I hoped were chicken bones on a dish.

Jesula seemed particularly taken by Lauren and had her sit next to her at the round table in the center of the room. Then everyone began taking their places.

Gulp.

I was wedged between Widelene and Tamara. I bent over to look under the table and when I sat up again, Widelene was giving me the stink eye. I didn't care. "I needed to check."

"He's absolutely right, Widelene," said Jesula. "He has every right to check. He doesn't know us."

"And we don't know him," she countered.

"But he is our best hope for reaching the spirits of the dead."

Lauren scooted forward eagerly. "Why do you say that?" She glanced at me curiously.

Jesula patted her hand. "The Lwa, the invisibles, trust him. They will lead us to these wandering ghosts. They don't know they are dead. But they should know who killed them."

"*Should* know?"

Tamara struck a match and lit the center candle. Widelene rose to douse the other lights. "They are mixed up," said Tamara. "They don't always know they are dead and so they don't know who was the last they saw. Especially traumatic death."

"Sometimes you see it still in their eyes," said Widelene, "but you have to catch them right when they die. An hour is too late."

Lauren leaned toward her. "Have *you* ever seen a murderer in someone's eyes?"

"Almost," she said, straightening her dress. "But it was too indistinct. And then the time was past."

Lauren flicked a glance at me before she settled in. Even with all the stuff I'd seen, sitting in the dark lit by one candle and waiting for a séance to begin gave me the creeps. *Me.* Of course my wolf vision saw just fine in the dark but I knew what could be lying in wait in the shadows, and it didn't make me feel any better.

"We are going to sit quietly while I call out to the spirits," said Jesula. "Maybe the Lwa will help us. There's never a guarantee. Let us join hands. And whatever happens, do *not* break the circle."

Oh man. I hated when they said stuff like that.

Her eyes glittered in the darkness. I felt the weight of midnight around us. These times of the day, the phases of the moon were no joke. The Wiccans in Maine told me that they had special significance, that power was stronger or weaker at these certain times, and you had to know when to do what. So it wasn't just a weird feeling. It was the real deal.

I kind of slumped in my chair but Tamara clutched at my hand, while Widelene just about strangled my other. I dared not say anything to her about it.

Jesula closed her eyes. Her head swayed back and forth gently on her neck until she really started getting into it. And then the...the other *kwer-koo* sisters—however you pronounced their name—started in. Jesula called out in a mish-mash of French and Haitian Creole to the spirits. I mean I guess that's what she was doing. I shot a glance toward Lauren and she was avidly watching the proceedings, looking from Jesula's face to the other ladies. I was looking toward the exit.

"The bones are walking," she said in English. That freaked me. She meant that the spirits were awake and listening, but man. She made some grumbling, gurgling sounds and her eyes seemed to flutter, closed as they were. Her voice seemed unnaturally lower when she announced, "The angels in the mirror!"

I actually turned to look at one of the many framed mirrors on the walls. It was all about letting the Lwa in, and they seemed to like traveling through mirrors. And when I saw something move from the edge of my eye, I whipped my head toward the mirrors on the other side of the room.

There was something there. In one of the mirrors. It was like a shadow, and I quickly glanced at everyone else but no one seemed to have noticed it.

The shadow had long spindly arms and it touched just the edge of the frame. And then, something like a face with nothing but shadow and the silhouette of a top hat on its head—tilted slightly to one side—and something like a cigar sticking out of its invisible mouth, looked both ways out of it.

I wanted to scream. I wanted to say something but I couldn't. I was a little too scared for that.

And then it turned toward me.

It was like a wraith, a shadow thing. Not three-dimensional but flat...like a shadow looks. It pushed through the mirror and stepped out with a long, slender leg.

"Hey," I gasped. Widelene shushed me, but I wasn't having it. "D-does anyone else see that shadow thing coming out of the mirror?"

Everyone turned toward me, but I kept my eye on the shadow thing.

Widelene tightened my hand in hers. "What do you see?"

"Sh-shadow thing. Long thin legs and arms. Top hat. Cigar. No face to speak of, but big glowing eyes. Stepping out of the mirror and coming toward me."

"Don't speak," hissed Widelene. "Lwa," she breathed.

It came right over to the table, barely even stepping along the carpet on its two-dimensional feet. It walked like a cat over something wet, lifting its feet daintily and making no sound.

It leaned over the table right next to me and stared like two inches away. I couldn't see it puffing on the stogie, but I could smell the acrid smoke. I did everything I could not to scream and to stay in my seat. I mean, I had faced down a god, a goblin, and an assortment of other weird shit, but this...

I breathed shallowly. So *that* was a Lwa. Man, I hoped it liked me.

It looked me over thoroughly, like it was sizing me up to buy me. Or eat me. It wasn't doing that to anyone else. It seemed to be ignoring them, in fact. Finally, I guess I satisfied it, because it smiled. I couldn't see a mouth before, just those luminous eyes, but when it smiled, its teeth gleamed like they were covered in glitter, rolling that cigar end in its mouth. It gave me a nod, reached up above the table, and proceeded to pull down some invisible string.

And that's when the foggy glob skimmed down from the ceiling.

I blinked. It felt like something was in my eyes, but no. There was something now hovering over the middle of the table, and I looked desperately toward Lauren. She saw it this time, and looked at me and then couldn't stop watching the fog beginning to form above the candle.

I hadn't noticed when the Lwa took off, but it was gone and the cigar smell with it. My eyes were suddenly glued to the foggy thing.

This mist wasn't like my ex's grandpa who appeared to us as a fully corporeal ghost. This thing — whatever it was — was thrashing around, like a cat fighting in a nearly transparent bag. A hand, then a face, then an elbow pushed out at different angles. And it seemed it was going to burst at any moment.

I hadn't realized I was getting out of my seat, but Widelene and Tamara both dragged my hands down and I thumped back into my chair. What in the world had I gotten myself into?

The thing above the table began glowing and I desperately wanted to ask someone what we should do. Personally, I felt running was the best option. But Tamara got a look on her face that seemed to say, "If you talk now, I'll stuff that candle down your throat" so I swallowed what I wanted to say and sat tight-lipped, staring at the glowing object.

Besides the flight reflex, I had to beat down the wolf, because it sure wanted to come out. I could feel my ears and snout tingle with the need to shift and I just gritted my teeth, forcing them not to get pointy. If something didn't happen soon, I didn't know how much longer I could control it. And then the game would *really* be up.

Jesula kept on droning on in French Creole, a mesmerizing sound that made my skin crawl. The glowing thing began taking form, and it didn't look like one thing, but several. To my horror, I realized it was all the victims of the Cutbacks, not just one of them. A face that formed, split into two, then three, then four, pulling apart like the sticky threads of a melting marshmallow. Their mouths were open in terror, mouthing their silent confusion. Their faces had separated, but their bodies were still conjoined in a horrible mass of misaligned ribcages, stubs for arms, malformed legs... "Jesus Christ," I murmured. I wanted to look away, but I couldn't. It was like the worst kind of car accident victims from something like a three-car pile-up, as if they had all melted together, except there was no blood, no color at all. White and transparent and sickly as they writhed in the air.

"What's happening?" came one of the voices. It was hollow, distant, like they were talking into a can from the next room. It kept fading in and out. The other voices joined the first. "What's happening? Where am I? Who are you?"

I turned to Jesula. "For God's sake ask them already...and then release them!"

Jesula didn't even give me the stink eye for talking. Her expression was sympathetic, if I was reading that right. She turned back to the slowly spinning ghosts, wrapped together in ectoplasmic cellophane. "Spirits, I call to you from a safe place."

"Where am I?" said one that looked like the homeless guy I saw that first night. His voice was light, like a whisper.

"You are in-between, child. Here, you are loved. Here, you are safe. Do you remember your name?"

"I don't know where I am."

"You are here. What do I call you, little one?"

"D-Daniel. Yes. That's my name."

"Daniel. *Mon petit.* Can you talk to me? I am Jesula."

"I...I guess so."

"Daniel. Something very bad happened to you. Do you remember?"

He seemed to sigh and I felt it like a cold breeze. "I don't...I don't want to remember..."

"Please, child. You must try to remember."

"I...I can't. I don't want to..."

Jesula turned to Tamara and she released my hand to jump from her seat, grabbing the little bell from the altar. She quickly sat again but instead of taking my hand, she rang the bell, its tinkling sound so much louder than the ghosts' voices.

But it seemed to calm the guy and he tried to work out what Jesula wanted. "You want me to remember? Okay. Well. It was night. I was on the beach with my cart, with all my stuff."

"Go on," she said.

"It was night. The surf was in my ears. Nothing but surf. Until..."

A whine started, like an engine, but it turned out to be the guy wailing and it crescendoed to a squeal almost unbearable to hear.

"All right, Daniel," said Jesula through the cry. "If you can't talk, let another speak."

"Who are you?" said the tinny voice of a woman as Daniel's cry faded away.

"I am Jesula, and we are in a safe place, a calm place."

"I can't see you."

"But I am here."

"Am I...dead?"

"Ah my sweet. Do not be afraid."

"Are you...an angel?"

A lump welled in my throat and I choked back tears. This was horrible. I vowed right then and there that I'd never, ever do this again.

Jesula smiled sadly. "No, little one. I am just a woman, like you used to be."

"But now I'm dead. Like...like these others."

"You see them?"

"Sort of. Why am I dead? And why am I here?"

"You must try to remember when you died. And then it will help you and the others to go on to where you must go."

"I don't know. I was on the beach. It was night."

"Yes..."

"It was night. There was a little bit of moon. You could see the surf. It was...beautiful."

"Yes..."

"And then...then...there was...growling."

I swallowed hard, getting that lump out of my throat. The initial sadness I felt was turning to anger.

Widelene tensed beside me. She squeezed my hand harder, probably without realizing it. She had some grip on her.

"And then...all I saw were bright eyes and sharp teeth. And pain. There was such fear and pain!"

"But *mon petite*, that is over. There is no more fear. No more pain."

"There *is* fear. I don't know where I am."

"You and your spirit friends are in-between the world you left behind and the one that is to come. You must go there, but only after I've talked to the others."

"I don't think they want to talk."

"You must convince them."

She fell silent, but then another man's voice came through, just as thin as the others. "You can't force her to tell you."

"No, no, little one. Only if you wish to. But we want to stop the killing. And you can help us."

"I didn't see anything," he said, his voice strained, frustrated. "It attacked me from behind. Claws and teeth. It smelled bad. And it growled. A giant dog."

"A dog?" she asked.

"And furry. A big furry dog. Lots of smelly hair. Powerful. I couldn't even turn around. I was gone before I knew what happened."

I couldn't stop myself. "Was there a person with the dog?"

Jesula gave me a harsh look, but the ghost answered anyway.

"I...I couldn't tell. It was big and furry and smelled bad. Like...like dead things."

"That's very good," Jesula assured. "You're doing fine."

"We want to get out of here. How do we do it? We want to go." His voice sounded desperate, shrill.

"Listen. Listen to the sound of my voice, all you sweet, sweet spirits. I call now upon the Lwa, our ancestor spirits and Bondye to help these lost souls to find their way. Help us, Bondye. Help us, Lwa. We are your servants. Help these souls."

The apparition of the conjoined ghosts still spun slowly, but now the faces and hands seemed more relaxed when they pressed against their ectoplasm. The faces looked calmer, their hands not as tense.

Suddenly, the Lwa was back, and it stood off in the corner grinning at me like the Cheshire Cat, a crescent moon of a smile that never changed, never wavered. And it pointed up into the corner of the ceiling.

A pinprick of light began to shimmer where it pointed with its flat finger, and the spirits suddenly turned toward it. They didn't seem to even notice the Lwa, but like a shot, they speared in that direction like a rocket tail, glowing and growing smaller until they and the light went out.

And then the Lwa, too, was gone.

The heaviness of the room lightened. I could breathe easier. And Jesula sat back with a sigh. I hadn't noticed when Widelene and Tamara had let go of me, but I found my face wet with tears. I wiped at it quickly.

Lauren wasn't as ashamed of hers. Her face was shiny with wet. She sat, hands in her lap, staring at the candle that barely flickered. When she looked at me, I couldn't read what was in her eyes.

Tamara got up and flicked the light back on. "Well!" she said, wiping at her own eyes. "That settles that."

"*Jé-rouges*," said Widelene. "The wolf."

"No," I cut in. "I saw that surfer gang. They're a gang of idiots who think they own the beach, and they have vicious dogs. Rottweilers."

Lauren slowly shook her head. "No. You heard what that one ghost said. He saw fur. Fluffy fur. Rottweilers don't have fluffy fur."

I stared at her, blinking. But dammit. She was right. It wasn't their dogs, unless some of them had other dogs... But no. I saw only the Rotts.

"Then it was..." I wasn't gonna be the one to say it.

"But that's crazy," said Lauren, coming to my rescue. "There are no wolves here." She was my hero. Until she said, thoughtfully, "But there was that blond wolf on TV."

Struck in the heart with a silver bullet. I *knew* I was going to be blamed for that!

Suddenly, Tamara was in my face. "You *saw* the Lwa."

"Yeah," I said uneasily. "I guess."

"You *saw* the Lwa."

"Yeah." I was getting a little freaked from her response. "Isn't that why you wanted me here, because the Lwa liked me?"

"You don't understand," said Jesula kindly. "No one *sees* the Lwa. One may serve as *chwal* for them and is possessed and speaks with a voice *for* them. But no one ever...*sees* them. That's why they are called 'the invisibles'."

My eyes darted from one face to the other. I was surrounded by the sisters and in their eyes was concern, not anger.

"Well...there's, uh, a first time for everything. Right?"

I was part creature. That's how I saw it. I was like it, in a way. And it recognized me. It did seem to like me, or at least see a kindred spirit. I had the feeling it could have wiped me out with one swipe of its two-dimensional hand. But it hadn't. It had smiled. And I wasn't the least bit comforted by that.

The sisters were convinced that a wolf had killed those people. I never heard anything like that from the news reports — except for that first one, when I saw the paw prints myself and smelled...something. I thought it had been wolf, then maybe dog, but now I wasn't sure of anything.

The Lwa hadn't outed me. I wondered why. It must have known I was wolf. And if werewolves were so bad in their culture, why did it keep silent?

"You heard them," said Tamara. "The spirits of those departed. It was as we suspected. A wolf."

I took in all their worried faces. "Why did you suspect a wolf?"

They exchanged glances but kept silent. Until Jesula spoke. "It has happened before."

"It happened before? Where?"

"In Haiti."

I had nothing to say to that. God knows what they think they saw. But we *had* seen the ghosts. *I* had seen the wispy wolf at the Voodoo ceremony. I guess it was time to go to a meeting of Jesse Vargar's pack.

CHAPTER SIXTEEN

☾

I WALKED WITH Lauren back to my truck after we said our good-byes. The QuoQuo sisters—whatever—were nice enough to invite Lauren to come back to talk with them about Voodoo. But something was up with them. They'd seen the wolf before back in Haiti, so they said. That didn't seem to be all there was to it. I also wasn't sure if they were being entirely honest with me.

When we got into the truck, I suddenly remembered the gris-gris bag. I pulled it from my pocket and handed it to Lauren. "Widelene came to visit me one night and gave me this. I don't know whether it's good magic or bad. I mean, if it was bad, why would she have given it right to me? She could have easily hidden it in my apartment."

She turned on the overhead light and opened the pouch. She moved the pouch this way and that to catch the light and finally took out the parchment. I got in close to her to look it over too. I could smell her hair. She used a nice shampoo because it smelled great. I watched her as she examined the contents. Her eyes were all alight with discovery, and brown like a doe's, with long lashes. She had a pert nose and nice lips, if I was honest. For some reason, the girl intrigued me. Not in a Jeff-on-the-make way, but in a…different way.

"According to this," she said, squinting at the parchment, "it's to ward off werewolves."

"What?" I snatched the parchment out of her hand, but it was written in French and I couldn't make out more than a few words. "Then why am I—" I shut the hell up. What had I been about to spill? *Why am I able to touch it when I'm a werewolf?* Yeah, that would have been super cool.

But then I thought about Lindsay. She had been ready to get it on with me again, and just as suddenly shied away. And I'd had that thing in my pocket. Was that why? Maybe it didn't work on me because they had made it *for* me? Maybe it *was* a useful thing to have.

I gently took it back from her, stuffed the scrap of parchment back in, and popped it in my pocket. "This whole thing has been weird," I said to the windshield, draping my wrists over the steering wheel. "I mean, they *hated* me when I showed up to their Voodoo ceremony. They wanted me to have nothing to do with them and Nadège, and suddenly they show up, giving me this and telling me I'm a Lwa's bff."

"Did you really see it?"

I nodded. "Yeah, I really saw it. It creeped me out. And I have seen some pretty freaky things. I don't know what to think, Lauren. What do *you* think?"

"I know there are things of this world we don't quite understand," she began carefully. "I've studied enough of it to know, to sift out the deeply superstitious stories from those with a little truth to them. To magic being real in some true sense in many cultures. And that there are...*creatures* out there that only a few have been able to see and comprehend." She turned to me in her seat. "You know, there are some theoretical physicists who conjecture that some of the things we claim to have seen—ghosts and other phenomena—are really other parallel universes slipping into our own. I mean, these are genuine scientists who are talking about this sci fi stuff, that it could be possible. Maybe that's what some of these other things are. Maybe it's something we can half-see slipping in on our plane that we interpret as a Chupacabra or Big Foot."

"Lauren...to be honest, the shit I've seen is not from a parallel universe. It's from another plane of existence entirely. Another world. I mean..." I faced her. Maybe a little truth was in order. "Gods. Goblins. Ghouls. Z-zombies. Really horrifying things. And you can see them plain as day. And interact with them. Fight them. Hand to hand. There's nothing theoretical about it. There are other worlds and it's really best they don't seep into ours."

By the look on her face, I could tell she was skeptical. I sat back and sighed before I started up the engine. Pulling out into the empty street, I slowly drove into one pool of street light after another.

"I'm hearing you," she said in her best psychologist voice. "But it's just...if you can't recreate an event, if there isn't any empirical data to study..."

I could show her an event to recreate. I could shift right now and show her, but I didn't want her to look at me like I was a freak. I really needed her. I couldn't alienate my last hope to figure all this out.

"I know it's hard to believe. But remember, I did know about that forget-me spell, and that worked, right? I mean you forgot some significant things, didn't you?"

Her hands on her thighs curled into fists. "Yes. I do recall that."

"So there is truth out there. And I've seen a lot. I wish I could prove it to you. And you *did* see those ghosts tonight. That was no parallel universe. That was this one."

She nodded, biting a nail. "I did see that. And hear it. It was...terrifying and enthralling at the same time. I don't know that I could make myself believe it at first. But there it was. I'd like to talk more at length about this with you, if that's okay. I'd like to get some of this down in writing."

"And I'll give you the phone number of the head of the coven back in Maine. I think he could help you a lot." I'd have to email Doc ahead of time, let him know to only go so far in his explanations, not to out me.

"That would be very helpful, thanks."

We sat in relative silence all the way back to her place. When I parked in front she got out and then leaned back into the cab. "Are you interested in coming in for a drink. Coffee?"

"I think I'm pretty beat for now. Raincheck?"

"Okay. Say, Jeff?"

"Yeah?"

"Do you really think there are werewolves around here? That they really exist? Do you think...they could have killed those people?"

I felt my face heat when I lied. "I don't know."

She nodded and then smiled. "Good night. Again, thanks for inviting me. It gave me a lot to think about."

Me, too. "No sweat. I owe you more surfing time if you're still interested."

She grinned at that. "You're on."

She slammed my door and I watched her walk up to hers and get in safe and sound.

Driving back to my place I pondered it all. Once inside my apartment, I stripped off my clothes — making sure I got the gris-gris bag out of my trousers and laid it on my bedside table. I slipped under the sheets and lay there, looking up at the ceiling. I had wanted it so bad to be those Cutback Boys. I wanted to see their dumb asses in jail for good. Because it was far worse if it was werewolves. Werewolves who had a taste for killing. I'd call Jesse Vargar tomorrow and insist I meet with him and his pack. I had to look these jerks in the eye. But I also had to admit, I was excited at the prospect of being in a whole roomful of wolves like me. Except that it was probably the most dangerous thing I could possibly do. I hated to admit it, but that thrilled me too.

☾☾☾

VARGAR WAS SURPRISED to hear from me on the phone. "How did you get this number?"

"I have my ways."

There was a pause. "Lauren gave it to you, didn't she?"

"That doesn't matter right now. What matters is that there is a werewolf killing people, getting a taste for it. So, who is the first guy I think of?"

"I never —"

"I know that, you idiot. It's your pack. I need to see them. I need to talk to them."

He clicked his teeth as he thought.

"Hey, you wanted me to join them before. Let's see what they're made of."

"You said you'd never follow my orders. And if you don't, you don't belong in my pack."

"Doesn't mean I want to hang out with them at Werewolf Night at Arby's. I just want to talk with them."

"I still don't know what makes you think it was one of mine."

"Let's just say that I know some supernatural stuff and it looks like there's a killer wolf out there. I know things, remember. Like forget-me spells."

He made a sound into the receiver.

"Are you growling at me?"

Sighing, he gave in. "Alright. Meet at my place tomorrow night, nine o'clock."

"There'd better not be any funny business."

"What does that mean? You think we get kinky or something?"

That was exactly what I was thinking, but I didn't want to admit it to him. "I just don't want to get jumped or initiated into something I don't want."

"Jesus, you're an asshole. I'm doing *you* a favor, right? Just be there."

"Okay!" I clicked off. Talk about assholes.

Luis was all over me when I finally made my appearance at the shop. "Are you okay, Jeff? The séance…" He shook his head.

"Yeah, how'd that go?" said Cam. "I bet it was bitchin'."

"Yeah, it was bitchin', all right." I took the necklaces off that Luis had given me. "Thanks for that. I didn't really need it as it turned out."

Luis draped the necklaces over his head and adjusted them on his chest. "So…why did you go? To get in good with Nadège?"

"No…it was…" I sighed. "Look, I'm gonna be straight with you." I glanced toward the door. No one was in the shop, but even so, I talked quietly. "I happened upon one of the people killed on the beach, and I was trying to figure out who killed them."

"Doing a little sleuthing?" said Cam, eyes all a-glow.

"I guess so. The Voodoo ladies offered a séance to ask the ghosts who killed them. I had those idiot Cutback Boys on the top of my list of suspects."

"Oh, man!" said Luis. "Those guys are nothing to mess with."

"I'm not afraid of them. But it turns out...it's not them."

"You...you saw the ghosts?"

I leaned back against the counter. "So...it looks like when I went to that first Voodoo ceremony, these spirits...took a shine to me."

I didn't think Luis' eyes could bug out much more than they were doing right now. But Cam was grinning like a fool. I guess he loved this kind of stuff.

"I mean, we sort of connected. They're called Lwa and they move through the spirit world and through ours by traveling through mirrors."

Luis was slowly shaking his head. I could tell that he'd not be looking in any mirrors anytime soon.

"The Voodoo ladies weren't too keen on a white boy in their midst, but they had to concede that the Lwa liked me. And...I saw it. Last night."

Cam clapped his hands so loudly it startled Luis. "All right! That is awesome!"

Luis spun on him. "It is *not* awesome. This is some serious shit. Jeff, you gotta promise not to do this anymore. It's Satan at work."

I was absolutely not going to tell him that my ex *met* Satan and it wasn't what he thought, but I didn't see the use in that conversation.

"It's a spirit world," I went on. "Like some of the magic I was involved in back in Maine. There was a coven I was friends with."

Cam got a quizzical look on his face. "I have a feeling you aren't telling us a lot of what happened back there. You just said you went to get Kylie back. What's with all this supernatural stuff?" Then he smiled slowly. "Are you shitting us? Is this all a punk?"

Luis almost had a hopeful expression. I hated to stomp on it. "No. It's real. It really is. Sorry."

I explained it all—loosely—the best I could, leaving out a *lot*. But they got the gist. That magic was real, that some creatures were real. Luis was going to shake his head right off. He seemed to be getting more religious by the moment.

"Jeff, man…"

"I know, Luis, but all that stuff being dangerous doesn't mean it's any less real or that we can't be involved. Sometimes you have to be in it for the good of the community. And that's why I went to this séance, saw the Lwa, and talked to the ghosts."

"What did they say?" said Cam, mesmerized.

I had to leave out about the werewolves. I just didn't want to go there. These two were taking in a lot and I didn't want them running for the hills.

"It wasn't the Cutbacks. It was…something else. Something … paranormal. I'm taking care of it."

"What is it?"

"Look, I was honest with you about all this supernatural stuff, but I don't think I should really go on about it."

"Are zombies real? Because that's cool."

"Cam. You are one weird dude."

I managed to hold off his questions. But Luis, he was properly freaked and spent a lot of the day clutching the gold cross around his neck. I didn't blame him.

That afternoon I took a call from Marlene and assured her the shop was doing fine. We talked around it, but it sounded like she was maybe getting ready to retire. That was probably a good idea. I'd miss her, but I knew she'd pop in every now and then just to say hello and to keep her hand in. At any rate, that was for another face-to-face conversation.

I bought the boys lunch from the Tequila Tiki cause I felt bad about revealing a world they may not have been ready to hear about. We had our burgers in the back of the store and talked some more. I told them what I could about spells and stuff, about some of the creatures I'd seen, and yes, even about the Zombie Vikings we had encountered. But I left out the wolf. I couldn't bring myself to tell them, even though it would have been easy to show them. The wolf was getting anxious. It wanted to break out and stretch its legs. And because I'd given away half my wolfsbane potion, I knew I'd have to brew more soon. I took my dose today so I was cool, but I was thinking that tonight, I'd run around a bit. Had to wolf out occasionally or I'd get fidgety.

I was glad the boys knew about some of it. I wouldn't slip up so much this way, and that meant only more helpers with what was going on. The truth was always simpler. But it wasn't particularly easier.

I was feeling bad suddenly about Nadège and I decided to give her a call too. She seemed cautious but glad to hear from me, as I stood outside the shop, watching the world go by and the sunset over the sea.

"I just wanted to talk to you," I said, "make sure we were okay. I don't know what happened last time, but I'd still like to see you."

"It's complicated. But I would like to see you, too, Jeff."

"Hey, I don't want to complicate your life. And I've made friends with your Voodoo ladies, if that's what's bothering you."

There was a pause. "You have?"

"Yeah, I think we're all squared away. They told me that the Lwa liked me. Weird, huh?"

"The Lwa...*liked* you?"

"That's what they said." I shivered. "I'd just as soon they ignored me, frankly."

"It is an honor, though."

"I've had better honors. Oh...I mean...shoot. I don't mean to insult your worshipping practices..."

"It's okay. You must be very sensitive to the supernatural world."

"I am a little. I told you about that coven in Maine, right?"

"So you did." We both paused for a moment, listening to each other breathe. "I wouldn't mind getting together tonight," she said, "but it would have to be late. After eleven."

"Hey, that suits me fine. Your place?"

"Yes. If that's okay with you."

"It's fine. And perfect timing too. I have something to do earlier this evening."

"Then...it's a date."

I clicked off the phone. Now I *really* needed to wolf, work off that extra energy till I saw her tonight. I'm glad she hadn't ditched me. Maybe she'd tell me why she cut out on me...or maybe she wouldn't. I'd blown off plenty of women too.

☾☾☾

WHEN NIGHTFALL CAME and it was time to close up shop, the boys didn't want to leave. Luis was scared and Cam just wanted more stories to torment his boyfriend with. I gave them the heave ho, though. Told them I had a date tonight and that tomorrow was another day and we could deal with it then.

I had a very rare steak for a late dinner—a big one, too—and by the time it was nine, I was ready to rock and roll. I figured I could be out and running for an hour and a half and get back in time for a quick shower and show up at Nadège's place. Time to strip down to nothing and shift.

Man, it was good to get my bones back into wolf alignment. I shook myself, ruffling the fur. Felt good.

I got to my porch, pulled the door closed with my teeth on the knob, and trotted downstairs. I just stood at the bottom step, sniffing the salty wind. I listened with my super-sensitive ears for people. It was a weeknight, so there were few around. The bars, of course, still had people, but it was also a cold, cloudy night with a breath of rain on the breeze. That would keep a lot of people away.

I stepped cautiously to the end of the driveway and looked both ways down the street. I wouldn't even think of taking the main street. I'd head down the back alleys to the strand and run on the beach. No one was likely to be there except some drug addicts and homeless.

I hurried down the alleys behind the houses and condos, in front of their garage doors and their trash bins. It smelled bad. Well, bad for a human, not so bad for a wolf. I could also tell where other dogs had marked their territory. And I began to sense the difference between dog and wolf. Dog smelled...how do I say it? More primitive. Less...*developed* than wolf. After all, my kind of wolf was also people, a subtle blend of the two. And appealing to my wolf senses. Not surprising, I guess. Vaguely I wondered if I shouldn't have called Lindsay, but I was afraid of us doing the nasty as wolves, and wasn't that how you made other little werewolves? No thanks. No litters for me.

It was good to get out as a wolf. Even trotting down the alleys, my pads scratchy on the rough asphalt, felt great, freeing. I stopped a lot to sniff the area, make sure there were no people. They smelled very strong. It was easy to discern them in the shadows. Once or twice I sensed them nearby, and I'd trot down a different way, making a circuitous route to the beach. There was a dark street that emptied to Pacific Coast Highway. The highway was still generally busy even late at night. It was a major thoroughfare north and south along the coast, after all. That would be well-lit, and I'd have to hurry across before anyone saw me.

I got to the street I wanted and loped along. I kept looking around as I went, bringing all the smells into my snout through my nose and mouth. The scents were colors and bits of information I processed as I moved along. I knew about how many people were awake and how many were settling down for the night; what they ate; whose car was leaking oil; if they had dogs in their yards or living rooms. You would have thought dogs would bark when I was near, but it was the opposite. They knew something was up with us wolves, and they stayed silent, hoping we'd pass them by. Safer that way.

I got to the end of the block where it met PCH. Yup, it was lit up, all right. I stayed in the shadow of a huge Bird of Paradise plant and waited. There weren't too many cars along the highway right now. That was good, but they were still constant. I had to measure when I crossed. I didn't want to be stuck in the middle, a target.

Finally, I saw my chance and scuttled over the asphalt, arriving to the meridian just as a bus went by. Off I went and hit the sand.

It was cold between my furry toes, and I headed away from the street lights along the strand and toward the surf. Out there in the dark, I could frolic. Hey, frolicking wasn't on my list of things to do as a guy. But as a wolf, it was heaven.

I ran full bore up one way and down the other, my tongue lolling out of my jaws. I licked the flavors of the scents. Sea urchin, dolphin, thresher shark, bass, sea lion...so many scents *in* the sea were open to me. It was the foam that brought the sea smells up. Amazing. But then I got a whiff of the oily scent of sea gulls and other sea birds, even though they were asleep in their nests. Still, their webbed feet and droppings left a visible trail to my senses, zig-zagging all over the sand. It was only at the waterline that the scent molecules began to disperse, purged by the relentless tide.

I was alive again. Surfing made me feel that way, but wolfing did too in an entirely different way. I wasn't afraid of being wolf anymore, not lamenting about my poor complicated life. It wasn't as complicated as I first thought it. It had its perks, like now. And I could forget for a brief time all the other things weighing heavily upon me.

Off I went, muscles moving smoothly under my fur, booking it along the surf line. I couldn't help myself and yipped a bit. But there was no one around. Maybe a person or two, but all they could do was watch me run by.

A splash at the surf and I saw a flash of silver, a fish trying to get back to deeper water. Before I could think, I had pounced on it and I had its slick body between my teeth. I chomped down. Raw, fresh, still squirming, blood oozing into my mouth. My sharp teeth made quick work of it, bones, fins, and all. I swallowed it, licked my muzzle. But then I stopped and looked down at myself. That was the first time I had ever eaten anything as a wolf. I didn't quite know what to think of it. I could taste the salty, slightly fishy taste still in my mouth. Capturing it had been a sort of thrill, and it was the most natural thing in the world to chomp it and eat it.

I had hunted. I mean...I really *had* hunted something.

Whoa. That was too close to creature status. That was wolf stuff. Not werewolf stuff, but the animal stuff. How easy it was to slip into that life. And if I hadn't been taking the wolfsbane, how much easier might it have been to kill and feel *that* blood in my mouth?

Yeah, I had to be careful. I had to be aware. *More* aware of what I was.

I didn't regret it, though. It was good. Tasty. Hit the spot.

I licked my jaws again, not just cleaning but tasting it again. Never thought of mackerel that way before. And probably not again as a man.

I took it a little slower along the surf, letting the foam spill over my paws. Even though I could reason perfectly well as a wolf, it was interesting how much of an animal I was. It was instinct pouncing on the fish. It was instinct sniffing the world around me and filing it away to remember it later. I…liked it. And…I sort of feared it, because I'd always been in control. Even surfing. You knew when it was time to bail off the board. You knew when to carve, the feel of the curl. Maybe that was instinct too. But, I supposed, it was mostly practice. I don't know. I didn't like that I was something other than Jeff all the time, that primitive instinct could suddenly take me over. WereJeff. It was kind of funny. And kind of not.

Just be aware, I told myself, keeping an eye on things around me.

I romped a little more, but some of the thrill had gone out of it. I felt a little guilty being out there after thinking about the ghosts we'd seen. They'd gone on to a better place, but they had been scared. It was good that the Quoiquou sisters were able to help them…and that Lwa dude. But what about the others who didn't have that kind of help? Were they stuck haunting places? Or maybe they went on eventually. Sucked, that's all I knew.

I was getting chilled even in my thick fur coat. I wondered if I'd shed a little come summer. Weird thought.

I trotted back up the beach, keeping an eye out. I totally thought I had. But when I got to the parking lot, it was clear I hadn't.

There were two cop cruisers and a truck from animal control. I was suddenly surrounded by dudes with guns and one with an animal catch pole, that noose on a stick thing. *Shit!* What the hell was I going to do now?

CHAPTER SEVENTEEN

❦

I GROWLED AT them, showing my fangs. I could have easily jumped them, torn them apart. Their bullets wouldn't have killed me. Might have hurt me, but not killed me.

At least I didn't think so. But now I wasn't sure.

And then I thought, *whoa, no. Chill, Jeff.* Everyone would get hurt. And I might bite someone. I already made one werewolf accidentally—my man Nick back in Maine—and there was no way I was going to do that again. I backed away, my hackles rose. I was scared, but I smoothed my face out to look less intimidating, even whined a little. I gave them the puppy eyes. I could see the confusion on their faces. They had thought I was a vicious animal...and then I wasn't.

I could tell I was de-escalating the situation but I could only do so much. If I tried to run, they'd shoot me. And if they had a tranq gun, I'd be out of it. Too out of it to know if they were euthanizing me. Or neutering. I shuddered. And wouldn't that be just peachy.

Then that guy with the catch pole was sneaking toward me. If I let him do that, maybe I wouldn't be shot.

I lay down, even wagged my tail. Now they were really confused. One of the cops said, "He must be someone's pet. You think that's just a huskie?"

"I don't know," said the other one, with his shotgun trained on me. "He really looks like a wolf. Damn stupid idiots with their wild hybrids. That's why it's illegal."

"Can you get him, Frank?" said the first cop to the animal control guy.

"I think I can. He actually seems docile." He came closer and it took everything I had to let him loop that noose around my neck. I felt it tighten. I tried being Lassie, panting, wagging my tail, just being charming. I walked with him to the truck like we were going for a fun ride. "You're okay, boy. No collar. No one's reported you missing. Maybe you belonged to the old man."

He was talking about Daniel, the homeless guy who was murdered. What could I do but follow along? He stuffed me into a cage and locked it. I just lay down.

The ride to the shelter didn't take long. But I hated the way the truck smelled. It was full of fear, from every kind of animal they had captured; cats, dogs, raccoons... I felt bad for all those guys. But I was beginning to get concerned for myself. What were they going to do to me?

It came to a stop and the guy with the catch pole came out and unlocked the cage. I did my Lassie routine again, even pretended we were going to play. "You sure don't look like a vicious dog to me," he muttered. Inside, I was locked down to an examination table. A vet or some guy in scrubs came up to me.

"This the one they think killed those people on the beach?"

"Yeah, but as you can see, he seems pretty docile."

"They can fool you." He cautiously approached me and petted my head. "I'm just going to take a little sample of your saliva, boy. Let's see if we can do this without tranqing you."

I was a good boy, a happy boy while he swabbed me. At least this would exonerate the big blond wolf.

"So, what kind of dog is this?" said the animal control guy.

"As far as I can tell, it's a wolf."

"A *blond* wolf?"

"Tawny. Must be a hybrid. But this is definitely a wolf cranium. Bigger head as compared to the body. Getting a blood sample..." I didn't even flinch when he jabbed me with the needle. Then he passed like a barcode gun over me. "No chip. Okay, you can put him in the cage."

I was released from the restraints and walked over to a room with concrete floors, drains in the middle, and lots of chain-linked cages. Everyone was barking when I came in and then all shut up when I passed them.

Animal Control looked around. "Damnedest thing," he muttered, looking around at the other dogs.

He set me loose in the cage with a water dish and an empty food bowl. No thanks, I already had my mackerel. But at least I wasn't going to be euthanized. Not yet, anyway.

He stomped away after locking the cage with a padlock, keys jangling from his belt, lights out, and door closed behind him.

Everything had gone quiet. The dogs weren't talking. Well shit.

I sat on the cold concrete. This was a problem. I didn't want to stand up Nadège, but what the hell was I gonna do?

I padded over to the cage chain-link door, pressed my head against it to get a good look at the door we'd come in through. Closed. No surveillance. No cameras.

I shifted.

And it was cold like a mother in that place, naked as I was. The dogs started snuffling and yipping. "Neat trick, huh guys?" I said to them. But the padlock on the door. That was some bullshit right there. I wondered if I could kick the door opened. I investigated in the dark. Still had wolf vision so it was no problem. I didn't see any way to kick my way through the welds. But maybe I could pry it open. With what?

I looked all around. Nothing I could use as leverage.

Then I looked up.

There were no roofs. All I had to do was climb. I stuck my foot in a link and hoisted myself up. Then they started to bark. "Shhh! Calm down, everyone. You don't want them to come—" And sure enough, I heard those keys behind the door. I jumped down and shifted again. The dogs quieted.

The light came on and Animal Control stood there in the doorway. "What the hell is going on?"

No one replied, of course. He shook his head, turned off the light, and locked the door again.

I shifted once more. "Okay, everyone. I'm going to get out of here. I wish I could get you out too, but I can't. So please all of you, chill?" I climbed again, curled my hands around the top and leapt down. I crept along the floor to the door and gently grabbed the doorknob, trying to turn it. Locked. Shit.

I looked around and there was a transom window over the cages. I'd have to climb a cage with a Doberman in there to reach it. "Now calm down," I told him as I approached his cage. He looked at me warily and maybe he was about to start barking. I morphed my face, just giving myself a wolf snout and ears, letting him get a good whiff of the werewolf.

He whined and crept back into the corner of his cage.

"That's what I thought," I said, snout in the air. I shifted back and climbed. I could barely reach the window when I got to the top edge of the cage. I prayed it wouldn't be painted shut, but it looked like they used it before. It squealed as I turned the lock but I was able to pull it open and down. But not all the way down. I could fit through it, I was sure, but wasn't excited about doing it naked. I was certain to get scratched up…but then I remembered I'd heal up real quick.

"Here I go. Wish me luck, guys." I flicked a glance at the Doberman and he looked like he would be glad to see me leave.

I had to press myself against the cold cinder block wall, edge over the top part of the cage, and shimmy up and through the thing. Sharp painted edges of the metal window frame got me and I'm sure I left blood behind, but I was half in-half out, looking at the ground below, a good twelve feet or so. I managed to maneuver my butt over the side and dangled by my hands. When I let go, I landed superhero style, bending my knees and then standing up. Asphalt parking lot with a chain link fence all around and razor wire. "Now why did they have to go and do that?" I stood, rubbing my arms to keep warm and scanned the area. There had to be some way to get over that. Ah! A gate. Maybe it was open?

I trotted over there, passing under the light and—shit. A camera. Oh well. Say hi to the camera, Naked Man. I tried to keep my face turned away from it as I headed to the gate. Locked.

I looked around. In the far corner was a shed right up against the fence. And it was in a darker area of the lot. I trotted over, got myself up on the roof of the shed, but it was still lower than the razor wire. I could leap over it if I shifted. I glanced back at the camera. I sure hoped it couldn't really see me from there.

I wolfed. Had to. And ooh. Warmth! I leapt over the wire, easy-peasy, and landed on the sidewalk outside the fence. Then I ran like hell, hitting the alleys and darkest streets I could think of. Peering over my shoulder, I could tell no one was following, and I made it back to my place. I slipped up the stairs, shifted, and opened the door.

Damn! That was stupid. I can't believe I got caught! I wasn't being careful...and I thought I had been. I couldn't let that happen again. But how would I be able to wolf out and *not* get caught?

Wait, what time was it?

Suddenly my priorities shifted. I had mere minutes to get a shower, change, and get myself over to Nadège's.

I scrambled around, getting cleaned up, dressed, grabbed my keys, and was out of there in ten minutes flat.

I was still late when I arrived but I apologized all over the place. Because she was one beautiful lady. She was wearing some kind of flattering long dress that clung in all the right places. And she had the most beautiful skin. You just wanted to touch it. *I* wanted to touch it.

"Come in. Sit down. Would you care for some wine?"

I could sure use something. I can't believe only a half hour ago I was in the pound. I couldn't let that happen again. It was sheer stupidity. I'd have to ask Vargar's pack what they did to wolf out, where they went.

Suddenly, a wine glass was thrust into my face. "Oh...thanks." I tasted the white wine. Kind of sweet this time. "You won't believe the day I had."

"Oh? Tell me about it." She settled into the sofa.

"Uh...I'd rather hear about your day. And let me just say, I appreciate you giving me a chance. I don't know what happened the last time, but—"

"It was nothing you'd done. Please don't think about it. Let's us just be glad we're here, together."

We clinked glasses. I drank some more. "So...what did you do today? Is fashion design as glamorous as they make it out in the movies?"

"Of course not. It's doing a lot of budgeting and checking inventory and an assortment of other mundane things. But I was making phone calls all day to Paris and Madrid."

"Oh. Well that's something. Are you going to show your clothes there?"

"I hope to.

"Wow. So this is a big thing. Do you have a studio, employees? I don't know why I didn't ask that before."

"Yes, there are people I have working for me. I can't possibly sew all these things myself."

"So you're going to be famous." I clinked glasses again and she smiled, shyly.

"You never know." She took a sip of her wine and set the glass down. "Actually, if you don't mind, I feel that we were doing okay together last time. And it was interrupted. I think I'd like to finish it."

"Finish...what?" I can't believe how stupid I was, twice in one day. She took the glass out of my hand and set it down, gazing at me from under her lashes. She slid toward me on the sofa and draped her arms over my shoulders. Oooh! Maybe I was a little dense at first but I catch up quick.

I smoothed my hands over her sides and pulled her in. "You mean...you want to continue where we left off?"

"What *do* you think?" she purred.

Her lips were suddenly on mine. And they were as luscious as I remembered. This was not like Lindsay. Lindsay was rushed and urgent and more instinct than my being aware of everything. But Nadège...she was slow and sinewy and... It was like she was slowly wrapping herself around me. I stroked her arms, running my fingers along her soft skin. It felt like it looked. So beautiful and sensuous. I eased my hands lower, giving her time to tell me to back off. But she didn't. I cupped her generous backside as I brought her in tighter, kissing deeply. Thoughts of the pound fled out of my head. My senses were full of luscious woman, the feel of her, the scent of her spicy perfume, clouding all my thoughts and woes. There was only her and the soft feel of the sofa beneath us.

I was in a bit of a lusty fog when she rose, pulled me along to the corridor, and to a bedroom lit with twinkly lights above the canopy of her four-poster. And that was all I noticed, believe me. I was touching her, all over, pulling down one corner of her shoulder strap just enough to kiss that shoulder. She shimmied out of the rest of it and there was miles and miles of perfect skin, toned with flexing muscles beneath, long shapely legs twining around me.

I had the presence of mind to grab the condom out of my trouser pocket before my pants disappeared entirely. She helped me on with it — a huge turn-on — and we were on our way.

She was on top of me, riding me, and suddenly her nails were biting into the flesh of my chest and just digging in, raking down me. Ordinarily, I wasn't aroused by that sort of thing, but this time...man! The sharp pain coupled with the feel of her around me, moving over me and I was popping my cork before I could help a lady out.

But I was a gentleman and gently lifted her off while I laid her down and kissed my way down to take care of her. Those long legs were around my shoulders and I was getting ready for round two, just from the feel of them.

☾☾☾

LATER, WHEN SHE was asleep nearly on top of me, I looked down at her. Her short hair, closely cropped to her head was sexy, even though I favored long hair. Hey, whatever, I guess. A beautiful lady was a beautiful lady, no matter how long her hair was. Her skin gleamed in the moonlight, all the amazing contours of it, the parts that weren't under the covers.

Then I looked down at my stinging chest. There were her nail marks. Dang. She got me good. Except...I hoped she didn't notice that by morning they'd be gone. Werewolf healing.

I decided to lay back and not worry about anything. Sleep. Sleep would be good. It had been a long, crazy day. We could deal with anything in the morning.

€€€

UNFORTUNATELY, SHE WAS up and gone by the time I woke up. And I was pretty disappointed, having planned a little morning activity with her. A note was there in the bathroom. Said that she had a lovely time but had an early appointment this morning, but could we get together tonight?

Shoot. Tonight was the wolf pack. Before I jumped in her shower I glanced at myself in the mirror.

Streaks from her nails were still there. I touched the raw skin with my mouth hanging open. What the hell? I was supposed to heal. My first thought was, what had those guys at animal control done to me? But they'd only taken samples, not injected me with anything. At least I didn't think so.

I touched the scrathes again. They still stung. What kind of Voodoo was—oh. Maybe it *was* Voodoo. Maybe she had…I don't know…magic fingers? Well, I thought with a chuckle, she certainly did, but…not like this.

I got in the shower anyway, did a little extra scrubbing with her sandalwood soap on the scratches, and hurried out the door. I texted her that I got her note but that I had a meeting myself tonight, but could we get together the *next* night? She texted me back just as I got to my place that this would be fine. Signed it with lip emojis. Girl!

I really wanted to tell someone what had happened to me. Not Nadège, but the animal shelter. I guess I could wait for this evening. I was a little tense about what it would be like, being in a room full of wolves. Would it be weird? Would it be cool? I hadn't a clue.

I was in the shop and I happened to let drop my night with Nadège. Cam was high fiving me, but Luis looked anxious. "I don't know, man. These Voodoo ladies concern me."

"Relax, Luis. I got this."

"You got plenty," sniggered Cam.

"I hope you know what you're doing," Luis muttered under his breath.

Oh, I did, homeboy!

Cam was cracking wise again when the bell above the door chimed. Lauren walked in and we both clammed up.

"Hi, Jeff. I wondered if you had a little time this morning for a cup of coffee. So we could talk."

She looked different. She'd done something with her hair. Instead of that pony tail she always wore, she'd let it hang loose, down to her shoulders. She kept sweeping it behind her, shook it out a lot.

"Sure. Can you guys handle the crowds?"

There wasn't anyone in the shop at the moment, so I guess we were cool. I wondered how Starlight Occult was doing in this off season, and how she could afford to carry Bliss. But having her there did leave Lauren time to study and do her research. I supposed some things were worth the trade-off.

We took it to the Mermaid and settled in with lattes. She swept her hair behind one ear and jumped right in. "That was a pretty intense evening, wasn't it?"

"Yeah. I'd never seen anything like it. And to tell you the truth, I never want to again."

"I've been to séances before, a couple of times, but I never saw anything like that. *That* was real."

"Are you sure? Maybe they had rigged something—"

"Did you feel it was faked? You being the friend of the Lwa, and all."

"Hey, that was freaky. And no, I didn't get a fake vibe from it. After all, I'd seen some pretty intense stuff before, like I said."

"Yes, I'm curious about that. You touched on some things, but never went into detail."

"I don't really know how much I should say. It all involved a magical book... Sounds weird now, but it was more reality than I've ever been used to. Take my word for it."

"You...don't seem to really want to talk about it."

I shook my head, toyed with the hot paper cup. "I guess I sort of don't. People...died. Magic can be...strange and unpredictable. And the creatures from these different planes, they play for keeps. They aren't able to reason, some of them. They're just creatures, bent on killing."

"Can you...give me details on some of the creatures at least? Some of the things you encountered?" She paused. "Were there any...werewolves?"

I tried to sip the coffee but it was too hot. I wiped my clammy hands down my jeans. "Um...no. Just some other kinds. There was a kelpie. And a ghoul. And then there were Draugr, zombie Viking dudes. And this goblin. It was big. And a tree creature."

She was staring at me with her mouth open and forgot to write down what I was saying. "Are you kidding me? Really, are you pulling my leg?"

I shuffled in my seat. "Honest to God, Lauren. I am not kidding you."

"Well, you really do look upset."

"I am. I'm still getting over it."

"I tell you what. Maybe we can focus on the magic itself. Do you feel comfortable talking about that?"

"Yeah, okay. What do you want to know?"

"You mentioned something about a book."

I licked my suddenly dry lips. Would this coffee never cool down? "There was this ancient book and my ex—she moved to Maine to open up her own shop. Well, she found this book bricked up in her wall and when she opened it—pow! All these things came out of it. But like one at a time. And she had to capture them and put them back."

"Did she know about this book ahead of time? Did she go there to find it?" Now she was writing furiously.

"No. It was all new to her."

"Did you go to help her with it?"

"I didn't have any idea either. I just went to win her back."

She looked up for second, quirked a smile, then put her head down again. "That's what you said. But then you got caught up in all this...magical stuff."

"Yeah. I thought I should stick around, do the gallant thing." *That was all a lie, Jeffy. You became a werewolf and then you couldn't leave.* Or so I had thought. "But she had her coven and they helped her figure things out and do spells. The book seemed to enhance what they could do. It was pretty gnarly."

She looked up again. "Gnarly. I didn't know surfers really said that."

I smiled, leaving some of my nervousness behind. I put my hand to the side of my mouth. "Akaw!" Some people turned to look, including the barista. "We say that too. Means 'awesome.'"

She chuckled and turned back to her notes. I noticed she clutched her pen like a little kid, fingers all tight on it, middle finger on top of it instead of the pen resting on it. I don't know why, but it made me smile.

"Before the presence of this book, could they do spells?"

"I don't know for sure, because it sounded like they did little things. And it's like that again, now that the book is gone."

"Gone?"

I held up my hands. "*That* is a whole other story."

She nodded, wrote. "What kind of spells? Like that forget-me spell?"

"Yeah. I mean, they could obviously do that. They said ley lines enhanced their power, and there were a lot of them around. I can see them." I said the last before I realized I shouldn't have. If I could have slammed my hand over my mouth, I would have.

I can only see them because I was a werewolf.

She looked up, pen stopped and poised over her notebook. "You can see them? The ley lines?"

"Uh...yeah. The magic, like infected me, and I can do some stuff. Just a little here and there. I don't, though, cause that's not my scene."

"You can do magic but you don't?"

"Um...yeah. But...I don't have any need to."

She raised her brows but looked down at her notes again. The pen moved once more. "But you could if necessary?"

"I suppose. Small things."

"Can you see any ley lines around here?"

"Actually, there might be, I just haven't looked for them."

"Do you feel them?"

I rolled my shoulders. "I guess so. Because I do think there are some here. I'm thinking more inland, though. That way," and I motioned vaguely with my hand sort of southeast. "That's weird. Never thought about it before."

She laid the pen down. "Seriously?"

"Yeah. I guess we could go look for them sometime if it means that much to you."

"Jeff..." She looked excited. "Are you aware of how much this would mean for my research? I mean...I've encountered the occasional shaman and Wiccan practitioner, but what you're saying sounds..." She seemed to be reaching for the words. "More...legit."

"Oh. Well...I'd be happy to help where I can."

"But I don't understand. If all that is true, you said yourself that the ley lines enhance magical power."

"They do. That's what the coven told me."

"So why wouldn't you go there?"

I shrugged. "Like I said, I'm not looking for power."

"But you went to the Voodoo coven."

"I was interested in the woman!"

That was the wrong thing to say. She stared at me. Her excitement, the animation in her eyes all seemed to shut down. She frowned, slammed her notebook closed, and stuffed pen and notebook into her bag. "Okay, I guess that's enough for now."

"Hey...Lauren..."

"Thanks, Jeff. I'll...talk to you later."

I swiveled in my chair. "Lauren..."

But she was gone. I don't know why she was so offended. I mean, I'm entitled to hook up. Even if it is a Voodoo chick.

I scratched at my chest. It itched where Nadège got me…in her *passion*. I smiled.

CHAPTER EIGHTEEN

☾

IT WAS A day of trying to reassure Luis that I wasn't dating the Devil, of side-stepping Cam's questions, and making some actual sales during the day. We had a flood of people in the afternoon. Some regulars were back for their tea refills; some older lady was there trying to book me to do a tea for her daughter's baby shower—that was a yes! And then there was an assortment of others interested in the spices and herbs. I did a lot of educating that day. It was fun. The way it used to be. My place. It got me to thinking that I needed to step up the promotion and outreach. The lady with the baby shower really got me interested in doing more like that; baby showers, bridal showers, birthday teas. Maybe some lectures at different organizations. Google some local covens and get them on our mailing list. To tell the truth, I stole some of these ideas from my ex. She always wanted to do this stuff and *was* doing it in Maine. I didn't see why I couldn't expand my base and do some of it too.

I guess I was busy on the computer when Cam came up to the counter and told me he was on his way out. I glanced at the window and it was dark! How did the day go by so quickly?

"I'll catch you, well, not tomorrow, that's your day off. Day after that?"

"Yeah. Luis is here tomorrow. Bye, Jeff."

"Later."

He locked me in at the front and I was in the place alone, in the quiet. I figured I should collect the wolfsbane stuff and bring it up to my place for some brewing. I had an iron Dutch oven—it would do instead of a cauldron in a pinch—and I gathered my things.

I set the alarm, turned off the lights, and headed out the back door and up the stairs to my place.

While I chopped and brewed, I thought about everything that happened in the last few days. Séances, ghosts, getting caught and taken to the pound, doing my own...pounding... It was a lot. "Just another day in the life of WereJeff."

I put the burner on low and the brew had to simmer for several hours. I threw a big T-bone on the grill on my landing, readied a baked potato, and set my table. Dreamily, I thought about Nadège. She was a real interesting lady. I wondered what the Qualcomm sisters would think of our getting together. Didn't really want to think about them. Wanted to think about Nadège and how sensual she was, how she wrapped those sinuous limbs around me, how she felt.

I ate my steak just barely grilled, devoured my potato, and sat back with my beer, staring at the last vestiges of the sunset. You could see the ocean from my front window, as well as the traffic of Main Street. It wasn't all that noisy except for the thump of music from the bars, so it wasn't a bad place to live. Plus, it was all mine. But I supposed that, someday, some woman would make an honest man of me and we couldn't stay in a man cave forever. But what kind of woman would marry a werewolf? Lauren had and hadn't even known it. I wondered if other wereguys—and weregals, I supposed—married and didn't tell their partners. That didn't seem right. Or smart. You'd *have* to tell them to keep them safe. What woman would want that in their life? Maybe they mostly married other werewolves. But that meant that your kid was one. That just seemed irresponsible. There was some coolness about being a wolf, but I wouldn't wish it on a kid of mine.

Every time I got relaxed about things, my mind would fill with all this other stuff. When I got captured last night, that could have really gone badly. If I hadn't thought it out, I could have gotten killed, or gotten someone else killed. This was a nightmare that wouldn't end. Not ever. I had to be smart. I had to be aware *all* the time.

There went my beer buzz.

I almost switched on my X-box but turned on the TV instead for the news. And crap. There I was again.

It was the body cams from the cops. "What appears to be a blond wolf was captured by animal control last night," said the lady newscaster. "This is the same wolf that might have a connection to the Sandman Murders on the beach in recent weeks. But sources say the wolf was apparently broken out of the county shelter by a *naked* man." The video switched to nighttime footage of yours truly—with my private bits fuzzed out for the more delicate natures of the viewing audience—running around the back parking lot. The video was pretty crappy, fortunately for me, because it wasn't going to be easy to identify my face. I had turned away most of the time, knowing the camera was there. And then I disappeared into the darkened corner where the shed was, and the next thing you saw was the blond wolf leaping over the fence.

"There was no comment from county animal control," the newscaster went on, "but the police say they are now looking for the man in question. If anyone has any information, you are asked to contact the Huntington Beach Police."

Oh great. Being wanted as the wolf wasn't bad enough, but now they wanted Naked Man. Awesome. How could one guy get himself into so much trouble and still be innocent?

It was getting late. Time to head over to Vargar's place and meet my...my tribe.

I glanced at the gris-gris bag on my counter. Should I bring it? Or would it end up being counter-productive? What was its range? How close did they have to be to me? You know what? Screw it, I was bringing it. I stuffed it in my pocket and headed out.

There were a lot of cars parked on his street and the house was ablaze with light. Okay, *now* I was getting nervous. I could take Jesse Vargar, but a whole pack of werewolves? Probably not.

I parked down the street and strolled down the sidewalk. I could smell them. There were lots of feathering trails of scent all curving toward his house. I could hear loud talking, but as I got closer the talking quieted until everyone had fallen silent. They knew I was there.

Before I knocked, Vargar opened the door. "You came. Come on in." He pulled the door wider to let me through.

As I walked over the threshold, their scents became stronger — sharp, acrid scents, softer scents, the scent of anger, the scent of trepidation. I wondered what they smelled off of me.

He closed the door and I stood there, looking into the front room. There were about ten guys there, and only two women. Please don't tell me they serviced these guys. I was already visualizing all sorts of kinks. I hoped I was wrong about that.

As I scanned their faces, I saw people of all races, all walks of life; guys in T-shirts, some in button-down shirts with ties, one guy with a polo shirt with some restaurant logo stitched on his chest. The women were just in blouses and jeans. They wore gold earrings and necklaces. Not surprising since silver was out. No one said a word.

"This is Jeff Chase," said Vargar. "Jeff, these are the Moonrisers."

I almost snorted. They had a name? Like a biker gang? Maybe it made them feel better. Maybe they didn't want to be known as Vargar's Boys ...just in case he was cut out one day.

I raised my hand, friendly-like. "Hey."

No one said anything back, but some nodded to me. I didn't see Jacob anywhere. I'd have to ask about that.

An African American guy in a suit stood up. "Jesse tells us you don't want to join the pack. Why not?"

I glanced at Vargar. "I don't know him. I don't know any of you, for that matter. I don't feel comfortable following orders in this kind of situation."

"What kind of situation did you come from?" asked an Asian guy in a blue T-shirt.

I shrugged. "Not a pack. From being bitten and left to fend for myself. It isn't a nice thing."

They all murmured with each other. I heard the name Jacob muttered. I guess they knew what he did.

One of the women, the red-head in some very tight jeans, leaned forward from her folding chair. "Jesse said some bullshit about you being bitten by the First Werewolf. How is that possible?"

I paused, thinking about how much I should tell. Just enough, I guess. "My ex-girlfriend was living in Maine and she found this ancient book, and when she opened it, a bunch of creatures from lore came out of it from wherever it is they were living; another plane of existence, another world—whatever. And the First Werewolf was one of them. He bit me. I killed him. The end."

The other woman, a blonde, looked to Jesse. "What does he mean by 'first werewolf'?"

I cut in on whatever explanation he was opening his mouth to say. "The very first werewolf. Centuries old. Thousands of years old. The Wiccan coven I was hanging out with and who helped me through it, told me that he was so old he wasn't even a man anymore. He didn't shift. Maybe forgot how. They think he was King Lycoan from ancient Greece."

That started another flurry of murmurs and whispers.

"Maybe you're lying," said a guy with a black beard and a man bun. "Maybe all that is bullshit. Whoever heard of some magic book?"

"Whoever heard of werewolves? I know of some people who know how to do spells," and I cut a glance at Vargar, who shuffled uncomfortably. "Didn't you get the memo that magic is real? I didn't come here to convince you. I came to get your help. About some murders."

"He's the blond wolf," said Vargar with a smirk I wanted to smack off his face. I guess he was getting his own back for my mentioning spells. "And the Naked Man on the news."

I rolled my eyes. I'm *so* glad he found out about that.

A few of the guys snickered behind their hands. "Yeah, well," I said, thrusting my hands in my pockets, "I'd like to see the rest of you escape an animal control compound."

"We're not dumb enough to get caught," said Man Bun.

I sighed, swallowing down my pride a bit. "I could use some pointers on how to stay on the downlow and still wolf out."

Everyone quieted again. I didn't know how you joined a pack. Did you have to posture a lot? Win a fight? I hoped I didn't have to fight anyone. This sort of thing just made me bored.

"Jeff's here tonight," said Vargar, "because he says he has it on good authority that the Sandman Murders were committed by a wolf. I've already cleared one of ours and he is gone for good." Everyone really got quiet at that, even turned their faces away. If they had wolfed, their tails would have been between their legs and they'd be whining. "So I need to know. Is anyone here losing control? Is anyone doing these killings?"

Naturally, no one spoke. "Seriously?" I said. "Like anyone here is going to admit that? They'd be confessing to murder. That's a capital crime. I don't know what kind of rules your pack has about that, but I'd think they'd be rather steep."

"We do have rules," said Vargar, his voice low, almost a growl. "And the penalty is death."

"Whoa," I said, holding up my hands. "No wonder no one's gonna talk. Are you crazy? A life for a life seems pretty severe."

"That's how a pack is run, Chase," he said in my face, pointing a finger into me. "Unless there's strict discipline, a Were can go nuts, doing whatever he wants to do. That can't be allowed. That's why one of ours was told to pack up and hit the road. If you don't follow the rules you're out, one way or the other."

"And what happens to a wolf who doesn't want to be part of your pack, who doesn't follow your rules?" I asked.

Oh, he didn't like that. His eyes wolfed and his fangs grew. I got a kick out of challenging his authority.

"Our rules *must* be obeyed," he went on. "Whether you belong to our pack or not. That's how we all stay alive. All the pack know that."

He didn't exactly answer my question, but I stared him down and scanned the rest of the "Moonrisers." I think I had a pretty good idea. For now, I was tolerated. But if I got too much out of line...or revealed who we were, they'd have no compunction about killing me. That was heavy. My throat was suddenly dry, but at the same time, the wolf wouldn't mind the action. *Chill, WereJeff. No one wanted to die.*

It didn't change the fact that a wolf had murdered those people for no reason. And they needed to be stopped. If I had to kill them, then so be it.

"So which one of you killed?" I asked. I'd pulled my hands from my pockets and I had allowed my nails to grow to claws.

No one said a thing.

"This is useless," I growled. "I wish there was a wolf lie detector."

Vargar rubbed his chin. "There is."

"Hey," said a guy in a plaid shirt. "What is this? Why are we listening to *this* guy?"

Vargar narrowed his eyes, probably doing that hypnotic thing, because the guy got a blank look on his face and sat again. "Because he's the one being blamed for this. And I believe he didn't do it."

I jerked my head toward him. That was something at least.

Vargar excused himself to go upstairs and everyone turned their eyes toward me. Man Bun got up and approached me. There was suddenly a lot of musk in the room. "You're bringing trouble to the Moonrisers. We don't like that."

"Who came up with that lame name? Vargar? You don't even need the moon to shift. Do you have club jackets with the name on it?"

Wrong thing to say. Everyone seemed to be growling, their eyes shifting to wolf eyes, their snouts elongating, they were rising from their seats and crouching low. I was slowly being surrounded.

"Hey, weredudes, chill," I said. "Okay, I apologize for making fun of your club name."

"It's not a club," growled Blonde Girl. Her ears were growing out of her hair. "It's our pack," she hissed between sharpening teeth. "You don't get to diss the pack."

"Okay, I'm sorry." It was in my words, but not in my body language. I wasn't backing down, and their inner wolves didn't like that. They expected me to whine, to cower, to turn away. I just couldn't do that.

Man Bun shifted in the blink of an eye and leapt. I shifted on instinct, ripping my jeans open from the waist down the leg. They slipped off and my shirt, too. I hunched over, my hackles raised, my teeth bared. The smell of them got me going, did something to my blood. Made it rush through me like adrenalin.

He charged. But as soon as he got within inches of me, I could tell by the look on his face that he'd changed his mind. Looked like he was smelling something bad. I realized it must be the gris-gris bag, though it was on the floor with the remnants of my jeans. The smell must have stuck with me, though. But too late, motherfucker. Instead of going high, I went low, with apologies to Michelle Obama. I went right for the back leg, chomping down hard on the tendons and muscle. He whined like a little girl...uh, girl-wolf? He tried to scramble away and simultaneously clamp his jaws to my neck. Too much skin and fur, dude. I tore flesh away and there was blood in my mouth...and man. If I hadn't had the wolfsbane, I think I would have gone crazy. The blood. It was like werewolf heroin. I was hopped up on it. I went even wilder. I got him on his back and I was ready to rip his throat out, his guts. I could hear others shifting around me, growling, barking.

But I held myself back. I saw the whites of his eyes, the terror in them and I knew right then and there, that I didn't want to be that wolf. He'd learned his lesson, that he couldn't challenge me, so I backed off him. He stayed on his back, tail curled up between his legs. He waited for me to give him the all clear. I did with a snort, forcing the blood out of my nostrils.

When I turned to the others who had surrounded me, I gave them a long howl before baring my teeth at them.

"ENOUGH!" cried Vargar from the stairs. He glared at all the pack but mostly at me. "I leave you for five minutes and you manage to piss off a room full of wolves?"

I shifted back and stood up, wiping the blood from my mouth with one long swipe of my arm. I was naked but it didn't bother me. The others were still wolves, but they were pacing restlessly, going in circles, head down, ears back.

I looked back at the guy I had pinned, and he slowly rolled to his stomach, but stayed low to the ground, ears down.

"He attacked me first," I said, like a twelve-year-old.

"I don't care who attacked first! This is pack territory. And no one asked *me* permission."

"I'm not gonna *ever* ask you permission."

Vargar's eyes got red. "Put your clothes on."

I grabbed my stuff from the floor. I pulled my shirt on. Nice big rip along my jeans leg. That was not fixable. I held it in place with my fist.

Vargar gave the rest of them the pack leader eye and they all backed down. That was a good trick. I wondered if I could master it. They each one shifted back, pulling clothes on. I was trying to be a gentleman and turned away from the women. I didn't know wolf etiquette but I figured what went for humans would also work for wolves.

Once everyone had shifted back and stood by their seats, they glared at me. Yeah, well. The same to all of *you*, too.

Vargar had a velvet bag in his hand. When he reached in, I wasn't sure what he would pull out, but it certainly wasn't what I expected. A piece of stone the size of a dinner plate. A corner of a bigger piece, it looked like. Thick like a slab of sidewalk, and in the corner was carved a wolf head in a circle.

"This is the Wolf Stone," he said. "No Were can touch it and tell a lie. You're all going to come up one at a time and I'll question you."

I'd never heard of anything like this. But then again, there was a shit ton of stuff I didn't know about being a werewolf. Like how did they get by without taking wolfsbane? And where did they do their wolfing out? And were any of them married to normal people? Did any have "cubs" of their own?

Everyone was hesitant. It was clear they were a tight bunch, but no one wanted to reveal any more secrets about themselves than they had to. I didn't blame them. But I had to know who was killing. Too bad Jacob wasn't here.

The braver souls came forward first. A burly guy in a tight T-shirt from some gym—and I believed that he got it from there and actually worked out—pushed his way forward from the back and glared at me the whole time.

He laid his hand on the stone and continued to glare.

"Tyler," asked Vargar, "did you kill those people on the beach? Did you have anything to do with those people?"

With big square teeth that were turning into sharp ones, he growled a defiant, "No!"

One by one, they got up, glared at me with their hand on the stone, and denied having anything to do with the murders. Even the idiot who attacked me, Man Bun, limped over to Vargar, swore on the stone, and appeared innocent. He didn't make eye contact with me.

When it got to the last few people, I turned to Vargar. "Are you sure this thing works?"

He growled at me, and with snout elongated, he put his own hand on the stone. "I just *love* Jeff Chase."

The stone glowed a bright green.

Oh.

He looked around the room, satisfied and stuffed the piece of stone back in its bag.

"Hold on," I said. "I didn't ask you."

If looks could kill, I'd be dead ten times over. But Vargar didn't hesitate. He took the stone out of the bag again, slammed his hand to it, and, looking me in the eye, said, "I did *not* kill those people on the beach."

I stared at the stone, daring it to glow. But it didn't.

He shoved it back into the bag with such force I heard some seams rip. "Satisfied?" he growled.

"It's too bad we didn't have Jacob here to ask," I added.

There was a gasp rippling through the room. I guess I put my paw in it again.

Vargar turned to me with a filthy look. "We don't discuss the banished."

Jesus Christ. This was such a cult! I was so not into this. The more I saw of these people, the less I trusted them. "Fine. I guess we're done, then."

I turned to go.

"Chase!" called Vargar.

I stopped and turned my head. I didn't like turning my back on these people, but it was a sort of last "fuck you" to them all. "Yeah?"

"I suppose you know you aren't welcomed in my pack."

"I'm crying big wolf tears over that."

"But...I will come by your shop tomorrow. We have...*things* to discuss."

"Whatever." I walked out of there; head held high. All the way to my truck and when I got in, my hands began to shake uncontrollably. What the fuck had I done? I almost killed a guy. I almost got eviscerated by a pack of werewolves. What the hell was the matter with me?

Whatever it is Jesse Vargar wanted to talk to me about, I hoped it would be useful to me.

CHAPTER NINETEEN

❦

WHEN I GOT back home it was eleven and I was exhausted. My brain hurt. There was so much to take in, I couldn't sort it all. Maybe I didn't need to.

I cracked open a beer and stood in my window, just gazing out to the ocean and the lights of Main and PCH. "I thought I could do this," I muttered. "I thought I could leave Maine and the coven and live my life, sort of be normal again. But…" I shook my head and took another long swig. I was mullering this whole thing. And I thought I had it handled.

"Shit. Maybe I *should* have stayed in Maine." But no. I *had* to have my own life, and that was back here, in HB, surfing, tending to my shop with my boys. I couldn't have lasted another month in Maine.

I tilted up the bottle but it was empty. I went to the fridge and grabbed another. I drank as I made my way to my bedroom and shimmied out of my ragged jeans. I looked them over. I'd have to toss them. Before I dumped it, I had the presence of mind to grab the gris-gris bag out of the pocket. It had slowed down the wolf attacking me. Might have avoided fighting at all if *I* hadn't gone for it. I set the beer on my dresser and grabbed some shorts, slipped them on. I tossed my ripped shirt in the trash, too, and stood there, bare-chested. I lightly touched the scratches that were *still* there. *Damn, Nadège. Girl, why'd you Voodoo me?* Had she somehow figured out why I left her at the dance club the other night? She didn't need to have sex with me to scratch me, though. Didn't seem like a revenge fuck.

I lightly touched the red and puckered scratches. They were still sore. I wondered now if they'd heal at all.

I looked up from my chest in the mirror. I was looking a little gaunt. Maybe from the stress, I don't know. Should have shaved too. I sported a little bit of beard these days. I liked the look. I leaned on the dresser and stared at the shadows on my face…and then something in the back of the room caught my eye.

I turned. Nothing there.

Back to the mirror, and there it was again.

When I glanced over my shoulder a second time, a shiver ran down my neck. There was nothing behind me. My breath caught as I slowly turned back toward the mirror. There was…*something*…in the corner of the room. A shadow. But only in the mirror that wasn't in the actual room when I'd looked behind me.

And then the shadow moved.

The smell of cigar smoke wafted toward me and I froze. It slid away from the wall and formed into the shape of the…the freakin' Lwa!

"Jesus Christ!" I watched in the mirror as it approached me, it's strange two-dimensional form seemingly impossible. My neck hair prickled bad, warring with my brain. I knew it wasn't behind me, but I *could* see it behind me in the mirror world.

Once it came to the frame of the mirror, those silver eyes staring at me the whole time, it smiled like it had before, a crescent moon of a smile that shimmered, a cigar hanging out of the side like a mobster. I stumbled back. My throat constricted but I still wanted to scream.

Its fingers came out of the glass over the frame and it climbed out of it, stepping over the low dresser and onto my floor. It cast no shadow. It *was* shadow. And there was no reflection of it in the mirror either as it came out of it completely.

"Shit!" I kept staggering back away from it, but it kept coming forward. It never moved its gaze from me and carefully stalked forward as I stumbled backward. It stopped when it seemed to think I would run. Cocking its head, it looked me over.

"Go away!" I barked. I had barely enough breath for speech. "Go away. I…I don't want you here."

One sharp edge of that crescent smile rose up into a smirk. He raised a hand, folded down his fingers one at a time till just the index finger was raised, and slowly ticked it back and forth.

Okay, I was out of there.

I spun around to run to the door, when an ice-cold hand closed over my shoulder. It was so cold it burned, and when I cried out and fell to one knee, it took its hand away. I looked back and it was ticking its finger at me again.

I tried to get to my feet but it was standing over me, looking down. It pointed at my chest.

I shook my head. I didn't know what it wanted.

It pointed again.

I stared down at my bare chest. The Lwa crouched over me and pointed to the scratches.

"What...what is it you want? What are you trying to tell me?"

It made claws out of its fingers and mimed scratching down me. Then it shook its head.

"Yeah, okay. I know they should have healed. You...you know what I am, don't you."

It nodded, with a wide grin again.

"So...what does it have to do with these scratches? Why are you bugging me about it?"

It cocked its head again, squinting now. It took the cigar from its mouth and very carefully tried to mouth something, even though it didn't appear to have any lips, just that crescent gash. I shook my head. I didn't understand...until I did.

It seemed to be mouthing...*Quoiquou.*

I knew my mouth had dropped open. It nodded to me, grinned again, and turned. A fresh puff of cigar smoke reached my nose, and when it turned and I saw its side, it almost disappeared. It was as flat as a shadow. There was no depth to it. It took its shadow-self back to my mirror, climbed in with one of its long, skinny legs, pulled itself in the rest of the way, and melded back into the Mirrorland's shadows.

I lay on the floor for several more seconds before I jumped up, threw a T-shirt on, and raced to the door. I don't think I was wearing shoes.

☾☾☾

I BROKE EVERY speed law getting to the Quoiquou sisters' place, caught the curb, and left the truck there hanging off it, before I stumbled to their door. I knocked at the same time I repeatedly jabbed the doorbell.

"Widelene!" I stage whispered to the door. "Tamara! Jesula! Open up! It's Jeff. For the love of God, open up!"

The door swung open, and Widelene, dressed in a long nightgown that buttoned up to her neck and carrying a baseball bat, stood in the doorway. Her sisters stood behind her. I ducked when it looked like she was coming at me with the weapon. "Chill, ladies! It's only me!"

"What kind of crazy white boy are you, knocking on our door in the middle of the night?"

"You gotta help me."

"Why we 'gotta' help you?" she asked with a frown. "What do you want?"

I took a breath and licked my lips. "I was visited by a...a Lwa."

Jesula pushed a clearly shocked Widelene aside and reached out and grabbed my arm. "Come inside. Close the door, Widelene."

She dragged me in and sat me down on their sofa. I realized I was in a state of shock. My hands felt cold and I was shivering. Suddenly, an afghan was dropped on top of my shoulders.

"You poor boy," said Jesula, rubbing my arms. "Tamara, get the boy some rum."

She ran to comply and I didn't even argue. Yeah, I'll take some rum. Or whiskey. Or vodka. Or all of it.

Widelene stood over me, just staring.

Jesula cooed softly to me in Creole. I didn't know what she was saying but it soothed. It was probably some kind of spell. I didn't even care.

"Where's that rum?" called Jesula over her shoulder.

Tamara thrust an arm forward, a glass of caramel-colored rum in it. She handed it to me and I tried to knock it back, but Jesula grabbed my wrist and controlled how much I got. "That's it," she cooed. "Just take a little. There's always more. Now then. You sit back and you tell us what happened."

It was pretty harsh rum, but I still appreciated the warmth and then the alcohol surging through me. I licked the taste of it off my lips. "I was just at home, drinking a beer and looking in the mirror…and it came."

Jesula urged me to take another drink, both her long-fingered hands on mine, and pulled the glass down again once I had sipped a bit.

"It climbed out of the mirror like it did the night of the séance. And it came at me. It was…it was trying to tell me something."

Widelene, eyes still wide asked, "It didn't possess you?"

"No, it just stood there, grinning at me."

They all exchanged glances with one another.

Jesula urged more rum on me and as she pulled it away from my lips, she asked, "What did it say?"

"It said *your* name. Your last name. So here I am."

Jesula glanced back at her frightened sisters again. "What else did it say?"

I shook my head. "It didn't say anything. It just pointed to my chest."

"Why?"

I felt like an idiot. But I grabbed the hem of my shirt and pulled it off, dislodging the afghan over my shoulders. They all stared at the scratches down my torso.

"Did the Lwa do that?" asked Tamara breathlessly.

"No. Uh…Nadège did."

"I told you!" said Widelene, trying to press past Tamara and Jesula. All she could manage was to stretch out her arm and shake a finger at me. "I told you to stay away from her."

"We were fine! She just got a little carried away. Although…this might be Voodooed. I mean they aren't really healing."

"Nadège," said Tamara uncertainly. She looked from Widelene's angry face to Jesula's judicious one. "Would she have done that?"

Widelene rattled off a bunch of scolding words in Haitian, Jesula barked back at her in the same language, and soon they were all arguing.

I put my fingers to my lips and whistled an ear-piercing sound. They all stopped and glared at me. "Hey! Remember me? What the heck was the Lwa saying to me? And is this gonna happen again? I don't want to see that dude come out of the mirror every time I'm trying to shave." Or anything else. That mirror was in my *bedroom* for cripes' sake.

Jesula put her hand to her mouth and thought. She took the rum out of my hand and drank a bit of it herself. "I...I have never heard of the Lwa behaving in such a way. You must understand, I am a mambo in my country...I *was*. And though I have seen many possessions, I have never met anyone who could *see* the Lwa at a convocation, let alone outside of one."

Great. Another one-of-a-kind deal with me. But it was probably because I was a werewolf, and I certainly couldn't tell them that.

"What am I supposed to do?"

"You did the right thing by coming here...as the Lwa told you to do."

"Okay. So what does it mean? Why am I here?"

Jesula took another swig of rum, knocking the rest of it back. "Sisters, we must talk."

They gathered together at the other side of the room, even though they spoke only in Haitian Creole. Every now and then they'd look back at me. I felt like a fish in a fishbowl. I slipped my shirt back on and meekly looked around, shying away from looking at their various mirrors on the walls. I couldn't escape them! They were everywhere.

After they'd conferred a while—and argued—it seemed they had finally come to a conclusion. They all came back to where I was sitting and stood over me. "It was decided," said Jesula, hands resting one over the another in front of her nightgown, "that we must summon the Lwa again."

I jolted to my feet. "No! No way. Uh uh."

"Now hold on," said Jesula, using that placating tone that somehow relaxed me. Damn them and their Voodoo! "Just sit, Mr. Chase, and listen. We must know what the Lwa wants of you. It is concerned—as *we* are concerned—about these scratches. After we see what the Lwa wants, we will prepare a healing poultice for you."

I didn't want to get Nadège in trouble, but if she was doing some unauthorized Voodoo on me, then...well. Something had to be done, I guess. "Maybe we should just call Nadège."

"NO!" said Widelene, scaring the bejeesus out of me. "We can't involve more people. The Lwa asked for *us.*"

"Yeah, but it pointed to *my* chest." I made the same clawing gesture that the Lwa made.

"I will make a poultice for you," said Tamara. "But after we summon the Lwa."

"Y-you said it doesn't always come, right? It may not show up?" I was sure grasping at straws. I didn't want it to come. I didn't want to face that shadow thing again. And I didn't know what her poultice could do to me. Maybe it wasn't good for werewolves. Maybe the Voodoo Nadège did was to ward *off* werewolves. Maybe that was poisoning me. Shit. Should I tell them about me? *Do you want to hang, Jeff?* And I had no doubt whatsoever that the three of them could cast a spell to make me go and hang myself. No thank you.

"We must," said Tamara. "We must know what the Lwa would have us do."

"I agree," said Jesula. She was all business now, moving furniture to the edges of the room, lighting the candles and incense on the altar. The three of them got busy, all in their long nightgowns, turning off lights, moving incense around to reach the four corners of the room, getting that gourd with the beads on it, the bell.

They positioned themselves before the altar. No churchy stuff this time. They did a few prayers in French and then got right down to it, ringing the bell, rattling the gourd, tapping the drum. They started to dance. Their bare feet spun on the rug laid out on the floor. The incense made me light-headed. Or was it the rum and two beers? Things were getting weird again. I was feeling the hairs on my neck rise. All I wanted to do was get the hell out of there.

When I rose to do it—I didn't care if they thought I was a pussy for running or not—the air in the room changed. I felt it. The women were dancing up a storm. They all looked like they were out of it, either eyes rolled back or closed with the intensity of their prayers.

And there it was again. The smell of cigar smoke and something moving within the mirror. I backed away. Sorry. Nope. Not gonna stay for this. I backed toward the door and grabbed the door knob. I pulled it open, but the knob slipped out of my hand and the door slammed shut. I tried it again but now it was locked. What the hell…?

When I turned toward the sisters, the Lwa was climbing out of the mirror. It circled the ladies in its tilted top hat that was as flat as it was and its enormous stogie, studying the women, walking around them.

In an instant, they all stopped dancing at once. They were breathing heavily, eyes closed…until they slowly opened them. I expected them to all look like zombies in a trance, but they were fully awake, looking at each other eagerly. I realized that they expected one of them to be possessed so the Lwa could explain what it wanted. But it wasn't happening. The Lwa grinned at them, before turning to look at me.

"Stay away from me!" I shouted. I backed up but hit the door. I had nowhere to go.

"Jeff," hissed Jesula. "Do you see it?"

"Yes! It's right freakin' in front of me!"

They couldn't see it. That was just great. "Can you talk to it?" I squeaked. "Tell it to back off of me?"

The Lwa was right in my face, with its strange silver eyes, no nose, and wide shimmering grin. The tip of the cigar might have glowed or it could have been my imagination. And I could sort of see through it. It had no substance. No *earthly* substance anyway. And when it had touched me before, its touch was like ice, like the cold of outer space. It wasn't *of* this place, that was all I knew.

"It's right in front of me, like, *inches* away." I was not afraid to admit that I was cowering. And terrified. Big bad werewolf was ready to wee in his pants.

"Great Lwa, spirit watching over of our ancestors," Jesula began.

It cocked a pointed ear toward her like a cat does, but was still staring at me.

"Keep going," I said. "It's listening."

"Great Lwa, tell us what you want, what you need? Use us as your *chwal*. We are willing to serve."

The Lwa turned toward them, looked them over again, but shook its head and got back in my face.

"It's not working," I hissed. "It doesn't want to possess any of you. It's...it's trying to say something."

It moved its mouth but I couldn't make it out. It was probably speaking Haitian. I could see the frustration on its otherwise blank, flat face. Finally, it looked straight at me, lifted its hand, and folded all the fingers down again in that strange, alien way, until the index finger was pointing at me.

And then it stuck its, cold, *cold* finger to my forehead. I screamed.

CHAPTER TWENTY

I MIGHT HAVE blacked out for a second. It had hurt so much. Like the worst brain freeze ever, and then real throbbing pain seared through my head. The Lwa had me pinned to the door with just an index finger pressed between my eyes.

But then...softly, like a breeze, like a wave hissing against the shore, I was beginning to hear words.

"W-wait a second," I gasped. "Wait. I...I can hear...it's talking to me."

I opened my eyes, and the Lwa was gazing at me. This time, not studying, but with genuine interest. I didn't feel any animosity. And it knew what I was. It was like...it was trying to calm me down, tell me it was my friend. I kind of shivered at that, but when it wasn't grinning so much, it looked like it...cared.

It was definitely speaking, but not in a voice. I heard the words, nonetheless. It was like my thoughts but *not* any thoughts *I'd* have. Very weird, but...not so bad.

"It's saying...the scratches will harm me if not healed." Nadège! What have you done? "That...it wouldn't have affected me if I wasn't a werewo—"

I froze.

Oh shit. Shit, shit, SHIT!

I cut a glance toward the sisters. Their eyes were wide. Their mouths hung open. No one was breathing.

"Please don't kill me!" I said all in a rush, my head still pinned to the door, with only my eyes darting toward the sisters. "I'm not a bad guy. I'm not! I'm not like your *loup-garou*. I swear. I'd never hurt anyone."

"But I gave you the gris-gris and you took it," said Widelene in the softest tone I'd ever heard from her. Her voice quavered. They were afraid of me. I didn't want them afraid of me. I would have gone to them, but the Lwa still had me pinned to the door with its finger.

"I don't know why I can touch the gris-gris bag. It doesn't seem to affect me. I...I even used it the other night. It did ward off the other werewolves... Dammit," I said to the Lwa. "Stop making me say stuff!"

It grinned and shrugged its shadowy shoulders.

"The Lwa is telling me to get healed. It clearly doesn't want you to hurt me."

Widelene suddenly frowned. "How do we know it is telling you that?"

The Lwa stepped back from me, taking its cold finger away, and turned angrily toward Widelene. It stretched out its hand and all the things on the altar were suddenly swept to the floor, including the lit candles.

Tamara yelped and ran to fetch the candles before they burned the carpet.

"It didn't like that you didn't trust me," I said. Hey, the Lwa dude *was* on my side. I'd've high-fived it if I wasn't sure my hand wouldn't just go through *its* hand.

It turned back to me with that wide, mischievous grin, Lwa to WereJeff. Was this really happening? I wondered if I needed a brain scan.

It turned and headed back toward the mirror. "Hey, uh, Mister Lwa!"

It stopped and slowly pivoted its neck, still with that crazy Cheshire Cat grin.

"Um...what does all this mean? How can I find the killer?"

It did that finger folding thing again, and with its index finger, pointed to its eye, nodding. Then it was off again, heading for the mirror in the large gold frame. Its long leg stretched longer to climb in, pulling the rest of its body with it. It stretched out its arm and flicked invisible ash from its cigar before it sank back into the shadows of the Mirrorland.

I slid down the door and lay back against it. My heart was thumping hard in my chest. But the Lwa was right. Now that the adrenalin was wearing off, I was starting to feel funny. And when I looked down at my chest, I could see these micro veins stemming from the scratches like black lines. That couldn't possibly be good. "Hey, uh, Jesula? Something's happening."

She began toward me when Widelene pulled her back. "You heard the Lwa. It made him confess it. He's a werewolf."

"And the Lwa trusted him. That means we can, too." She shrugged off Widelene's hand and knelt beside me. Her fingers touched my skin. They felt cold, but only because my skin was burning up.

"She wasn't trying to poison me, was she?" I croaked. "Please say she wasn't."

"If she didn't know you were a…a werewolf, then no."

"I'm…I'm not feeling too good."

Tamara came at me in time with a trash can and I emptied my stomach into it in convulsing heaves. I felt terrible. My temperature was rising by the second, and my head was pounding. My stomach cramped. There was nothing left to heave.

"I'm dying, aren't I?" I said weakly. So this was it. Of all the things that happened to me, I was going out like this. I never pictured it. I thought it might be doing something heroic, like back in Maine, fighting the bad guys. Not like this on the floor, dying of fever.

"You are not going to die," said Jesula sternly. She barked out orders in Haitian to her sisters and they ran to comply, even Widelene. I was getting a little fuzzy by then. I think I slid further and ended up lying on the floor. I was probably delirious, because all about the Quoiquou sisters, I saw these things flying around, like rainbow-shimmering-transparent creatures and they were throwing sparkly dust everywhere. So that was weird. My head was drumming and I was so hot, I just closed my eyes.

After a while I was drifting. I was a wolf, running free; no worries, no fears. I was running along the surf line and it was bright daylight. I could smell the salt and the sand, and a thousand other things, from the fish in the ocean to the bag of French fries a seagull was flying away with. And it was glorious. The sun seemed so bright. And I was running toward it, because the warmth felt so good on my fur. But then everything started to get darker and colder. I couldn't find the beach anymore. I was wet and cold, shivering, trying to curl into myself and my fur...but then all my fur was gone, and all I was, was just a naked guy again.

"Where's my fur?" I muttered.

"You are all right, Jeff. Here now, drink this up."

I didn't remember who that was, but she sounded nice enough, so I did as she told me. Fingers held up my head as I drank. The thing I was drinking tasted vaguely of coconut milk. Was this a piñacolada? "Not enough pineapple," I slurred to...whoever. She kept urging me to drink it, so I did.

Now I was feeling a little clammy, like I'd gone in the ocean and sat around too long in my wet suit. But nothing smelled like the ocean anymore. I smelled...patchouli?

I woke with a start, snapping my eyes open. I was soaking wet and lying in a puddle. They'd poured cold water on me to lower my temperature, I guess. I blinked as the room came into focus. There were no more flying things, no more fairy dust in the air. The sisters were bending over me with worried expressions and I still had the taste of coconut in my mouth.

"What...what happened?"

"You were very sick," said Jesula, soothing back my wet hair off my forehead. "You were burning up with fever from the poison. How are you feeling now?"

I looked down at my chest and the scratches were finally disappearing and healing over. Jesula watched the process with interest. The other two, with horror.

I scooted back against the door and sat up. "Thank you. Thank you for saving me. I was a goner for sure." I glanced up at the other two and sighed. "I'm not dangerous. I'm just a...a guy who turns into a wolf occasionally."

"But you are *jé-rouges!*" said Widelene.

"But I'm *not*. Whatever you've been told about werewolves is wrong."

"We are not wrong," said Tamara, still breathing a little quick and short. "Werewolves in Haiti *do* kill."

"And slavers just make you think they do when they kidnap kids to sell. It's not werewolves."

"Hey, White Boy," said Widelene, getting back her attitude with her hands at her hips. "Don't tell *us* about Haiti. We know all about the slavers. But we also know there are werewolves. Skinwalkers."

I was feeling back to my old self again and I stood. "I don't need an animal skin to shift. Watch." I turned away from them to take off my shirt and my shorts and shifted in seconds. As a wolf, I sat down, wagged my tail, and did the Lassie routine.

They all screamed, so I shifted back, trying to keep my dignity while slipping my shorts back on. "See? No red eyes, no blood-curdling howl...no animal skin to put on. I'm me. I'm Jeff. With...a werewolf problem that isn't my fault. I didn't ask to be bitten."

"You are the blond wolf they're after on TV," said Tamara, hands still pressed to her cheeks.

"Um...yeah. But that's circumstantial. When I was wolfed out, I found the guy already dead. It was a wolf that did it, but I can't find the one who's guilty. I will, though."

"You are the blond wolf," said Jesula, "*and* the naked man they are looking for." She smirked a little.

"Yeah. I was stupid enough to get caught by animal control. So much for your big bad wolf."

"But...Jeff," said Jesula. "What are you doing here in Huntington Beach? You could hurt someone."

"No. See, that's just it. I won't hurt anyone. I take wolfsbane. It calms me. I don't get all wolfy when I smell blood like I would if I weren't taking it. Don't you see, it's under control. There are werewolves like me everywhere. We're just...people trying to get by. And this is my home. I belong here. If people would just stop trying to find me and kill me." I swept my gaze over them. "So...so you aren't going to kill me, are you? I mean, you just went to the trouble to save my life." I looked at Widelene particularly. "You can trust me. You can."

"You take wolfsbane?" said Widelene. "What's that?"

"It's a potion made with a flower...more commonly known as monkshood. Aconite. It was something discovered in eastern Europe centuries ago to calm werewolves."

Jesula nodded. "He's right. I have researched it."

"And he owns a *herb* and tea shop," Tamara pointed out.

"Yeah. Easy access. There are other things that go into the potion but I carry all that too. Look, I've only been a werewolf for six months. The only things I've killed are demons and bad magical creatures. I have a coven who will vouch for me back in Maine."

"That is all very well," said Widelene. "But why didn't the gris-gris bag send you away? It was to protect you against werewolves, but since you *are* one, it should have made you too uncomfortable to stay."

I began to shiver. Soaking wet, I was cold, and hugged myself for warmth...until Jesula ran to get the afghan and laid it over my shoulders. I gave her a grateful smile. "I don't know. I might be slightly different, werewolf-wise. I was bitten by the *First* Werewolf. The first-*ever* werewolf, from centuries ago? I think that made me just a little different."

They were hearing a boatload all at once. There were a lot of stares with wide eyes and parted lips. I looked away from them, rubbing my arms and finding a wooden chair to sit on so I wouldn't soak their sofa. "Look, I know it's all a lot to take in, especially with your belief...uh...*knowledge* of the kind of werewolves you have in Haiti—"

"They aren't true werewolves in the sense that *you* are one," said Jesula, following me and sitting on the sofa. "They are Skinwalkers. They are evil shamans who put on the skin of a wolf and enchant themselves. When they kill, it gives them more power. That is why they murder children, because their innocence gives them greater magic. This is why we kill them on sight in Haiti. But there are many in Haiti who kill the wrong people. People who they don't like or they only suspect. And yes, we know about the slavers who rely on the superstition of my people to do their own evil. You *are* different."

"So…you *won't* kill me?"

She smiled, leaned over, and patted my knee. "No, Jeff. I give you my solemn oath that we will not kill you."

I turned to the others. "Even Widelene?"

She had the most stubborn look on her face, but she rolled her eyes and kept her arms firmly folded over her ample bosom. "I won't kill you. I don't know if I trust you completely, but I won't try to kill you."

Tamara rushed over and bent to hug me. "Oh, poor Jeff. I won't kill you either. I want to help you."

So now I had three aunties looking out for me. That was better than three Voodoo witches trying to kill me. Yeah, I'd take that any day.

"And so," said Jesula, getting all business-like. "Tell us about the other werewolves and who you think is killing those people on the beach."

CHAPTER TWENTY-ONE

THEY BROUGHT ME hot tea. I recognized it as *Te Jenjanm*, a spicy ginger tea from Haiti that really made me feel better, as I told them about my investigations. I felt I had to lay it all out to them and so I spilled about the Moonrisers. I was sure that was breeching pack etiquette but since I wasn't part of that pack, I didn't feel guilty about it.

Jesula sat with her hands together in prayer, fingertips pressed against her lips. "And you say this Jesse Vargar brought out something he called the Wolfstone?"

"Yeah, said it was like a werewolf lie detector."

"I have never heard of that. Was it a small stone, like in a ring?"

"No. It was more like a piece of sidewalk. Wait, let me call someone." I had Lauren's number ringing before I realized what time it was.

"Do you know what time it is?" she croaked from the phone speaker.

"Dude, I am so sorry. But I have an important question."

"It had better be."

"Have you ever heard of a 'Wolfstone' as a werewolf lie detector?"

"What? What is it with you and werewolves?"

"I just...um...do you know about it or not?"

"Yeah, I know about it." There was some rustling and muffled movement. She was probably sitting up in bed. "A wolfstone was a big slab of stone they used to lay over graves in the early New England colonies. Wolves were such a problem that they put these on the graves to prevent the wolves from digging up the dead.

They killed the last wolf in Connecticut in the mid-eighteenth century, so they stopped making the stones."

"So...it's not a werewolf thing?"

"That depends on who you ask. There's some research that I just scraped the surface of that seems to suggest that the wolves killed in Connecticut were, in fact, werewolves."

"Oh. Then if someone had part of a wolfstone, it could be used for some kind of magic for werewolves?"

"If it was created to deter werewolves, I imagine it was more than stone, otherwise, werewolves could have dug up the corpses as men and then shifted to eat the dead, right?"

"Ew. Yeah, I guess so."

"Is that all? Is that what was so urgently needed in the dead of night?"

"I'm really sorry, Lauren. I didn't realize it was this late. Thanks, though. I owe you dinner."

"You don't have to do me any favors," she said, suddenly sour.

"It's not that. I'd like to. You've been really helpful to me. I'd like to take you out. Can I call you tomorrow?"

She sighed. "Yeah, I guess so."

She clicked off and I stuffed my phone back in my pocket. "You heard?"

"I thought you were dating Nadège," said Tamara, narrowing her eyes.

"I was. I am. Lauren's just a friend."

"Mmm hmm," she said in that way that means, "Oh, right."

"She is!"

"Never mind that!" said Widelene.

"It might be a good idea not to see Nadège again," said Jesula. And before I could object, she touched my arm. "You don't want a repeat of the scratches. And...if this wolf knows you are hunting him, he might try to hurt you."

"And Nadège could get hurt too," I said. I hadn't even thought of that. Jesula smiled indulgently.

"It's for the best," said Widelene. The others gave her a meaningful look.

"Guys," I said, glancing at the clock on the wall. "It's two-thirty. I'm pretty beat. Mind if we pick this up tomorrow?"

The sisters seemed reluctant to let me leave, but Jesula made the decision, as always. "Jeff is right. He's had a very hard day. He must take care of himself. You go now, Jeff. You sleep well. We will talk to you tomorrow."

"Okay. And really. Thank you all for saving me. Thank you for believing in me. We'll get through this."

I staggered to my truck—which, remarkably, didn't have a ticket it on it for the way I'd parked it on the sidewalk—and climbed in.

I got home at a more leisurely pace, making sure I followed all traffic laws and speed limits. I dragged myself upstairs and fell into bed. I didn't even take off my clothes. I slept like the dead and awoke sometime around seven-thirty. It could all have been a dream...if it weren't for the torn jeans hanging out of the trash can and the clothes I was still wearing that weren't quite dry.

I looked down at my chest. It was scratch-free. I lurched into my bathroom and looked in the mirror. I startled back a bit, thinking a Lwa might come out of it, but there was nothing there. "Dude, Lwa," I sighed, before throwing back the shower curtain, "just don't make a repeat appearance in the mirror, okay? My heart can't take it."

I scrubbed everything, and shaved around qmy beard in the shower. That way I wouldn't have to look in a mirror. Then I wondered how a vampire shaved. And then I wondered if vampires were real and then I stopped thinking about it because I didn't want to know.

Clean, shaved, combed, I started my day, which meant stuffing the gris-gris bag into my pants pocket and heading downstairs for some tea.

I got there way early, earlier than Cam who would arrive in an hour. I made the tea for the urns—deciding on a ginger spice, thinking of the Quoiquou sisters from last night—and drank my own mug full.

It was still too early to call Lauren to apologize for last night, but it wasn't too early to hear from Nadège who had texted me earlier:

Let's get together tonight. The moon is full and arouses feelings of romance in me.

Well hell. The sisters told me to stay away from her. And they were probably right. I mean, what was I going to say? "Don't scratch me like you did, cause it could kill me?" Because, to be honest, it was hot as hell. Though another bout of getting an antidote from the sisters didn't appeal to me. Maybe just dinner. The sisters couldn't object to *that*. But damn, that lady was *hot*.

I texted back, *Yes!*

"So smooth, Jeff. So smooth."

"What's smooth?" said Lauren, coming through the door with an aluminum coffee cup.

"I didn't realize I unlocked that."

"Maybe you're as tired as I am." She looked at me pointedly.

"I'm really sorry. I just didn't realize—"

She waved at me. "Doesn't matter. I spent another half hour wondering why a wolfstone was so important. And then, funniest thing, I remembered my ex had something like that. When I found it one day, he hit the roof that I was touching it. Just another reason he and I are splitsville."

"Ha, that's funny." I wasn't laughing.

"The man had his secrets. It wasn't appealing."

"That's not a basis for a good relationship." Did that just come out of *my* mouth?

"You're right. Mmm. What is that tea? It smells really good?"

"Ginger spice with something a little extra I like to add. Wanna try some?"

"Sure."

I got her a little sample cup. "Mmm. I can certainly taste the ginger. But it's got something else in there. Some kind of floral thing."

"Dried quince. It adds that floral scent and flavor."

"That's really nice. You know your teas and spices."

"I should open a shop!"

We laughed. It was good to see her in a good mood. "Hey, Lauren. I'm sorry about whatever it is I said last time we met. If I offended you in some way, I'm sorry."

She lowered her face into her tea. "No, it was me being in a mood. Don't take offense. And hey. You're taking me out, I hear?"

"Yeah. How about...tomorrow night?"

"You got a date. I mean a dinner. Um...a night...out...shit. I'll stop talking. I gotta get to my shop. Bye."

As she flounced away—her hair down once again—I was beginning to get the feeling she maybe had a bit of a crush on Old Jeff. I smiled. It was cute. She was better-looking than I'd first thought. But I'd try not to lead her on. It was cool to have a friend who was a girl. I'd never tried that before. *New days, Jeff. New things.*

Cam arrived not too long after. "Hey, did you hear the news?"

"What now?"

"That blond wolf the cops captured...and then lost? They did some tests and exonerated it from the murders. It wasn't the right wolf...dog...whatever."

Whew! Well, that was something at least. "Maybe they'll stop looking for it now."

"I don't know about the wolf, but they want that naked dude. Why would you go to a pound to break out an animal and not wear any clothes?"

"So you can't be identified by them?"

Cam looked at me for a moment before he burst out laughing. "Right. You are a riot, Jeff."

Yeah, I was a riot, all right. I felt scared last night that I had spilled the beans to the sisters, but now I felt better with some knowledgeable people to get help from. I thought it was going to be all right. Maybe I didn't need a pack. What I had needed all along was a coven.

The bell above the door jingled and I looked up. Shit! Just what I needed. "Hi, Lindsay."

"Hi, Jeff."

Cam smiled and shook his head, and drifted to the back of the shop.

She tucked some of her blonde hair over her ear and looked at me coyly from under her lashes. I could smell her pheromones. "I, um, haven't heard from you in a while, and I thought..."

"I know. I'm sorry. How's it going?" I glanced at Cam and started to reach for her arm, but thought better of it. "Why don't we go to the back and talk?" I led the way to the back room and closed the door. "How's it going with the lost time thing?"

"I'm chaining myself up at night, and it seems to be working. But it sure puts a damper on my personal life. Know what I mean?"

"Oh, I do, girl. Uh...what, uh, did you want from me, exactly?"

There was a pause. "Well...you know what my problem is."

And now it's *my* problem, apparently. "I know. Did you contact Jesse Vargar again?"

"Yeah. He thinks the best thing for me is to join his pack. Are *you* joining his pack?"

"Nah, I'm giving it a pass. Me and Jesse...we don't get along."

"Oh. Because...you know. I thought we sort of...clicked? You and me."

Yeah. I was clicking all over the place. I was doing all I could to *not* shift right there. Or tear off my clothes. "Oh...about that. You know, it may not be the best idea for us to get together again. I mean...you feel it, right?"

She stepped closer. "Yes," she said breathlessly, pupils blown. If she kept that up, that wasn't all that was going to be blown...

I reached into my pocket and closed my hand on the gris-gris bag. I pulled it out and she immediately lurched back.

"What *is* that?" she snarled. I could tell she felt suddenly trapped in the small room. I stuffed it back in my pocket.

"It's werewolf deterrent."

"Why would you have that?"

"Because! If we lose control, we could get jiggy as wolves and—not to put too fine a point on it—that's how you make baby werewolves."

"Oh! Oh my God! I don't want to do that."

"I didn't think so. Whatever is affecting the two of us isn't something we can deal with on our own. And if it doesn't affect the others in the pack, then maybe that's the best place for you to be. Where you belong, I mean."

"Then...does that mean we won't be seeing each other again?"

"I'm thinking it's best we don't. Not without this." I showed her the bag again and she shied back with a grimace, like I was holding a steaming pile. I put it away again.

"You just seem like a nice guy, is all. And you were there when I needed a friend."

But you got much more. Then I started to think about her missing time, and wondered about the timing of that. Was it possible that Lindsay was our killer wolf and didn't even know it?

What could I do? It was no good using the wolfstone on her if she couldn't remember. Maybe good old-fashioned hypnosis would work. Or maybe the Quoiquou sisters knew a nice little ritual. "Listen, Lauren—I mean Lindsay!" *Keep it straight, Jeff.* "We need to get to the bottom of your memory loss and what you might have been doing during those times. Talk to Jesse about it for sure, but...I might have some other people for you to talk to. Is that all right?"

"Yeah, I guess."

"Good. Can we get together tonight? Around five? I'll give you an address to go to. I'll be there, too. There are some ladies, in a coven. They can help us."

"A coven?"

"Yeah, a Voodoo coven. Look, it's complicated to explain but they can help you with your missing time, get to the bottom of it. Maybe stop it. And maybe stop our weird—" I gestured between us. "This thing."

She nodded. Reluctantly, I thought.

"Okay. I'll call you."

She leaned in to kiss me, but must have gotten a whiff of the gris-gris and backed off.

I started to think about all the balls I had in the air; Nadège on the downlow, since the Quoiquou sisters didn't want me seeing her. Then there was Lindsay, and I don't know what the heck was up with that. And then this murdering wolf that I was still sure was part of the Moonrisers.

Lindsay left and I fell against the backroom wall. Whew! And I thought Maine was crazy.

CHAPTER TWENTY-TWO

☾

I GOT ON the phone quick to Jesula, and she agreed we should meet. Then I got on the phone with Nadège and agreed to meet *her* at ten. Hey, just like the old days, juggling several women at once. Except this time, it didn't seem as fun as it used to be.

Cam kept giving me looks all day, and winking. Dude! If you only knew.

Finally, I left early, leaving him to lock up and get the register straightened away. I wanted to call Lauren to talk, but what would I say? She couldn't help because she didn't know about me, and I really wanted it to stay that way.

I made sure I got to the Quoiquou sister's place before Lindsay. I didn't want her walking into that on her own. She was probably freaked enough by circumstances.

"So we're bringing another *jé-rouges* into our home," said Widelene, looking at me with narrowed eyes.

"I told you, these werewolves are different from the ones you knew in Haiti. We're all just stumbling around trying to figure things out. Now, I need to tell you some stuff before she arrives. I met her one night at a bar, and we had this uncontrollable need to...you know. Hook up. And it's still pretty strong. I'm just barely holding her off with the gris-gris bag."

Tamara cocked her head at me. "When you say 'uncontrollable need', do you mean..."

"I *mean* we would have done it right then and there on the dance floor if we hadn't gotten out of there. It's no secret that I like the ladies, but I usually have a little more control than that. But this was...animalistic. Primitive. Lauren told me that if we had done it as wolves, she would have gotten pregnant with a werewolf."

"A rutting pair," said Jesula, her brow slightly furrowed.

"Yeah, something like that. How do I stop it? I don't want to get with her. It's kind of like...rape, you know? For both of us. We're both unwilling." Mostly.

Widelene blew out a loud breath. "A neutering charm?"

I grabbed myself unconsciously. "Let's not go overboard."

"A *calming* charm," said Tamara, giving Widelene a withering look. She went to the altar and grabbed an old book. The handmade leather cover was stained with wine, cigar burns, and candle wax. But it had parchment pages like the Booke of the Hidden. It kind of scared me a little. "I can find a charm to calm you both. It will go against your natures, so it's best you don't see much of the young lady afterwards."

"No problem. As long as it won't...you know. Cramp my style."

She looked down her nose at me over the pages with just a hint of a smile. "No. Your style will remain...*uncramped.*"

"Good." I fidgeted. Stuck my hands in my pockets and paced a little, until Widelene handed me a glass of rum.

"Oh, thanks."

"Just take a little. It's for the ceremony."

I sipped and clutched the tumbler in my hand. "So...what sort of ceremony is this? Like hypnosis? The Lwa doesn't have to be here, does it?"

"It shouldn't," said Tamara, finger tracing over the handwritten lines in the book. "What we will do, is have her walk through the instances she lost time. She'll tell us what she did, what she can't remember."

"Oh, okay. She'll be all right, won't she? I'm kind of worried that...well. That she might be the killer wolf and just doesn't remember."

The sisters all looked up at me from wherever they were in the room. They exchanged some silent thoughts with one another, before they went back to their various tasks. Widelene was arranging the room, pushing back sofas and chairs, and placing one big threadbare chair in the middle of the room. Tamara read in the book, while Jesula lit candles and incense.

"You still have the gris-gris Widelene gave you?" asked Jesula over her shoulder.

"Yup. Got it right here. It still works on her. It was sort of the only thing keeping us away from each other."

"Good. Put it on the altar."

"Uh...don't I need it?"

"Not for this ceremony. Leave it here."

I pulled it out and laid it carefully on the altar. I noticed there was still a silver knife on the table beside the incense. I stepped carefully away from that.

"What should I be doing?" I asked, feeling a little lost.

"Stay out of the way," said Widelene.

Jesula shook her head and sighed. She offered me a smile. "You make the young lady feel comfortable."

And just as Jesula said it, the doorbell rang. She nodded to me to get the door. Lindsay was standing there, hands crushed together nervously. She offered me a quick, distracted smile before she came in and looked around. I could feel her discomfort pouring off of her.

Jesula was there first, a colorful *gele* wrap around her hair. "Welcome, Lindsay. I am Jesula. That is Tamara, and over there is Widelene. We are going to help you try to remember what you did during your blackouts."

"So...you know about...about...Jeff and me?" She swallowed nervously.

"That you're werewolves?" hissed Widelene. She was also wearing a colorful *gele* and a flowered dress with a big bow at the back. "Yes, we know." She didn't bother hiding her sneer.

"You sit here," said Tamara, gesturing toward the chair in the middle of the room.

Lindsay gave me a deer in the headlights look. "You'll be here the whole time, won't you Jeff?"

"The whole time. Don't worry."

She sat gingerly in the old chair. It looked a little like a shopworn throne. Tamara handed her a glass of rum. "Drink a little of this."

Lindsay stared into the glass. "What is it?"

"Just rum. It will help you relax."

She nodded and took a sip. Tamara gestured for her to drink more. Oh, she was going to be relaxed, all right. That stuff was strong.

Wide-eyed, Lindsay knocked it back, emptying the glass, and Tamara took it away.

Jesula put her hand on Lindsay's shoulder. "We're going to dim the lights, and then we are going to hypnotize you, of a sort. All right?"

"Yeah," she said, curling her hands nervously over the chair arms.

"Now," said Jesula, "close your eyes."

Man, I really hoped it wasn't her. Though at the same time, it would be nice to get this over with. Except we'd have to figure out what to do about it. And I didn't like what we might come up with. Vargar would want to know, and if it *was* Lindsay, I sure wasn't going to tell *him*.

Jesula took up some of those burning incense sticks and waved them in front of Lindsay, leaving wisping trails of smoke and scent. It was strong for my nose that picked up the least of scents, even when I wasn't wolfed out, and Lindsay was feeling it, too. She wrinkled her nose and kind of shied away from it.

Next, Jesula motioned Tamara close. She had little brass bells in her hand and tapped them together lightly. They resounded with a gentle *ting*. "Lindsay," said Jesula in a soothing voice. "Are you listening to me, child? Nod your head."

Lindsay did. She was still clutching the chair arms for dear life.

"Relax, child. Listen to the sound of my voice." Tamara tinged the bells every now and then. "Listen to the rhythm of your breathing; the beating of your heart. This is your life force within you. The blood flows from your heart through your veins, giving you life. Your breath fills your lungs and releases again. You feel the breeze on your skin, through your hair, touching you like a caress. Breathe…in and out…in and out. Good. You're doing very good, child. Can you lift your right arm for me?"

Slowly, Lindsay's right arm looked like it floated upward.

"Good," said Jesula in that calming tone that was putting *me* to sleep. I shook it out of my head. The incense was getting heady. I wasn't sure if it wasn't laced with something. But I did notice Lindsay's other hand on the chair arm wasn't clutching it anymore, and instead lay relaxed and loose on it.

"Child," said Jesula, walking all around the seated Lindsay. She still carried the incense sticks, and they sent a wreath of smoke around Lindsay's chair, that created a sort of spicy mist surrounding her. "Put your arm down. Your whole body is too heavy to move. Too heavy with weariness. It's nice just to sit there, listening to my voice, smelling the incense, feeling the chair under you, cradling you."

Lindsay's head suddenly lolled to her chest. I jolted toward her, but Jesula saw me and raised a finger for me to stop. Oh. Lindsay was under. Cool.

"Now Lindsay, child, tell me about the first time you lost hours. Tell me what you felt, what you saw."

She said nothing, just kept on breathing as if she were asleep, left her head on her chest, her hair falling forward and covering her face. When suddenly, I noticed something happening to the mist over her head. Like a movie projector, an image began to form in the mist, in full color, of the world through Lindsay's eyes. I watched it with a slackened jaw, staring like a fool, at the magic before me.

Lindsay was obviously a wolf, as she was low to the ground. It was night, and she trotted along the sidewalk, turning her head this way and that, raising her muzzle to sniff the air. It was down on Main. I recognized the shops she passed, and she was heading toward the pier.

She was brown as a wolf, and really kind of cute. She looked down at the sidewalk below her from time to time and we could see her little brown wolf legs. She would easily be mistaken for a dog.

She crossed PCH without much trouble, and there wasn't anyone around, so it was probably late. It was more or less the same path I'd taken before, and when she got to the beach, she, too, headed for the surf line and the foamy tide. She trotted along and when she got to the barnacle encrusted pier, she simply stood in the shadows for a while. I heard a noise behind me and looked, but it was the image, not anything in the room. Instead, I watched as WereLindsay turned her head.

There was Daniel, the homeless guy with his shopping cart loaded with his worldly goods. He was rolling it along the strand. It rattled and skidded on the sandy sidewalk. She watched him and sniffed the wind.

No, I thought, I prayed. *Lindsay, don't do it. Please.*

She hesitated, watching him for some time, before she took off in the opposite direction, trotting along the sand.

Whew! Then maybe it *wasn't* her. But now I was glued to the weird video of her life that played out above her head in the mist. It showed another day, and another of Lindsay as a wolf, exploring the back alleys and streets of Huntington Beach, sniffing in trashcans, sniffing at fences where dogs whined and fell silent behind their gates, even those with the "Beware of Dog" signs.

Once she was on the beach when the Cutback Boys showed up. Hiding in the shadow of the pier, she watched them harass with their big Rottweilers an old man who had a tiny poodle. The poodle was giving them what for, as small dogs were wont to do, and the Rottweilers were straining at their leashes. Suddenly, one of the Cutbacks released the leash and the big dog was all over the poodle. It never had a chance. I winced and looked away. The old man was crying and yelling, over and over, "Why did you do that? Why? It's just a little dog."

"Now it's a dead one, old man," said the asswipe. I wanted to leap into that mist and show my displeasure with my fists...or claws...but the scene changed again.

Daniel was under the pier, sitting in a dark corner, eating what looked like a corndog. The Cutback Boys were walking along the strand, dog leashes in one hand, tequila bottles in the other, and they were swigging away, tossing the empties out to the beach, trying to break the bottles. They didn't notice Daniel at first, but the dogs did.

I didn't want to watch. I didn't want to see.

And just as I was about to turn away, Lindsay started to growl. The Rottweilers immediately snapped their heads toward her, tucked in their tails, and backed away, much to the consternation of the Cutback Boys. They ended up being pulled behind the dogs on their taut leashes, leaving the old man alone.

Daniel stared into the shadows at Lindsay, and just as I thought it was going to get bad, she, too, turned away and trotted along the beach in the opposite direction from the Cutbacks.

What the hell?

And scene after scene, was WereLindsay, just sniffing around and exploring the region. That's all she did. She wasn't a killer. Thank God.

The smoky incense faded along with the images, and Jesula slowly brought Lindsay out of her trance. She raised her head, opened her eyes, and blinked at me. "I was just wolfing," she said in awe. "I saw everything. And I sort of remember now."

"Your memories will all come back to you," said Jesula, "and I don't think you will lose time anymore. You were simply afraid to be what you are, and your consciousness would not allow you to think about it."

Lindsay took her hands and with tears on her face, thanked Jesula. "You guys are the best," she said to them, even as Widelene continued to frown at her. "And you, too, Jeff!"

Before I had a chance to stop her, she leapt up, grabbed me, and planted her lips on mine. It was instant fireworks in my head...and other places. We must have been getting into it good. She wrapped a leg around me, and I was thrusting into her. But the next thing I knew we were suddenly covered in ice cold water.

We both tore away from each other, shoulders at our ears, mouths open in surprise at Widelene with her empty bucket. She gave one satisfied nod before she wandered away in the direction of the kitchen.

Tamara surreptitiously insinuated herself between us. "And now we need to do the charm that will keep you both...from losing your heads. Jeff, you stand over there. And Lindsay, you go over there."

Tamara picked up the book from the altar along with the silver knife.

"What are you going to do with that?" I said.

She didn't answer. Jesula took up a drum and began to beat it. Then Tamara started up a call and response out of the book. Soon she was muttering in Haitian faster and faster, the same words over and over, until she was convulsing with her eyes rolled back. She dropped the book and came at me, grabbed my wrist in a steely grip, and slashed with the silver knife. The pain was like fire, I howled. Not a human one either. I partially shifted. I couldn't control it, and my muzzle had grown without even thinking about it. I stared down at the slash on my arm, and it bubbled and sizzled.

Widelene was sprinkling my face with what I hoped was water from a tied-up bunch of flower sprigs, repeating Tamara's prayer. Tamara finally let me go. I saw the bruises she left behind and the cut on my arm was still on fire, and I mean literally. There were blue flames coming up from it. I howled again.

I was in so much pain, I crumpled to the floor, rolling around holding my wrist, still half-shifted. I heard Lindsay howl, because the same thing probably happened to her, and then we were both rolling on the floor.

Someone put a glass to my lips and I automatically drank. It was some kind of milky drink mixed with rum so it wasn't too bad, and as it heated its way down my throat it suddenly felt like a cool liquid flowing down into my veins, cooling at last the fire in my wrist.

I lay back on the ground, panting. I shifted back to human, just letting the throbbing ache in my wrist settle down. "You could have warned me," I said to the ceiling.

"I didn't want you to tense up," said Tamara, normal-eyed again.

"Didn't want me to...never mind." I rolled up to my elbow and glanced over to where Lindsay was lying. She was recovering too. "You okay, Lindsay?"

She breathed deeply and turned her head toward me. "That really hurt."

"I know, babe. Sorry."

She sat up, rubbing her wrist. The scar was already fading on my skin. "What was all that for?" she asked.

Tamara offered her a hand up, and she took it. "It was so you and Mr. Chase could keep away from one another."

She was blushing hard, almost as much as I was. "Oh."

"But it's also best, child, to stay away from him."

She cut a glance at me. "Oh! But...Jeff's been good to me..."

"You are a mating pair. That will not change. Only until one or both of you finds someone you are in love with."

"True love," I said, perhaps a little cynically as I rose. I don't know if I believed in that. I thought I'd been in love with Kylie, my ex. But I guess I wasn't. When I saw the way she looked at the demon she'd hooked up with, I guess she hadn't been in love with me either, because I don't remember her looking at me like that. I felt a little...well. I don't know how I felt.

Lindsay had a horrified look on her face. And I knew exactly what she was thinking. We were monsters. Who would ever love us?

"You're beautiful, girl," I told her, even as tears rolled down her cheeks. "You watch. Someone *will* love you."

In her eyes was a brief flash of gratitude. But it didn't last. Maybe she didn't believe that any more than I did.

Lindsay left soon after that, not saying anything, not looking at me. I guess I wasn't going to see her anymore. And that made me feel pretty bad. She was alone in this, no help except for maybe

Jesse Vargar and his lame Moonrisers. I wished her well. Maybe the Moonrisers was what she needed. Maybe they *could* help her.

The sisters were observing me closely. I looked at my watch. "Ladies, I want to thank you for helping us out. That was...really great of you. I think she'll be okay now." I glanced at my watch again. "I, uh, have a date tonight, so I guess I'd better get out of here."

"With Nadège?" asked Widelene, blocking my way.

"You know what? Yeah. I do. I don't get why you are so down on us together except for the *white boy* thing. That's pretty racist of you."

Widelene drew back with an expression that seemed to say, "You are *such* a white boy!"

"Now, Jeff," said Tamara.

"What? Nah, I'm not listening to any more speeches about this. Nadège is cool. She's exciting. She's a real lady. I just won't let her scratch me, is all. I'm sure she'll agree to that. So, if you don't mind, I'd like to go now." I stared down Widelene until she let me by her. I reached for the doorknob, but then Tamara said something that stopped me in my tracks.

"We think...we think Nadège is a killer."

CHAPTER TWENTY-THREE

❦

"WHAT THE HELL are you talking about?"

The sisters congregated together, each with their own signature expressions; Tamara with dark, determined eyes; Jesula, stone-faced and calm; and Widelene with a twisted mouth and furrowed brows.

I stepped toward them. "What. The. *Hell* are you talking about?"

Jesula, of course, spoke first. "Back in Haiti, before the days of the earthquake, my sisters and I did our best to track down and hunt shaman-werewolves. Skinwalkers."

"We are good at what we do," said Widelene, her chin tilted upward.

"After the earthquake," continued Jesula as if Widelene hadn't spoken, "there was chaos. We had to first fend for ourselves before we could help others far less fortunate. People lost entire families, their homes, their way of life. There was disease, thievery, murder. And the kidnappings and killings began again. We knew some of them were slavers, but we also found some of them *were* Skinwalkers. Still more eluded us. And we suspected one of the most powerful had fled the country. We followed him here, to the United States, but soon lost him."

"We used all the power at our disposal," said Tamara. "But the Skinwalker eluded us. Finally, one day, with the help of a Lwa, we found him. Well. *Her.*"

"No one is certain it is Nadège," Jesula rushed in to say.

"It can be nobody else!" barked Widelene.

Tamara's weary expression looked as if this was an old argument. "Be that as it may, we got to know her. And though we cannot penetrate her defenses, we have reason to believe it is her."

"We don't have absolute proof," said Jesula, shaking her head. "I counsel caution."

Widelene huffed. "We've been cautious for months and look what happened? She killed again, over and over."

Jesula faced her with a stern and steely look. "And what if we are wrong? Then another refugee is hurt by us."

Widelene backed down, glancing off to the side.

Jesula squared on me again. "We were wrong once about someone we suspected of being a Skinwalker. We ruined his life. His wife and children left him and he...he committed suicide. We can't be wrong again."

My heart was racing. I longed to shift, to run and howl. I barely kept it together. "Well...what do we do? How can we...prove or disprove it?"

Jesula suddenly brightened. "Sisters, we have been going about this the wrong way. We should not have kept Mr. Chase *away* from Nadège. He is close to her now. He will be able to use the charm."

Tamara's eyes lit up. But Widelene was digging in, shaking her head. "He'll do it wrong and mess everything up!"

"Hey! I've done magic before. Well...at least seen it done. My coven back in Maine. They're the people who helped me and taught me how to make the wolfsbane. I helped them make charm pouches, do spells."

They silently conferred. A blink, the raising of an eyebrow, all seemed to convey a well-worn conversation. "We must at least try it," said Tamara, speaking at last.

"If we try and fail, we are back to the beginning again," said Widelene. "She'll flee."

"What choice do we have?" said Jesula. "She is a powerful mambo. Soon, she will suspect about us and then *we* are in danger."

I was beginning to rethink this date with Nadège. "Look, maybe you're right. Maybe I should just forget seeing her."

"No!" Jesula was suddenly in my face. "No, now is the time. If it is her, she cannot be allowed to kill again. If she kills again, she will be too powerful to stop at all."

"But you're not sure. If you do this charm and it isn't her, what happens?"

They all fell silent. Oh great! "She's damned if she is and damned if she isn't? That isn't very good odds."

Widelene made her case by smacking her hand into the palm of the other. "We must be willing to sacrifice the one to save all."

"That's easy to say if *you* aren't the *one*."

She clamped her mouth shut, but she still glared daggers at me.

I blew out a breath, pushed my hair off my face. "What does the charm do?"

Jesula straightened her dress, smoothing it out though it didn't need smoothing. "It will strip the power from her. The power to do the skinwalking. She will have no more reason to kill because she cannot gain magical power from it any longer."

"And if it isn't her? If she isn't this Skinwalker?"

"It...it might cause irreparable damage. She could go blind. Mute."

"And *you're* willing to take that chance," I said, pointing into Widelene's stubborn face. "She's a designer. This will ruin her life."

"And what if she is a killer?" said Widelene, walking forward. I took a step back. "You talked to the victims yourself. You saw how their throats were torn open. How confused they were. Do you want that to keep going on? Do you want her to be unstoppable?"

"I don't know. I don't know if I believe you."

"It is a dangerous choice," said Jesula. "But we are losing the war. If she isn't stopped, she will do unimaginable damage. A shaman who kills for power does not care who they must step on, or at what cost. If we are wrong, it is a small price to pay."

"For *you*. Not for *her*."

We were at an impasse. They looked imploringly at me, and I stared dumbfounded at them. How was I supposed to make that kind of choice? It was worse than deciding who would live and who would die. In that, I was a terrible wolf.

"You guys," I said, lowering unsteadily to the nearest chair. "How can you ask *me* to do this?"

Jesula crouched next to me. "We can't."

"What...!" Widelene began, but Jesula held up her hand and Widelene's voice cut out. Was it a spell or just the power of her presence?

Jesula pressed her hand on my arm and gently squeezed. "We can't ask it of you, Jeff. We can give you the charm and you must decide for yourself whether you use it or not. You must be very close to do the charm effectively." She looked up at Tamara. "Bring me the bag."

Tamara disappeared into the shadowed kitchen, and returned with a small palm-sized pouch and handed it to Jesula. She held it in front of me. "You must reach into the bag, take the herbs in your hand, and throw it in her face. And say the charm as you do it. Listen carefully. You say —"

I shot to my feet, shaking my head. "Don't do this, Jesula."

Gathering her dignity about her, she slowly rose. She suddenly looked like some sort of avenging goddess with her patterned dress and colorful *gele*, with her braided hair sticking out of the top like a broom. "You say these words. *Sa ki mal, ale! Sa ki mal, dwe detwi! Mwen mare ou, mwen mare ou, mwen mare ou!*"

"What? I can't remember all that! What does that even mean?"

"It means, 'evil, begone! Evil, be destroyed! I bind you, I bind you, I bind you.' Now. *You* say it."

"I...I don't even remember the first line."

"This boy is useless," said Widelene in disgust. She marched over to me and slapped her hand to my forehead with a loud smack. It hurt. But then I made the mistake of looking in her eyes and I suddenly couldn't move. "Remember the words," she said in a monotone. "*Sa ki mal, ale! Sa ki mal, dwe detwi! Mwen mare ou, mwen mare ou, mwen mare ou!*"

I couldn't help it. I was like a puppet. I couldn't stop myself from repeating the charm aloud. The words felt strange on my tongue and lips, but in my mind — in the place where her palm was pressed — the alien words took root, swirling there, waiting to be used like water in a pipe. I repeated it, every weird word.

Widelene, satisfied, nodded, and pulled her hand away. I swayed and stumbled back into the chair. "Wha...what did you do to me!"

"I enhanced your memory. You're fine."

"Don't ever do that again."

"You were wasting time."

"I'm not doing that spell."

She shrugged. "Fine. Let it be on your head when she kills again."

Tamara looked worriedly from me to Widelene. "*He* must decide. We don't know for sure, Widelene."

"*I'm* sure. I'd do it if I could."

They fell silent, looking at me anxiously. Even Jesula, who wasn't sure Nadège was guilty, wanted me to do it. They were leaving the fate of this woman — who could just as easily be innocent of their charges — in *my* hands.

I was *not* going to do that charm. No way. There was no way I would blind her. Because I knew in my heart of hearts that she was innocent. I don't know what got them so convinced it was her, but *I* wasn't convinced. She could have easily killed me at any time and gotten power that way. She had a million opportunities. I wasn't buying it.

But I didn't say anything more as I rose, rubbed my cold arms, and left their house. It was eight o'clock. I had time enough to take a much-needed shower and dress nice for my date; for a date I now dreaded.

I could break the date, I supposed. I could just not go. Ghost her, leave it at that. And it was really tempting. I'd certainly done it tons of times to girls I had tired of. Yeah, and wasn't that a nice thing to admit to myself.

I got home and just sat in the dark, not moving. How much better would life be if I just sat here in the dark and never moved again? I'd never have to deal with Jesse Vargar and his stupid Moonrisers, or Nadège, or the Quoiquou sisters, or any magic shit ever again. Which was fine by me. It was better to just disappear than to do this crap.

I wish I hadn't met them. I wish I hadn't met Nadège. I wish…I wish I was just…*Jeff* again.

"It's your own fault, dude. You *had* to go to Maine to try to get Kylie back. You weren't even in love with her. What was it? Pride? Stupid, useless pride?"

I dropped my head in my hand, rubbing my fingers into the tightened muscles on my forehead. What was I going to do? I pulled the charm bag out of my pocket, untied the drawstring, and looked inside. Smelled like citrus and dust. Mummy dust? God knew what was in there. I trussed it up again and shoved it deep into my pants pocket.

I had some time to kill. But there was nothing I wanted to do but sit as I was in the dark.

☾☾☾

ENOUGH TIME HAD passed that I had to get cleaned up. Now or never. I voted for never. But something compelled me to my feet and into the shower. It wasn't some spell from Widelene, either. I guess…I just couldn't leave it. I needed a way to prove Nadège's innocence. Could I just ask her? If she was this big bad Skinwalker, then she'd kill me and that would be it. And if she wasn't, well. That would be the end of us anyway. But she'd still have her eyesight.

If she was innocent.

"Goddamn it!" I was so pissed off at those sisters. I scrubbed my anger into my hair, my body, until I was raw, and rinsed off. I wrapped a towel around me as I got out and scrubbed the terrycloth over me, until I was raw all over again. I never knew a date could feel like going to the gallows.

I dressed, checked the hair in the mirror, and looked back at the charm pouch on the bed. Take it, don't take it? "Jesus," I muttered, as I snatched it up and stuffed it in my pocket.

Even as I was heading over there in my truck, I still debated with myself. *Five miles away. I could turn around. Three miles. One mile.*

I pulled up in front of her place and sat in the truck with the motor off. I tried to think of the few times I was with Nadège, if there was anything amiss about her. I mean, as a wolf, I had certain extra sensory perceptions, so to speak, and I tried to remember if I smelled anything off about her. But all I could recall was her strong perfume that smelled of exotic places. True, it was so strong it masked her own scent but that wasn't suspicious in itself. Or *was* it?

Damn. Now I was second-guessing everything we ever did, everything she ever said. But she'd been straight with me, I was sure of it. Except...that one time when we were getting all into each other and she suddenly took off on me. What had *that* been all about? I had thought it was maybe a spell from the Quoiquou sisters. But had it been something else? And if it had been her figuring out I was a werewolf, why did she want to see me again? Unless...it was to poison me with her scratches.

I was doing it again. Second-guessing. But now all of our interactions seemed to be drenched with double meanings.

I guessed I had sat there a long time, because I saw the front door opening, and Nadège's long, sinuous limbs stood silhouetted against the doorway. With measured strides sexier than any runway model, she made her way down her path, got to the passenger side of my truck, and leaned over at the window. "Just going to stay out here?" She smiled, cocking her head. "Or are you going to come in?"

Wow, she was so beautiful. Lit just by ambient porchlight, her features were perfection, from the shape of her short nose, to the lusciousness of her full lips — and I knew personally just how *how* luscious those lips were — to her high cheekbones and the sensuous gleam in her eyes.

"Yup. Sorry. I was just a little distracted." I unbuckled the seatbelt and slid out of the car. And it was then I remembered I didn't bring any flowers or wine or anything. Just that little old pouch for blinding the nice lady. *Smooth, Jeffy.*

I turned my burning face away and followed her inside. She'd turned up the ambience, with soft music, a little incense in the air, and lit candles. Two wine glasses sat on the coffee table in front of her sofa, with a bottle of wine.

I swallowed.

I had barely turned around when she was suddenly in my arms, breasts against my chest, a leg sort of hugging my leg. Did I mention what a beautiful woman she was? I felt perspiration beading on my forehead.

"Hi," she said softly, before leaning in and pressing her lips to mine. Before I could say anything, her arms twined around my neck, she pressed even closer, and I found myself sucking on her tongue. I used superhuman willpower to gently push her back.

"What's the hurry?" I managed to croak.

She smiled. She made her way smoothly to the sofa and uncorked the wine. "I'm glad you weren't late."

"Me too. I mean...I never mean to be late."

"That's okay. You're here now. No worries." She poured me a glass and handed it over. She sipped her wine—which made her lips glisten—and gazed at me from under her lashes. You know, this really wasn't fair. I wasn't good at holding back like this.

I gulped my wine and set the glass down. Nadège took that as her signal to move in, sliding toward me on the sofa, leaning forward, shoulders first, and placing a manicured hand on my chest.

I nervous-laughed a little and grasped that hand. "You know, you scratched me last time."

"You seemed to enjoy it."

"Yeah, well. I think it got infected a little. So maybe, let's not do that again."

"Oh!" She reached for my shirt buttons. "Let me see. I can give you something for it."

I pulled her hand away. "No, it's okay. It's cleared up. But...we'll have to ease up on poor old Jeff."

"'Poor old Jeff'," she purred. "Such a defenseless man."

"You don't know the half of it."

She was edging toward me again, raising her face to kiss me when I pushed away. "No, look, um..." I took both her hands. "We...we need to talk."

She looked at me strangely, shrugged, and leaned back, taking up her wine glass. "Talk about what?"

"Well...tell me about your life in Haiti. How did you become a...what's the word? Mambo?"

She narrowed her eyes slightly and took another drink. "Why do you want to know that?"

"Um...I'm curious. About the whole Voodoo thing. I told you about the Wiccan coven back in Maine, didn't I? Well, they did some pretty remarkable things, and I just wondered how different Voodoo might be from Wicca practices."

"You...want to ask that...*now*?"

"Yeah," I settled in, trying to look enthusiastic for the conversation.

She took another drink, more like a swig. "As I understand it, Wicca differentiates from Voodoo because it looks to the magic of nature. Voodoo looks to ancestor spirits for its power."

"Like L-Lwa?"

"Lwa make it possible for the Voodoo priestess to open the door. *Vodouisants* must have no fear about entering through the door."

I eased forward, noticing I had pressed myself deeper and deeper into the sofa back as she had talked. "What's behind the door?"

"Power. Magical power."

"Sounds like there's a price to be paid."

She gazed at me steadily, running a long-nailed finger slowly around and around the rim of her wineglass. It was hypnotic. "There is always a price to be paid."

"What...what *is* that price?"

All of a sudden, she laughed, startling me.

"My, what a deep conversation for a date," she said.

I tried to laugh, too. "I know. I guess I felt we should get to know each other better."

She set down the wine glass and reached for me again. "I can think of a good way."

I slipped out of her grasp and stood, then tried to hide the maneuver by sauntering over toward the altar and looking it over. "There's a lot of interesting things here. You know, the Wiccans didn't pay any kind of price. They're just sort of at one with the universe."

"It can't be very strong magic."

I thought of the magic they could do when the Booke of the Hidden gave them that power, by holding open...oh. A door. A gateway. And that let the power flood in. Because after the Booke was gone, they couldn't do as much magic as they had with the Booke around.

"It was," I said. "But...like you said...they had opened a gateway."

"Ah. You see. It is a dangerous thing."

"And...how do *you* get more power?"

I didn't turn my head, but I felt her rise behind me and come closer. "More power? Why should I want that?"

"I don't know. People get mad with power sometimes. They want more than they can handle."

"What makes you think I can't handle it?"

I shrugged, glanced over my shoulder at her. "I've heard that some people in Haiti...some people who call themselves shamans really drink up the power. And they have to do some pretty bad things to get it."

"That is true. Some do."

I turned then, licking my suddenly dry lips. "Do *you*?"

She blinked at me for a few seconds. "Jeff...who have you been talking to?"

"Oh, you know. You hear things. Bits of stuff here and there."

I glanced at her again and her eyes had gone fun\
was gone. It was like a blink when they looked odd li\
and then another blink and they didn't. Was it th\
candlelight, or just my overactive imagination? Whateve.\
the hair on my neck stood up, tried to grow. I pushed it back.

"Here and there," she muttered. "There is a lot of w\
information coming out of the internet. People mistake ceremoni\
for real things. I wouldn't give much credence to loose talk about\
someone else's culture."

"Oh, I know. There's so much false information out there."

"Exactly," she said, getting in close again.

I turned back toward the altar and hovered my finger over the gourd with the beads on it. "It's uncool to believe that stuff. That's why...that's why I'm asking you."

"You ask...a lot of questions."

"So...when you lived in Haiti, did you ever hear rumors of shamans who did bad things?"

The cloth on the altar had hundreds of tiny round mirrors sewn onto it. The light flickered over them, and I raised my head to one of the round mirrors in a gold frame hanging behind the altar. I caught the slightest of movements in it. But it wasn't the flickering candle flame.

And then I saw Nadège in the mirror. She looked different. Shadowy. Darker in a way I didn't understand. I fumbled around, grabbing for the gris-gris in my pocket...but it wasn't there. Shit! I'd left it at the Quoiquou sisters' house! And suddenly, I remembered. The time she shied away from me and left abruptly...I'd had the gris-gris bag in my pocket.

I spun. Nadège was frowning. "I don't like your questions. They are an offense to me."

"I'm sorry. I didn't mean to...mean to..."

She strode to the sofa. On it were different colored cloths, some patterned cotton, some batiked, and a scroungy hide that was strewn across them all. "Do you really want to know what price is to be paid by opening the door of power?" She grabbed the hide d draped it over her shoulders. It looked like an old coyote. Death."

"What are you doing?"

She straightened the hide, fur side up, over her shoulders, getting it even, before she pulled up the desiccated dog face over her head.

In an instant, there was something like a glittering waterfall cascading over her, passing from the hide down to her feet. But they weren't feet anymore. They were paws. She'd turned into a wolf, and not a nice, furred-up werewolf, but a scraggly, emaciated *thing* that seemed to have the face of a wolf but not. Its ribcage was enlarged and you could count all the ribs, like a walking furred skeleton. The eyes were wild-looking, and the jaws were open and snarling, revealing glistening fangs. She wasn't on all-fours. She looked like what werewolves were supposed to look like in movies. And all around her, the smell of the dead. That's what the ghost had said, too. She smelled like dead things. Maybe that's why she wore so much perfume...

I just stood there, utterly shocked. *Oh, Nadège. No.*

She growled and stalked toward me. My brain finally clicked into gear. Shift? No! If I shifted, I couldn't get the charm pouch. I struggled getting it out of my pocket as I backed away, wondering if I could get it in time.

She leapt. I dropped to the ground and shifted, ripping my clothes. She tried to grab my neck with her jaws but my powerful paws pushed her back, keeping her an arm's length away as she snapped her jaws and barked at me.

I looked down. My pants were in tatters, but the pocket was still intact, bulging with the charm pouch. I needed to hold her off long enough to get it, and that meant shifting back. I couldn't hope to hold her off as a man.

She suddenly pulled away from me and shimmered back into a woman, holding the wolf skin off of her. "So," she said, somewhat surprised. "You are a *real* werewolf. I did not expect that."

I shifted. "Don't do this, Nadège. You can come back from this. You don't need to kill anymore. Be the person you're trying to be."

"But this *is* the person I am trying to be. I'm trying to be invincible. And killing a werewolf...well. That will give me great power indeed."

"But...you and I..."

"It was very pleasant. I won't give me pleasure to kill you. But it will give me power. So, all in all..." She shrugged.

"You don't care at all, do you? I saw the ghosts of your victims. I *talked* to them!"

"That's very interesting. You seem to have unusual powers for a werewolf. Who made you?"

"I'm not going to stand around and *chat* with you. I'm going to stop you. Any way I can."

She smiled and then laughed. "I don't see how that's possible. You might have special magic about you, but I have so much more."

Before I could say anything else, she draped the skin over her head again and shimmered into the monstrous wolf. There was only a half second between that and when she attacked again.

I shifted in an eyeblink and tried to go for her throat, but she was slippery and sinewy, not like a normal wolf, and she slipped out of my grip. I had to just use the strength of my paws again to keep her jaws away from my jugular.

There was suddenly a weird shift in the air and...the smell of cigar smoke? I glanced at the mirror. It was the Lwa crawling out of it, headfirst, getting down on all fours by the altar, top hat still firmly on its head in a rakish tilt, stalking around us both like a spider with elbows and knees bent unnaturally outward. Whose side was it on? I hoped it was on mine. After all, it had gone to the trouble to try to save my life.

With all my might, I suddenly shoved her back and ran to the other end of the room, shifting the whole time. When I had fingers, I dug deep into the pocket to grab the charm pouch, but she was on me again. I shifted my muzzle to snap at her but she wasn't deterred.

The Lwa was standing upright now, walking around her like a paper doll. She didn't see it! Even as powerful a shaman as she was, she couldn't see it.

The Lwa finally looked at me. It made its fingers do an explosion motion into his face, nodding like a grinning idiot, switching its stogie to the other side of its moonlight mouth.

All very well for you, Mister Lwa, but I've got my hands full! Care to give a little help?

Maybe it psychically heard me, because it raised its hand to the altar and everything swept off of it.

That must have been too much for Nadège. She turned to look, and in that instant, I shifted my hands and got the charm pouch out. When she turned back to me, I tore open the bag and hurled the herbs in her face. I unwolfed my head and reached into my brain and pulled out the words Widelene had put there; "*Sa ki mal, ale! Sa ki mal, dwe detwi! Mwen mare ou, mwen mare ou, mwen mare ou!*"

Her eyes grew wide, her jaw fell open and suddenly the house was full of screaming. It wasn't just her. It came from every corner. The disembodied sound came from the very paint on the walls. Everything was screaming like all the souls that were ever cursed, all the deaths she had ever committed.

She snapped back instantly into human form, but something was happening. She was aging. She was growing as old and wrinkled and as desiccated as that scraggly wolf hide. Her eyes bulged, her teeth rotted out right before my eyes, and her hair grew long and white, all in a matter of seconds. She threw back her head and screamed, joining the horrific screams of all the other souls, whirling around her. And they suddenly rose up like a tornado. Things in the room started flying around; pillows, napkins, the wine bottle, the things that had been on the altar, pictures on the wall.

I cowered back, stuffing myself into the corner of the room and holding on with claws extended into the plaster walls.

The whirlwind captured her, and she and the things, and the wind were all heading toward the mirror. They zoomed toward it and passed through it like it was water and I watched as the whirlwind with the now ancient Nadège passed through into the Mirrorland room until the shadows closed it up and the mirror suddenly turned black.

Everything stopped. The wind. The sounds of screaming. It all just stopped and I was standing alone in a room full of the detritus of a tornado—wine strewn everywhere, papers stuck to the walls with it, broken furniture—and I suddenly sagged with relief. Because I was alive and not dead, not a helplessly lost ghost.

A movement in the corner of my eye startled me. It was the Lwa.

It raised its paper-flat top hat to me and then set it back down at the same angle on its head, giving the top hat a final tap. It glanced at the black mirror that seemed to remain black, and turned to one of the other mirrors. It hopped up onto a frame and stepped in--didn't even give me a backward glance—and vanished.

CHAPTER TWENTY-FOUR

MY CLOTHES WERE in tatters. I just stood there, shaking. The wolf in me told me to get the fuck out of there and the man thought that was a good idea too.

I ran out the door, letting it slam shut behind me, and made it to the truck. My hands were shaking so badly, I couldn't get the key in the ignition until I finally did.

I peeled out of there. Looking back at it through the rearview mirror, I thought the whole neighborhood would be out there after all that horrific noise. But maybe it hadn't gone beyond the walls. I wasn't sticking around to find out.

I automatically headed home. I threw myself out of the truck and flew up the stairs. Maybe I should have gone to the Quoiquou sisters' house, but screw that. I needed to be *home*! After I poured myself a big whiskey and my hands didn't shake so much anymore, I called them.

"Well?" said Jesula, anxiously.

"It's...it's done. It *was* her."

Silence. And then, "Oh, Jeff. Are you all right?"

"Um...not so much, but I will be. She...she turned real old."

"Ah. As I suspected. She was very much older than she looked."

"Oh yeah? How much older?"

"Maybe a hundred years or so. Each death not only gave her power but the life that they would have lived. She might even have been *two* hundred years old. Or even older."

Crap. I'd hooked up with a two-hundred-year-old witch?

"Jeff? Jeff, are you there?"

"Yeah. Just...thinking about stuff."

"Have a drink and calm down. Do you want us to come over?"

"No. I think a little alone time is what I want. Thanks. And…Jesula?"

"Yes?"

"I'm glad no one else had to make that call. It was hard enough for me. But…no one else could have done it. Not when she had turned into the Skinwalker. Maybe what was needed was a werewolf."

"I see. Maybe what was needed…was *you* all along. Goodnight, Jeff."

I clicked the phone off and tossed it to the table. I didn't think I'd be getting any sleep tonight.

☾☾☾

I WOKE UP in my chair at dawn in front of the X-box, the play paused and the one-shooter was standing around like a guy who lost his date.

I'd lost my date. And I still couldn't make out how I felt about it. I couldn't figure out all night what I felt about it, what I *should* feel about it. I was glad the killings would now stop. The cops would never find the killer wolf, but at least I was exonerated. That was something to celebrate. I guess.

Not that I felt like doing much of anything. I sure didn't feel like going in to work. I didn't feel like seeing Lauren tonight either. But I owed her. What I felt like doing was surf. I needed to.

I slipped on my trunks and wetsuit and got the board from the shed. I drove down and parked. I saw a few surfers braving it down the shore, but it looked like I had this beach to myself.

I waxed, stuffed the board under my arm, and ran across the cold sand. I belly-flopped onto the board and paddled out, feeling the cold sting of salt and water in my face and hair. The sea and the horizon were almost one what with the fog just offshore, and it was cold, but it felt fresh, renewing. I wanted the waves to wash away what I'd seen in the last twelve hours.

There wasn't much by way of waves. Mostly, they were ankle busters, so I let the ocean lift me and lower me with the swells. My eyes tracked the shore, taking in all of Huntington Beach I could see, even a little of Newport off to the south. All the cars buzzing along PCH, the houses, hotels, restaurants. My hometown spread out before me; the rich guys, the surf bums, the middle class just trying to make it...and some werewolves. I had never known that. How I wish I still didn't know.

I suddenly felt it and looked behind me. A wave. Like it was coming in just for me. I readied for it, took it, rode it. I got up and man! A barrel, like it was custom ordered. I rode that baby, at one with it, teasing it and it teased back, swelling, curling, letting me ride her like she was a woman. I came into shore smooth as you like on the most perfect wave I'd had in a long time. "Akaw!" I yelled into the wind. "That was awesome!"

"Great," said a voice on the beach. "Now you can get off our beach."

Fuck me, not this shit again.

I grabbed the board, walked out of the surf, and held it upright, glaring at Darkhorse Richardson, Cutback Boy. "You picked the wrong day to hassle me, Cutrate."

"Hey, dude. For the last time, it's *Cutback*."

"I *know*, douche. It's *meant* to insult you. But I guess you're even too dense to be insulted." I swung my board at him, barely missing, and headed toward the parking lot.

"Hey asshole, I'm talking to you!"

I swung back at him, dropped my board, and got right in his face. "I know what you and your twat friends are doing. And I'm giving you a warning right now. Get out of town. All of you. Get out now or I won't be responsible for what happens to you."

"We're not afraid of the cops," he postured, trying not to look as nervous as he smelled.

"Who said anything about the cops? You're gonna be dealing with *me*. And I play for keeps." I wolfed my eyes just enough to scare him. And he *was* scared. Stumbled back and everything.

I gave him one more long look before I bent to retrieve my board and turned my back on him.

"Y-yeah?" he called after me. "Well...we'll see about that. I know where you work, dude. You...you just watch yourself!"

I didn't even turn around as I stuck my arm upright, hand in the air, giving him the universal salute of the middle finger.

I waited for him to come after me. *Come on, come on, douchebag. Let me show you what messing with me is like.*

But he didn't. I made it to my truck and glanced back. He was storming up the beach, maybe looking for his balls.

"I'm not done with you yet, you and your asshole gang," I muttered. But right now, I couldn't care less. I busied myself, stripping the wetsuit off under my towel, and got my sweats on before getting back in the truck. I just sat there, looking out to the waves. Yeah. That had been good, therapeutic. I needed to listen to my inner surfer and do more of that. Maybe even convince Lauren to go out again. She had been good out there. It made her smile. I had the feeling not much made her smile lately. I didn't mind taking that on.

In the end, I did go to work that day. It seemed like a better idea than wallowing alone in my apartment. Things needed to be done and it took my mind off of it. The boys seemed to sense my mood and left me alone. Which was just as well. I got a lot done. I checked on the inventory — making sure I ordered the ingredients for the wolfsbane — and followed up on some calls from vendors. I'd hooked up with a local potter and a local glassworker to get a few art pieces in the shop. They were expensive so I didn't have much. Just to give the place an artisan flavor, and the tourists liked shopping local.

The shop felt good today, smelled like herbs and hope. Maybe Nadège had sort of cast a pall over the place and I hadn't even noticed. Or maybe it had been just over me. I was feeling better, that was for sure and anxious to go out with Lauren.

When my crew heard about that I got a world class ribbing. "So Lauren now," said Cam, straightening up a shelf of barbeque rubs in cannisters. "What will Nadège say to that?"

"She won't know about it," said Luis, rearranging the window display. That was his thing.

"No," I said. "Nadège is out of the picture. And Lauren and I are just friends."

Luis whipped around. "No more Nadège? I thought you were into her."

"Well, you know me. I was, and now I'm not."

"She dumped him," said Cam in a stage whisper.

"She did not dump me," I said, ruffled. "We just...didn't get along in the end."

"Dude," said Luis, "would it kill you to stick with one woman for a change?"

This one would have. Killed me, that is. But aloud, I said, "And that worked out so well with Kylie."

"That was your own fault, man," said Cam. "And you know why."

I sighed. "Yeah. I know. But I'm trying to turn over a new leaf."

"With Lauren," he said.

"For the last time, she is just a friend."

Cam and Luis exchanged looks.

"Just a friend," I mumbled. "Can you guys close up? I gotta go upstairs and get ready."

Luis turned to me, a hand at his hip. "You're taking her out?"

"As just a friend."

I left out the backdoor and went up to my place. Jeesh. Those guys were unrelenting. Couldn't a guy have a girl strictly on a friendly basis? *Maybe not you, Jeff.* But I would. I wasn't interested in Lauren that way. She was cool, like a dude. I remembered her ninja moves with the Cutback Boys. That was some gnarly stuff.

I skipped the cologne and headed down to my truck. When I got to her place and went up the walk, I paused. Lifting my nose in the air, I sniffed. Was that a...a wolf nearby?

The wind shifted and I lost the scent. I scoped around into the dark with my wolf vision, but I didn't see anything. Maybe I was just jumpy. That shit with Nadège went down only last night. It was enough to make anyone jumpy.

I knocked on the door. When she answered, she was wearing a tight sweater and skinny jeans. She'd put on a little make-up, too. Uh oh.

I couldn't help but open the car door for her. I was acting in date mode. *Cut it out, Jeff. That's not what this is.*

I drove us to this place I liked overlooking the beach. It was casual and not upscale, but the burgers were great. "You know," she said as we were walking to the restaurant, "I haven't been out in ages. It's nice to feel like a person again."

"Oh...you mean...since breaking up with..."

"Yeah." She tucked her hair over her ear and looked around. "I've been here before. I do like this place. I like the ocean view."

"I was surfing this morning, and I was thinking we should do that again."

"Yeah," she said with a smile, "I'd like that."

We were taken to a table by the window and ordered beers. "Now then," she said, leaning forward with her hands threaded together in front of her. "What the heck happened with the ghosts and the Voodoo ladies?"

Here we go. Just as I was beginning to try to forget Nadège...

"I, uh...found the killer."

Her mouth fell open just as the waitress came by with our beers. She shooed the waitress away, asking her to come back in a few minutes before Lauren took up her pint glass and gave it a good gulp. "What happened?"

How much to say? "So, uh, it was that other Voodoo lady. The one you hadn't met, I guess. She was what's known as a Skinwalker."

"No shit! She could really turn into a werewolf?"

"Sort of. She had the magical ability to drape a wolfskin over her and become a wolf. A sort of Scoody-Doo version. And killed those people."

"Why?"

"To get more power." I slid my beer mat back and forth across the table. I really didn't want to relive it.

Her hand was suddenly on mine and I looked up. "Are you all right?" she asked.

"To tell you the truth...no. If it's okay with you, I'd rather not talk about it."

"Oh. I'm sorry. I didn't realize..."

"How could you? But...when I'm over it, I'll tell you. It'll be great for your research."

"Right now, I'm thinking more about you."

I sat back with my beer and couldn't help a smile creeping along my face. "You are?"

She fumbled, blinked at me, and straightened her sweater. "You know what I mean. I'm concerned for your welfare."

"Oh, yeah. Right. Should we order now?"

Once we got off the subject, we eased into more conversation. I asked her about her ninja skills and she told me how she decided to take lessons after breaking up with Vargar.

"You said he didn't get violent with you." My hand curled under the table on my thigh, claws flexing out of my fingers.

"He didn't. Some of his friends, though. I don't know." She dipped a fry in a pool of ketchup on her plate. "They were kind of...how should I describe it? Overly macho? Toxically so? Even some of their girlfriends were over the top. You want to know what I think?" She was using the French fry to gesture. I watched the red-tipped fry bounce in front of my face. "I think," she said, her voice dropping in volume, "I think they were white supremacists. KKK."

I nearly choked on my burger. I set it down, coughed into my napkin, and looked up at her. "Really? Is that a thing around here now?"

"Why not? The world's getting stranger by the minute."

She didn't know the half of it. They were super macho because they were werewolves. So how come I was so mellow? Is that what belonging to a pack did to you? Then no thanks, brah.

"Why would he be hanging around with those people?" I couldn't help but say.

She shrugged and popped the end of the fry in her mouth. Chewing thoughtfully, she cocked her head. She was sort of cute when she did that. Her hair fell to one side and it gleamed and shimmered in the low light. It looked smooth and touchable. "I don't know," she went on. "For the last few years, I sure couldn't get into the head of my ex. That's why we broke up. Too much strange behavior. Too many secrets. I wish him well, but...it was sure disappointing."

"I can imagine."

"You were dating someone recently, weren't you?"

I shrugged. "Kind of fell through."

She nodded, grabbing her burger. "I suppose you're used to it, flitting from one woman to the next."

That pulled me up short. Is that what she thought of me? Is that all I was? "Hey dude, that's not cool."

"It's true, right? I mean, didn't you say that your ex became your ex because you were fooling around?" She bit into her burger and chewed, cheek bulging with food.

I spread out my hands, looking for the words. Finally, I grabbed my beer and took a big swig. "So okay. Ya got me. I was trash. I *was*. But that's over. I have learned the error of my ways."

She snorted. "It's okay. People don't change."

Don't they? "*I* can. I'm done with that. I've seen the harm it can do. I'm woke."

She snorted again and set the messy burger down. She grabbed her napkin and wiped her lips and her hands. "Jeff, there are just some immovable forces in the world. And once a philanderer..."

Ouch. "Seriously. I'm going to prove to you that a guy can change. He can have experiences in his life that make him not only *want* to change, but *force* him to. I want a life. And some day, when I meet the right girl and fall in love, I want to get married and have kids. And you can't do all that when the dude is out trolling the town."

She raised her brows and drank more beer. "Wow. You sound serious."

"I am serious. Really. I've had some life-changing events lately. It makes you think."

We both ate in silence for a while. She put her burger down, wiped her hands, and folded her fingers together, resting her chin on them. "You do seem a little different from when I first met you. A little more...mature, maybe."

I guess when I first came to town, I was flush from Maine and the Wiccans. And when I got to know what was going on here, it kind of pulled me up short. I mean, I thought I could just pick up where I left off. But Lauren was right. Things had changed. *I* had changed. I had to be vigilant, because there were always magical things I didn't know about that could turn around and bite me in the ass. Literally.

I wanted to be the kind of man I should have been all along. Not the one my ex left California for. The kind she should have stayed for.

"I think it's going to be a process," I said, cradling my beer with my elbow on the table. "A process I'm still going through."

And it meant keeping being a werewolf to myself. I knew that meant keeping secrets, like Jesse Vargar did so unsuccessfully. But it had to be done. The last thing I wanted to see was a woman I loved look at me in fear. I vowed right then and there that no one was going to know. Not even Lauren. No. I couldn't stand the idea of her being afraid of me.

She clinked her glass with mine, startling me out of my thoughts. "Well, here's to it."

"Thanks." I drank it down and set the glass aside. "Ready?"

"I think I'd like to walk this off a little. Walk on the beach?"

"You're on."

We argued over who would pay the bill, and settled on splitting it in half. Then we bundled in our jackets and started walking along the strand.

"I've only lived in HB for about five years now," said Lauren, walking beside me and glancing out to the ocean. "But now I can't think of anywhere I'd rather live."

"I know what you mean. I guess I took it for granted a little. When I went to Maine, I thought I might be stuck there."

Her hands were thrust deep into both her jacket pockets. "Why?"

Oops. *Because, girl, I'm a werewolf and I didn't think I would be able to leave the Wiccans who took care of me.* "Uh...there was a business proposition that I thought would keep me there. But it turns out it fell through. And I was much happier about it. Now I have a whole new appreciation of my hometown."

She smiled, tilting her head toward me. "Surfer boy in Maine?"

"Yeah, that was harsh. I've never been away from surfing for so long."

She laughed. "I guess *my* passion is research. You're never too far from a computer or a library."

"True. Do you travel much for your research?"

"Yes, I do. And I get to learn about local superstitions. I buy things for my shop. There's a special corner there of rarities from different locales."

"Really? I missed that last time. You'll have to show me."

"I will."

"Did you ever get any vampire stuff from Transylvania?"

"Actually, I did. And I checked it out. It's the real deal."

"What is it? A stake?"

"Something like that. A Victorian vampire slaying kit."

I flicked my glance at her. "Dude!"

"I swear. Now mind you, I haven't found any evidence that vampires are real, but it would be interesting to —"

A voice behind us bellowed. "You said you weren't dating her!"

We both whipped around.

"Jesse!" cried Lauren.

"What the hell is this? The minute my back is turned —"

Laruen had gone red in the face and got right up to Jesse, jabbing him in the chest with her finger. "You don't have anything to say on the matter. And what are you doing? *Stalking* me?"

Vargar eased back. "I...I..."

"Dude," I said, shaking my head.

"Shut up, Chase. I want you to stay away from my wife."

"I'm not your wife," she said. "And I can see who I want to see."

"We're just friends," I said, but then Lauren cut her gaze at me.

"Yeah. Just friends. Of *course*, we're just friends. Why would I be another notch on your bedpost?"

I stared at her, taken aback. "What? Are you crazy? Whoever said that? Lauren, I—"

"Oh, save it. You're just as bad as he is."

Vargar moved closer to Lauren but she took a step back. Then he glared at me. "Stay out of this, Chase. This is between Lauren and me."

"Excuse me," I said, doing my own glaring at Lauren, "but I happen to be the injured party here. I'm being accused of something I didn't do."

"And just what is that?" cut in Lauren. For a short chick, she sure had a lot of moxie. It seemed she took turns getting into my face and then Jesse's. "What is it you didn't do? Make a move on me?"

"Cause we're just friends—"

"Wasn't I attractive enough? Blonde enough?"

"What a minute. *Wait a minute!* I just asked you out as a friend. I'm trying to be a nice guy. As for your ex, here…"

"You don't get to talk about me, Chase."

"And *you* don't get to talk about *me!*" I yelled. "Lauren, I'm kind of confused here. We obviously need to talk." I took her arm.

"You want to talk," she said angrily, though as she clutched my arm with her fingernails, I wasn't certain who she was madder at.

We started to turn when Vargar put his paws on me. And I do mean paws. I saw them shifting from hands to hairy paw-like hands, and his snout and ears were growing. "Chill, Vargar," I hissed out of the side of my mouth.

But it was too late. He'd gone full wolf. And he was going to tear me apart. I shifted in a blink, and growl-barked back at him. I don't know who leapt first, but we were all over each other.

Our clothes were being ripped apart, and though I wanted to tear into him, I held back, just going on the defensive. We rolled and rolled on the sand, our fur flying in all directions as we tangled. I shoved him off and put my head down, snarling and growling, when all of a sudden, he got this shocked look in his eye. He slowly turned toward…oh shit! Lauren!

We both looked at her. And she stood stock still, eyes as wide as I'd ever seen them, her mouth hanging open. Vargar shifted first, trying to hold his tattered clothes in place.

"Lauren, sweetheart. Look, it's okay — "

"Oh my God…" she whispered.

I shifted back and stood breathing hard behind Vargar. "Lauren. Shit. I…we…"

For some reason, she looked the most hurt while looking at me.

"Jesse," she said in a strained voice. "I can't believe this. I can't believe you. Is this…is this why all the secrecy?"

He lowered his head and shook it. "I'm so sorry. Let me explain — "

"Just get out of my sight. Go."

"But Lauren…"

"Just *go!*"

He turned, gave me a filthy look, and ran off.

"And you!" I desperately tried to hold my clothes together so I wouldn't embarrass myself, but I think it was a lost cause. "All this time. You knew. And you knew about him. So *that's* why you wanted so much to learn about werewolves. Were you *mocking* me? Was this all some sort of joke to you?"

"No! I was trying to keep it *from* you. I was trying to protect you!"

"Oh, that is some laugh. You knew about Jesse all along and you knew I didn't."

"I just met him a week ago."

"But you knew."

"I didn't know he was married to *you*. Until later."

"Okay. Well. I guess you had your laugh."

"Laugh? Believe me, I'm not laughing at anything."

"Believe you? That's the biggest laugh of them all."

"Lauren, what was I supposed to do? Tell you? And wouldn't that have been the biggest line ever. 'Hey girl, I know you're interested in the supernatural. And guess what? I'm a werewolf.'"

"You lied to me."

"I never lied to you. I never *told* you. And I was never going to tell you."

"I don't deserve the truth?"

"Of course you do. But it's...it's not a truth most people really want to know. Tell me honestly, would you have wanted to know? Would you have wanted to know about Jesse?"

"That's not the point."

"Oh yes, it is, and you know it. You'd be afraid. And I didn't want you being afraid of me. Because..." Because...oh shit. Lauren.

"Don't you think *I* get to decide that?"

"No. I didn't want you to look at me...like you're looking at me now. Like I'm a...a thing. A creature."

"No. I'm looking at you like you're a liar."

"That's not fair. I tried to spare you."

"I'm a big girl."

"And I'm a monster!" I was breathing hard, harder than from the fight. And my eyes burned.

Her expression didn't change. "Maybe you always were," she said softly. If she had shot me with a silver bullet my heart couldn't have hurt more. I even took a step back.

She shook her head, looking at me disgustedly. "What makes a guy like you a guy like you? Always trying to make your move. Always looking to score. Why was I such an idiot to think we could be friends. That we could be..." Tears welled in her eyes and spilled down her cheeks.

What was she talking about? Why was I now somehow the butt of all her pain? I was beginning to think it wasn't the werewolf that was pissing her off so much, but Jeff the Lothario.

"Lauren," I began softly. "I don't think you realize —"

She wiped at the tears angrily and lifted her chin. "I guess we're done," she said.

"What? Lauren, wait..."

She got right up to me, her finger in my face like a gun. "Don't ever talk to me again. *Don't.*"

As she turned away and stalked toward the parking lot in the distance, it was that instant — and I'll never forget it — *that* instant that I knew for sure. I had had hints all night and yes, even before, but I had ignored all the little signs. She was getting a thing for me and not just as a friend. But worse. And it was something I couldn't deny anymore.

I was already falling in love with *her*.

Well shit.

To be continued in BAYING FOR BLOOD

GLOSSARY

Aggro – aggressive surfing/surfer.

Ankle busters – no waves to speak of.

Backdoor – going inside the curl of the wave, from behind its peak.

Barrel – Just about the most perfect wave, the hollow part of a wave when it's breaking,

Benny – a person who is not a local.

Boglius – adjective like "cool" and "awesome".

Bondye – (BOND-ee-ay) the good God, the Creator in Haitian Voodoo practices.

Brosef – term for "bro" or "brah" in Hawaiian slang.

Carve – a sharp maneuver on the face of the wave.

Curl – the wave where it's breaking.

Cutback – a surf move done sharply in the shoulder or the wave or on its flats to get back on the surf line.

Deck – the top surface of a surfboard.

Donk – stupid, like a donkey.

Dude – a surfer, a friend, anyone.

Hodad – a person who hangs around the beach and doesn't surf.

Jé-rouge – (jheh-ROOzch) French for "red eyes", specifically as it relates to werewolves.

Leash – the piece of material that ties the leg to the surfboard.

Loup-garou – (loo-gah-ROO) French for Werewolf.

Lwa – (l-WAH) Haitian Creole for ancestor spirit

Mon petit – French for "my little one."

Mullering – wiping out

Namer – a surfer who shares a secret surf spot with others.

Shaka – a sign surfers use, made from extending the thumb and the little finger.

Shorepound –unsurfable waves that break right on the shore.

AUTHOR'S AFTERWORD

❧

JEFF HAD STARTED out as a not-too-nice character in the Booke of the Hidden series. But for dramatic purposes, I wanted to bring him into the story, the boyfriend who cheated. Some editors told me not to do that. But some romance writers said I could, as long as I redeemed him. And I wanted to. Once Jeff became a werewolf, we saw a different side of him, a reformed side. And now he was a tragic figure, never sure he could go back to his old life. And that's when I began to think that he could make a fun spin-off series with a lot of humor and a lot of pathos.

Having never written a character quite like him, I thought it would be a fun challenge to delve into his psyche, not just the werewolf but the bro!

I hoped you enjoyed this first entry into WereJeff's tale. Two more books to go. If you enjoyed the book, please review it. And sign up for my newsletter to get all the news about events, including virtual ones online, by going to BookeoftheHidden.com. Thanks for reading!

ABOUT THE AUTHOR

JERI WESTERSON is the author of the critically acclaimed Crispin Guest Medieval Noir mysteries. She also writes historical novels and several paranormal series. An award-winning author, her medieval mysteries were also nominated thirteen times for national mystery awards, from the Agatha to the Shamus. Jeri lives in Menifee, CA, mother to a grown son, a gray cat, and a laconic tortoise.

Bookofthehidden.com
JeriWesterson.com
EnchanterChronicles.com

Made in the USA
Monee, IL
06 February 2020